Skeletons

Beyond the Closed Door

A NOVEL BY

Nanette M. Buchanan

ISBN: 978-0-9793883-3-0

Published by

I Pen Books

www.NanetteMBuchanan.com

Acknowledgements

To my husband, the journey has proven worth it.

I want to thank you for traveling this road with me.

To my son and daughters, thank you for understanding my desire to fulfill my dreams, your input and support has carried me through.

To Adrienne, my sister, you've never skipped a beat and that alone keeps my heart flowing. Our love is truly, one of a kind.

To my readers and book club members, there is a new beginning in each novel so sit back and enjoy. Thank you for your support.

To Ella Curry, of EDC Creations, Urban Knowledge Books, Rising Sonz, and Rob's Books thank you for your continued support. You opened the door made room on your shelves and welcomed my books. I thank you for seeing my vision and giving me an opportunity to be a part of your literary world.

Chapter 1

Sage Monroe looked at the clock on her desk and silently thanked God it was four o'clock. She was looking forward to a weekend with no showings or any scheduled meetings. It had been a quiet day with only two closings and no new prospects. Corporate property leasing and sales was a new avenue for the group but the clients often scheduled appointments later in the day. Her last appointment was at four fifteen, and she began to clear her area preparing to leave shortly after her client's departure.

Sage worked with her best friend Karen Berger. The two women were co-owners of the Berger Realty Group. They began the company ten years prior and business was lucrative. Karen, Sage and Corrine Taylor were mortgage brokers and worked the earlier hours. Marcie Tremble, Sandy Swartz, Carmen Lopez, Cheryl Landing and Deidre Morgan were realtors. The group worked well together. Sage and Karen counted their blessings. They took on the challenge of working in an office with all females three years after opening. They had yet to regret their decision. The ladies agreed to keep their business affairs away from their personal affairs, although office talk tended to get personal. In the seven years that the team was together no customer could repeat anyone's personal business. Bickering and gossip would not be tolerated. They were friends and partners, each owning a percentage of stock in the business and respect for each other.

Sage and Karen went through their college years together and decided after acquiring their business degrees to start their own business. Their friendship had survived high school, college, the birth of their children and the end of Sage's marriage. Sage had a sister, Sierra, who was four years younger than her and since the death of their parents the distance between them had grown. Karen was closer to her than Sierra.

Sage cut off the coffee pot in the small kitchen and wiped off the counter and table. She didn't mind keeping the office opened until six, but she couldn't wait to relax at home. Sage had called everyone to let them know after her 4:15 appointment, the office would be closed and they could check their voice mail for week-end showings or cancellations. Sage checked each office door and smiled as she noticed Karen walking past the large stenciled window in the reception area.

Karen walked in the door bringing the cold from outside. It was the colder months of winter and every night brought a reminder that spring wasn't around the corner. Sage dreaded the chill that would bite at her face as she went to the parking lot to her car.

"Hey girl, whew it's getting cold out there. I thought you were leaving early today?"

"I'm still waiting for the four fifteen. "

"Sage, if you want to leave, I'll talk to the guy. Where's he from?"

"I'm not sure. He said he got our card from a business associate. He's looking at the strip mall over on Madison. There's two openings over there I'll talk to him about both."

"What does he want to put there?"

"Karen, I told him to stop by. I really didn't get into it over the phone. The purchase price is listed in our book, but he didn't sound as though it mattered."

"On Madison, I thought those were leases? I'm thinking about the wrong property. Wait, I think Carmen has a contract on one of them."

"It was posted. I told them to mark them when they have a property under contract. I think he wanted the double lot."

"Let me check the paperwork she gave me."

Karen went into her office. Sage continued to close the blinds, preparing the office for her departure.

"Karen girl look at this one here."

The office was located on one of the busiest streets in downtown Baltimore. Parking in front of the office after four in the afternoon was easier than the morning hours but the meter maids worked until six. Most drivers forgot to deposit the meter fee before leaving their vehicles. Sage and Karen watched the arguments from the office window daily as the drivers disputed their twenty-five dollar tickets.

"Who got caught without change this time?"

"Girl, look across the street, he's putting money in the meter in front of the drug store."

"Whew, yeah, that's a looker. Well dressed too. He's not from this area that's for sure."

"Karen, you can't say that. That law office has a few lookers."

"You said that right, a few. But that brother has them beat."

Sage turned away from the window no longer interested in the site.

"Sage, he's crossing the street. I think he's the client."

"Get out the damn window then!!"

"Oh, yeah you're right."

Karen moved from the window and made herself look busy. As the door opened Sage couldn't help but be mesmerized by the man that entered the office. As he took off his Fedora hat his dark chocolate skin showed an even tone from his baldhead to his overly attractive face. His mustache was well trimmed over lips that were moisturized. His appearance said he was well taken care of. As he stepped toward the reception desk where Sage sat he removed his gloves and unbuttoned his cashmere coat revealing a blue wool suit. Sage had discreetly looked him over from head to toe noticing he had accented his wear with matching shoes. She watched him as he crossed the floor to approach her, and she marveled at the fact that he had a walk that showed a man filled with confidence.

"Good afternoon."

"Good afternoon, Ms. Monroe?"

"Yes, you must be Mr. Randall."

"Yes, pleased to meet you."

"This is Ms. Berger. If you step this way we can go over the specs in my office and set up a showing for you."

"Sage, we can talk to Mr. Randall in the conference room if you like."

Sage looked at Karen realizing her claws had come out, and it wouldn't be long before she started to purr. Karen was single and used every opportunity to alert men that she was available. Her business sense was second to none but as far as her sense in love, she had none.

Mr. Randall stood looking at the two women enjoying the added attention. He didn't let his ego get ahead of him. Kris Randall had been told many times that he was a visual delight. He'd wait for the compliments. As he listened to the women give reasons for the better location to sit and talk, he made several observations. Ms. Monroe's physical characteristics fit what he had imagined from their conversations over the past few days. His interest in the property had become second to him wanting to meet the lady behind the sexy professional voice. Sage Monroe had no outstanding beauty but her cocoa skin and deep brown eyes matched the arousal her voice gave him, whenever he called. Although, she was shorter than he expected, he was sure he wouldn't tower over her height of approximately five foot six inches.

Kris assumed Sage had been married before. He could see her desk from the door of the office and various pictures of a young man and woman who resembled her were displayed on her book-case. He hoped they would meet in her office, if so he would look for the picture of the man in her life. Karen Berger didn't impress him much. She was very attractive and could fulfill his tempo-rary fantasies, but he knew immediately, Karen wouldn't hold his attention long. She was lighter than Sage and looked as though she was biracial. Kris dealt with a few women of mixed races and he concluded, they all had problems with relationships. Karen openly showed her interest in him and Kris didn't like being chased.

Lately, he had been focusing on his business ventures, which included renovating and building properties for various investment groups. After his last relationship ended, he vowed to remain single and just date off and on. Although he went out once in a while with close friends, the touch of a woman was surely missed. Kris thought about it. Sage Monroe could change his mind about a serious relationship.

"You're right Sage. Let me just check that paperwork for you." Karen walked to her office hoping Mr. Randall was noticing the walk was for him.

"I'm sorry Mr. Randall. I have the files set up in my office. Please step this way."

Kris followed Sage into her office, although Karen's exit had caught his eye. The office was larger than it appeared to be. There was a large conference table with eight plush chairs for seating. A flat screen television was at the end of the office separating the bookcase that started at the office door and extended around the room to a PC, fax machine and file cabinets. Kris admired Sage's taste in furniture as he wondered why her desk sat in the middle of the office. Plants and pictures gave her office a comfortable feeling and Kris smiled taking his seat.

"I like your office. I see why you're at ease when you talk on the phone. If I may ask, why is your desk in the middle of the office?"

"Thank you, there are stressful days spent here but when I'm surrounded by what I have acquired here I am comfortable. I work better when I'm comfortable."

They both smiled. Karen brought in the paperwork on the strip mall interrupting Kris's response.

"Thanks, Karen. Were you correct about the location?"

"Yes, I'm sorry I don't know why it wasn't posted."

Sage let out a sigh knowing she would have to explain the situation to her new client and hope it wouldn't cause him to be upset. Karen saw her reaction and took the opportunity to talk to Kris.

"Mr. Randall, can we interest you in other properties. It seems the location you were looking into is under contract."

Kris smiled. He would welcome the opportunity to work with Sage and get to know her better.

"That will be fine. Ms. Monroe I understand that given the situation you wouldn't possibly have a location in mind today. Should we set up another meeting? I do have to let my investors know their first choice isn't available, but I'm sure they'll be interested in looking at other sites."

Karen looked at Sage realizing Mr. Randall was indicating he wanted to work with Sage. Karen took the folders and materials Sage had on the Madison Strip Mall and left Kris and Sage in the office to discuss business.

"Thanks Karen. I'm sure I have all the information Mr. Randall needs. I'll call you over the weekend and wrap things up with you. I'll lock up as planned. Mr. Randall, I'll show you a few sites similar to the Madison Strip, and we can set up another appointment if that's okay with you."

"Sure, Ms. Berger, perhaps we'll see each other again."

Karen was surprised to see Sage pulling out the listing book for Kris Randall's review.

"Most definitely, I'm sure you'll be satisfied with our services."

Sage smiled and Karen understood she would have to make her own time with Mr. Randall.

Chapter 2

The meeting lasted two hours. After talking to Kris Randall it was apparent that the investment firm wanted a decent location, an office space in the strip mall and the opportunity to purchase more property as well. Sage and Kris agreed vacant land would be best. The investors would have the option to build or lease, as they needed.

Kris was pleased with the plans for the purchase. Sage had explained she wouldn't be available until the following week to discuss showing him the sites.

"You did say you weren't working this weekend, and I can truly understand. Sometimes you just want to rest. When can I look forward to the two of us viewing properties?"

"Mr. Randall it wouldn't be fair for me to say I will be the only representative from our office showing you the properties we have available. We have a team of realtors who will take you out as often as you like for viewings. Don't hesitate to call us if you see something that you like."

"Ms. Monroe. I'm looking forward to you being the representative. I don't always have this feeling of confidence in realtors, but I think you are quite different. I must insist that you sell me the property."

"Well, in that case Mr. Randall...."

"Kris, call me Kris."

"Kris, in that case, let's agree to talk on Monday."

Sage could insist that Mr. Randall deal with the realtors but there was a good commission linked to the sell of the properties he chose to see. She had already thought about future prospects. Kris told her he had a few contracts with clients looking for property in the area.

"That will be fine. I'll look forward to your call. If I'm not in my office, please call the alternate number on my business card."

It was dark outside and Sage looked past Kris through the office door and noticed the parked cars in front of the building were gone. She knew it as a sign that the parking lot attendant wouldn't be in the lot. Sage didn't like walking the parking lot at night.

"Mr. Randall, I mean Kris would you mind walking me to my car. I'm certain the attendant is no longer in the lot."

"Sure, do you have anything to carry to your car?"

"No just me."

Chapter 3

Sage walked in her front door and kicked off her shoes. The television could be heard in the hall where she hung up her coat and scarf. As she walked toward the living room she heard voices that told her she had guests awaiting her arrival.

"Ah, Dionne, I forgot you were coming over tonight." Sage said as she recognized her daughter's voice.

Sage looked at the clock on her mantel as she entered her living room. It was now close to seven thirty and relaxing would now turn into a hot bath, getting to bed early and sleeping late in the morning. Sage's daughter, Dionne, and her fiancé, Jarad, were surrounded by wedding magazines and samples of invitations.

"Jarad and I brought over the books for your input. We can't decide which invitation would be appropriate. I mean, they're so beautiful. We can't decide."

Jarad smiled and turned his attention back to the program on the television.

"Hello Jarad. Dionne I hate to do this to you tonight honey, but I am beat. I don't know if I'm catching a cold or what but I am tired and there's no way I can choose an invitation tonight. I'm off on the weekend. What are you guys doing tomorrow?"

"I thought you were coming home early. Wow, let's see…"

Jarad and Dionne, Sage's youngest, were to be married the second week in June. They set the date to be a year after their engagement but couldn't find a hall for June nineteenth. The date was moved to June tenth. They had less than six months to walk down the aisle and Dionne was beginning to show signs of bridal anxiety. Dionne and Jarad had been dating two years and both worked and saved for their big day. Sage admired her daughter's persistence in following the charted preparations given to her by her chosen coordinator, but she wasn't as enthusiastic about her daughter being married and lately it showed.

"How's tomorrow afternoon, will say around three or four. Jarad is that good for you?" Dionne asked hoping Jarad would say yes.

"Hmmm no, I can't, I promised to take my nephew to my parent's house for my sister. If I take him there I might as well handle that other business for my father then."

"Well do you mind if my mother and I pick the invitations, and I show you what we picked? "

"Dionne, it doesn't have to be this weekend. You won't be mailing them for a while. Go with Jarad and help him with his father's papers and business. Jarad, how is your dad doing?"

Jarad was told he was the executor of his father's estate. His father was suffering with Alzheimer disease and there were legal issues that needed to be managed before his death. Jarad's parents lived in Towson, Maryland, and he tried to get there on the weekend to visit with them.

"He's hanging in there Ms. Monroe. It's a day-by-day thing. I'm worried about my mom you know, being tired from dealing with this thing daily though."

"I can only imagine. Dionne it's up to you. We can wait or you can come by Sunday." Sage hoped she would come by later in the week.

"Is this your way of avoiding the conversation about us getting married?"

"Dionne, I'm tired. I really forgot about you coming over. You're not getting married until June. You have other things to be done. If you want to do something this week, do them."

"Dad said you were handling this well, but I'll let him know what he thought was true."

"What does your dad have to do with this?"

"Everything, you don't want to talk about this wedding or give your input because of your divorce from dad."

"He said that?"

"He said you were taking this well."

Sage didn't want to discuss her ex-husband, and what he thought about marriage.

"Dionne, you're grown, twenty nine to be exact. How else would I take it?"

"Then why is it every time I want your opinion you somehow avoid the conversation. We told you we would be here tonight. You didn't even call to say you would be late. But now you're home and you're too tired to even look at the invitations. Come on mom, you don't want me to get married."

"I'm just tired. I have been tired all day."

"Not too tired to work though. Jarad, I'm ready when you are!"

Dionne didn't wait for a response. She gathered the magazines and pictures as she headed for the front door.

"Ms. Monroe, we'll talk and call you if that's okay." Jarad felt he owed her an explanation.

"That will be fine Jarad, I'm sorry."

"She's been real upset lately. I don't know what it is? Maybe your husband knows, she talks to him a lot."

Sage walked Jarad to the front door. Dionne was sitting on the passenger's side looking out the front window. She didn't turn to look at her mother or Jarad in the doorway.

"I'll make sure she calls you."

"Thanks Jarad. I'm really am sorry."

Jarad got into the car and pulled off. Sage locked the door and turned off the television. She went to the bathroom and ran water into the tub. She mixed the hot water with bath beads and salt. After her bath, she would have a cup of hot tea. She didn't have much of an appetite. She would skip dinner. Sage drank her tea and was in the bed before ten o'clock. She didn't give a second thought about Dionne's comments about her ex-husband.

Chapter 4

Karen hadn't heard from Sage, and she was anxious to find out if Mr. Randall decided to look at other properties. Karen also wanted to know how long the meeting between Sage and Kris lasted. Sage hadn't dated seriously since her divorce. Karen watched her friend as she went through the aftermath of her divorce, and it seemed Sage didn't get over her love for Brian. Karen had never been married. Her relationship was an on again off again romance with Vince, the father of her twenty-one year old daughter Kandi. Vince fulfilled her needs when she needed a decent escort or a night of teasing pleasure. Karen had told Sage that's what she was missing. Karen described her girlfriend as a woman who wouldn't let go of her past. Sage's only effort to separate from Brian totally was her use of her maiden name Monroe. The name Drakeford was stricken from all her legal documents, and she refused to answer to the name after their separation.

Karen invited Sage to outings hoping she would enjoy herself and maybe find a companion to relieve any feelings of loneliness. Karen told Sage that every woman needed a man, even if he was only a friend. Sage didn't agree. Karen finished the papers on her desk and decided the rest of her afternoon would consist of shopping. She picked up the phone to invite her best friend for a relaxing shopping spree.

"Sage its Karen; call me when you get this message. I was wondering if you wanted to do some shopping." Karen left the message after the tone as instructed on Sages' answering machine. She called Sage's cell phone and after two rings she realized she would be leaving another message. Karen smiled to herself thinking Mr. Randall had broken down the walls that Sage had built.

Karen packed her briefcase with materials she would need to review at home and left the office for the day. Her cell phone rang with a jazzy tone that told her it was Sage.

"Hey girl, I thought maybe you were too busy to answer the phone."

"Karen, I feel sick as hell. I don't know if I'm coming down with the flu or what. When you called, I was in the bathroom getting reacquainted with my toilet. We met early this morning and have been together ever since."

"What? Do you need some soup or something? I can stop by with it on my way home."

"I ate soup for lunch, and it took awhile for my stomach to settle. I took some cold medicine, but I still feel awful. Girl, I'm getting ready to lay down again. I haven't been out of the bed all day. I didn't feel too good yesterday either, I should have known I was catching something."

"I called to ask you to go shopping. I hope you'll feel better later though do you have enough medicine?"

"I have over the counter medicine. I don't know if it will be strong enough to fight this mess though. I'm taking it every four to six hours. Girl, go on shopping. Call and check on me later, I'm going to try to sleep."

"Sage, I'll be there in an hour or two. I'll use my key. You don't sound good at all."

Sage didn't answer. She needed someone there with her. Sage hadn't been that sick in years.

"Go lay down. I'll see you when I get there."

"Okay, thanks. Listen can you bring some orange juice."

"Sure, I'll see you in a few."

Karen hung up the phone thinking twice about her shopping spree. She decided to go to her house and pack an overnight bag. She would stop at the store for juice and other items she would need to help Sage recover.

Chapter 5

The weekend wasn't long enough for Sage to shake the flu. Karen told her on Monday, she would take her to the doctor. Sage had a fever off and on that was accompanied by a deep cough. The cold rattled in her chest and Karen thought it had developed into Bronchitis. Sage told Karen to go home so she wouldn't catch it but Karen ignored her request. Karen called Dionne only to find out she had gone with Jarad to Towson. His dad had taken a turn for the worst, and they left early Saturday morning. Karen didn't call Trevon, Sage's son. She knew he would worry and Tulsa, Oklahoma was a long way to travel if Sage had only the flu. Karen didn't tell Sage about the call she made and convinced her she didn't want to worry anyone else. She would stay with her until her doctor gave them further instructions.

Sage was given a prescription for Bronchitis and was told to stay home until the medication was gone. She had pills and liquid antibiotics and they both would make her drowsy. Karen told her she would be staying with her and leaving from her home going to the office. Sage tried to argue about it but her condition wouldn't let her. She drifted off after coming home and taking her first dose of medicine. Sage went into the kitchen to prepare their lunch.

Karen called the office to retrieve their messages and have the calls forwarded to Sage's home line. One of the messages was from Mr. Kris Randall. He left a number for Sage to return the call. Karen wrote down Sage's messages and put Mr. Randall's on the top. Karen put the messages on the tray with Sage's lunch. She walked into Sage's bedroom and was glad to see Sage was sitting up.

"How are you feeling? Were you able to rest a little better?"

"Girl, my head feels so heavy. I'm beyond miserable. But complaining ain't gonna help. I'm glad you convinced me to go to the doctor. This thing could have gone into pneumonia if I waited the seven days they tell you to wait on the medicine bottles."

"What seven days?"

"You know they tell you to take the medication for seven days, and if you still feel bad call your doctor. Well, I usually wait to see if the medication works. This thing I caught would have had the best of me by then."

"Well, here's your lunch. I'm going to get my tray and join you. Those names and numbers on that paper are your messages. I don't expect you to call them back. I'll return the calls for you just tell me what's been done with each one."

Karen left the room and Sage looked over the names as she sipped the tea from her cup. Karen had prepared beef barley soup. She gave Sage a glass of orange juice and a cup of tea. Sage looked at the clock on her nightstand and realized she had an hour and a half before her next dose of medicine. Her cough had subsided but the tightness in her head and chest let her know she had a lot of cold that had to leave her system. Karen returned with her tray and sat in the wing chair beside Sage's bed.

"Karen thanks, I don't have much of an appetite

I don't want you to think I don't appreciate you doing this for me."

"Girl please, eat what you can, or what you feel you can. Did you look at the names?"

"Yeah, most of them can be rescheduled with Sandy or Carmen. They've spoken to them already. I contacted them as follow ups. The other three need to be assigned as new viewings. The files are on my desk. I'll deal with Mr. Randall myself."

"You'll deal with Mr. Randall? Must have been a good meeting."

"He's interesting. But he wanted to set up the viewings with me only. I'll tell him I'm sick and then assign him to one of the girls."

"I'll call him for you and take him out to see the properties. I mean his business is worth me taking the time right?"

"Karen...." Sage started coughing and it took a moment for her to continue her statement. Karen got up to help her cough up the mucous that built up in her throat. The cough was raw and showed signs of pain as it rattled in sound.

"Karen, you can take him out after I call him. I need to call him though to keep his business. It's just like you to want to show him your properties."

"My properties? It's our properties Sage. Oh, Damn girl, I wasn't even thinking like that."

The statement brought a smile to Sage's face as she began to cough again. They ate lunch discussing the messages and the results of the meeting Sage had with Mr. Randall.

Chapter 6

Kris called the Berger Group on Wednesday only to find that Sage Monroe was out sick. Sage called him Tuesday and left a message on his phone that she would be out of the office and would try to reach him later. Kris had spent the night entertaining guests, a celebration of a deal the firm thought they wouldn't close. The night lasted longer than he thought with most of the guest leaving early Wednesday morning. Kris wasn't pleased with his social life because it was slowly evolving around the business he worked in. Although he desperately tried to keep his business and personal affairs separate most of his affairs started from the business associations he had made.

Kris picked up the remains of the gathering the night before. His thoughts drifted to Sage again, and he decided to ask where flowers could be delivered to her. As he dialed the number he decided to as for Karen Berger.

"Good Morning, may I speak with Ms. Berger please."

"May I ask who's calling?" The voice on the other end was overly pleasant, which gave Kris the impression that the regular receptionist wasn't in the office.

"Mr. Randall, Kris Randall."

"Please hold sir. I'll connect you shortly."

Kris waited no more than two minutes and then heard Karen's prepared answer.

"Mr. Randall, I'm so glad you called. Ms. Monroe has been out of the office, and I wasn't sure she could contact you. I would have called you myself, but I believe she must have your file."

"Yes, good morning Ms. Berger, I did speak with Ms. Monroe. I was calling to get information from you. I want to send her flowers, a get-well wish. I don't know when she'll be in the office, and I wanted her to enjoy them at home."

"I see." Karen was impressed. He could have sent them and wondered if she got them. Karen wanted to offer to deliver them for him, but if he was going out of his way to order flowers his kind gesture should be recognized. Karen thought the surprise might spark Sage's interest. Karen was hesitant about revealing Sage's personal information. It wasn't normal to give clients the address of employees, even if it was an act of kindness.

"Mr. Randall, can I put you on hold a moment?"

"Sure, I'll hold."

Karen put the call on hold and called Sage on the other line. Sage was up and around, although she still had a cough. The medication would be complete on Monday. She told Karen she would work from home on Thursday and Friday. They agreed she wouldn't do any showings on the weekend and pick up the pace on Monday feeling refreshed.

Sage answered the phone winded from climbing the stairs.

"Hello, Karen?"

"Are you okay?"

"Yeah, I thought I missed you. What's up?"

"I've got a client on the line who wants to send you a get well wish. You've gotten a lot of warm wishes and calls of concern. Anyway they wanted to deliver flowers here thinking you would be in. I want to give them the address and have them delivered to your house. I mean you won't be here until Monday."

"Karen my name is in the yellow pages."

"It's under Drakeford, not Monroe. So is it okay?"

"Who is the client?"

"It's supposed to be a surprise."

"Who? Kris Randall?"

"How'd you know that?"

"It's not what you think. Give him the address that's fine."

"Hmmn. Maybe there's more to this than you think."

"No, he's just being nice. Yeah, give him the address."

"Okay, I'll see you later."

Karen returned to the blinking line hoping Kris was still on the line.

"Mr. Randall?"

"Yes." Karen could tell by the echo that he had put the call on the speaker.

"Do you have a pen? I'll give you the address."

"Thank you. Yes, I'm ready."

Karen recited the address and Kris repeated it to her. He thanked her for her help and said goodbye. Karen shook her head as she hung up the phone. Her thoughts were the same prayer she said for all the clients that showed interest in Sage.

Kris called Sage at eleven before going to the florist. He wanted to be certain there would be someone to open the door and accept the delivery.

"Hello." Sage sounded a lot better than she had on Monday, although her voice wasn't as sexy or professional as it had been in prior conversations.

"Good Morning Sage, its Kris. How are you feeling?"

"A little better thank you. Have you scheduled your showing with one of the girls in the office?"

"That's a joke right? I'll wait for you to handle that business. It's no hurry believe me. My clients have to talk to their clients and so on and so on. They told me to move forward and give them the information on the land as I get it. They'll look at the locations and make their determination, and we'll still have to wait for others to agree. It's a process. I'm calling to see about you, I mean if you allow me. Is there anything I can get you or help you in anyway?"

"I'm a lot better, I know I don't sound like it though. I could have worked at the office, but I'm still taking medicine. I really appreciate the gesture though."

"Listen, we've been talking for more than three weeks now. It's been business as usual but my interest is going beyond the Sage Monroe owner of the Berger Group."

"I see. Well, I can't say that I haven't had questions about you. But the reality is you are a client, and I don't mix business with pleasure."

"Okay, I guess now I do want to schedule an appointment with another realtor."

"What?"

"Yeah, I mean if that's what I have to do to get to know you. Oh well."

"Kris, I don't think you understand." Sage didn't get the humor in Kris's response. When he laughed, she let out a sigh of relief.

"Money talks huh? I can't help it if I'm attracted to you. This contract is not my contract. I'm negotiating for my client. They're your clients put the contract in their name if you like. Listen Sage, I'm not a person who goes after every woman I meet. I can honestly say I haven't had that type of relationship in at least three years."

"That's hard to believe but if you say so."

"Why? I've been to dinner and had a couple of drinks but none of them have been with a woman who could say we had a relationship."

"Okay, I hear you. To answer your original question Karen brought a few things over so I'm stocked for right now."

"Oh, you and Ms. Berger are close?"

"Yeah, we're good friends. Most of us at the office have been friends for years now." Sage made the statement letting him know any of the women in the Berger Group would be unavailable to him if he truly wanted to pursue her.

Kris listened recognizing Sage's wall of defense. The challenge perked his interest more. He would be working at breaking down her wall. "If you need anything, please call me. I'll be happy to pick something up for you or come and sit with you while you nod off from your medication."

"Now why would you want to sit with me while I nod? Never mind don't answer that."

They both laughed. The conversation ended without Kris telling Sage he would be delivering the flowers to her door.

Chapter 7

Dionne spent the morning writing and rewriting the invitation list for the wedding. Jarad had given her the names of his family and friends, and she was preparing a completed list for him to review later. There weren't many problems with the seating arrangements but Dionne wanted to talk to her mother and father about her father bringing a guest. Brian hadn't mentioned it, but Dionne didn't think it would be fair to invite her father and not offer an invitation to his guest. During her parent's divorce, there was never any mention of the "other woman". No one ever spoke her name or mentioned seeing her in public. Although her parents had been divorced for seven years the marriage broke down years before Trevon graduated from college. Dionne could remember the arguments they had about her father's late nights and weekend business trips. Neither Dionne nor Trevon took sides, but their mother was right. Sage was not a part of Brian's business world. She never was invited on any of his outings or business events.

Sage would beg to travel with Brian wanting to spend more time with her husband and the response was usually an argument that sent him out of the house for two more days. Sage stopped asking after Dionne's first year in college. The Berger Group became her outlet and as the company grew so did her mother's confidence.

She didn't look back and continued to become independent of her husband's finances, attention and love. Dionne and Trevon came home during the Thanksgiving break during Dionne's sophomore year in college and Trevon's last year in high school to find their father wouldn't be joining them for the traditional Thanksgiving dinner.

Dionne asked questions her entire break. Trevon couldn't answer any and it was only a matter of time before divorce papers were being discussed. Sage didn't talk to Dionne or Trevon and there weren't any family members that wanted to discuss the separation or a divorce.

Brian remained a devoted father and didn't give any reason other than misunderstandings between a husband and a wife for the lost of his marriage. As the years passed Brian's relationship with Dionne strengthened. Trevon joined the military and was stationed in Tulsa, Oklahoma with his wife and son. Brian made attempts to stay in touch with Trevon, but he was Sage's baby and wanted no parts of his father's excuse for breaking up the family.

Dionne wasn't sure her parents didn't give up on their love too soon. She believed her father when he said it was filled with years of misunderstandings. Dionne didn't know how her mother felt but as her wedding date got closer she could see her mother's fear of another marriage that could possibly lead to divorce. Dionne was determined to get her mother to let the past go and live as her father had done. She didn't want to do the separate visits when she and Jarad had children. Dionne dreamed of Christmas's for her children with both grandparents, something she missed since the death of Sage's parents.

Dionne and Jarad had been in Towson since Saturday. Jarad's father had to undergo tests and Dionne stayed with Jarad at his parents awaiting the results. Jarad and his family went to talk with the doctor leaving Dionne time to finish the guest list and call her coordinator about other plans. Dionne called her father as she did once a week. Brian was always glad to hear from her.

"I didn't pick the invitations yet. I tried to include Mom, but she made excuses on Saturday about it being too soon to pick invitations."

"Dionne, your mother will help you. It is early. You've got six months."

"Now you sound like her. Dad, I want to get this stuff done. I'll rest better knowing everything is in place."

"What are you going to do about Jarad and his parents?"

"What can I do? His father is sick, we'll deal with it."

"Jarad can't possibly be making wedding plans and helping his mother with his sick father. That's pressure and stress."

"So, what are you suggesting? We don't get married. Like you said we have six months. If his dad remains sick, what, we don't get married?"

"Dionne, listen, I'm just saying the same thing your mother said. You've got plenty of time. Go with your girls and pick out the dresses. Get other things done."

"Dad, please. Are you sure you didn't talk to your wife?"

Brian hesitated before answering. Just the thought of talking to Sage gave him a twinge of guilt. He wouldn't know what to say. They hadn't spoken in more than five months. It was the last time Trevon and his family visited. Brian wanted to see his grandson and spend time talking with Trevon and his wife. Trevon made arrangements for them to have dinner at a local restaurant. The surroundings were nice and the dinner was handled well by Sage and Brian but Brian hadn't spoken to Sage since. Brian called Trevon off and on since the dinner but the conversations were always short. Conversations with Sage were non-existent. Brian had the same desire as Dionne. He wanted to be with his family for celebrations and holidays without being overwhelmed by guilt. Brian had convinced himself that time would heal the pain he had created.

"Your mother wouldn't discuss your wedding with me. She'll come around, give her time. The closer it gets to the date she'll give you the help you need. She's probably as nervous about you getting married as you are."

"I'm not nervous. And what would make her nervous? She got married."

Brian didn't know how to respond. He couldn't explain the ups and downs, the uncertainties of marriage. Sage had expressed her feelings about marriage and how she couldn't trust another man. Brian couldn't tell his daughter, he was guilty, and he was responsible for Sage feeling the way she did. New brides don't see divorce in their future. New brides don't think about cheating husbands.

Dionne wouldn't acknowledge the excuse Sage gave for her divorcing the man she fell in love with in her early years of her college. Trevon told Dionne that Brian was caught cheating by Sage and there was no need to ask questions. There were plenty of questions that needed to be answered but Dionne didn't think that her father's affairs should keep him away from his family forever.

"Your mother will have to explain her views on marriage to you. Women have different opinions than men. You know the Venus and Mars thing."

"Dad, you're good at avoiding the point. Mom is condemning my marriage before I get married. She hasn't even tried to date because of what happened between you two. It's ridiculous. It's been years." Dionne added another point. "I think, deep down, she still loves you."

Brian knew better than that. He smiled to himself and hoped if Dionne ever found out the truth, she would be open-minded and still keep her relationship with him. He had betrayed his wife in the worst way, and he knew it left remnants of bad feelings.

"I love her too, but it's different when you get hurt. I don't know how to explain it. Your mother is strong. She hasn't said a word about our problems to anyone and that takes a lot of strength.

Most women talk about the man like a dog and make sure he loses more than his home and his wife. Your mother made sure I kept a relationship with family, friends, you and your brother. I appreciate her letting me have parts of my life that other women destroy after divorce. It sounds like you're looking for an alliance. It's between you and your mother. Give her a chance to talk to you woman to woman."

"I just don't understand. I mean, even Trevon is still angry with you."

"Really? I can't tell. I would hope not."

"Do you talk to him?"

"Yeah, not as much as with you, but we talk."

"Hmmn."

Brian never thought about Sage telling Trevon about what finally caused their divorce. It was obvious that Dionne didn't know. She promised not to ruin his relationships. She told him he would destroy each relationship just has he had destroyed theirs. She promised she would sit back and watch. A question began to haunt Brian. *"If she told Trevon, who else would she tell?"*

"Have you talked with your mother about this lately?"

"No, she's not feeling well. The flu or something, I'll see her this weekend. That's the reason for my call. I almost forgot. Will you be bringing a guest to the wedding? I don't need to know a name or anything, but I just need it for the count. Dad, you're living your life, that's good. Trevon and I are grown, and you're divorced from Mom. There's no reason why you can't bring a guest with you. It may help Mom to move on too. I know we don't talk much about you dating, but you are right?"

Brian wasn't dating as often as he liked, but he was dating. He had two serious relationships since his divorce. They lasted for a little more than two years. Each ended when he refused to display his affection in public or attend different business functions with them. Brian didn't feel the need to make himself a public spectacle.

Since those relationships his dating was limited. Many times he called an escort service or attended functions by himself. Those dates didn't require commitment; it was all business.

"I date off and on, nothing serious. In six months who knows, I may not be dating anyone then."

"Listen, it's just a count, but I wanted you to know your guest would be welcomed."

"Thanks but your mother may object to my bringing a date. I don't know, it may seem like a slap in her face."

"Dad, think about it!! It's been seven years. Mom needs to let it go. The invitation stands for you and your guest. I'll tell Mom."

Brian didn't argue. He knew his daughter would bring it up. Sage would think he wanted to bring a guest. He didn't want that. Now he had a reason to talk to Sage.

Chapter 8

Brian gave a lot of thought to when he would call Sage. Since Dionne's marriage wasn't until June, he wondered if he should wait to talk to her when the date was closer. He understood his daughter's concern but his feelings told him he needed to let Sage know it wasn't his idea to invite a guest. He called his secretary letting her know to hold all his calls. As he picked up the phone he leaned back in his leather seat, trying to get comfortable before Sage answered. The seat didn't give him comfort, and he realized it was his nerves that wouldn't allow him.

Brian looked around his office as the phone rang, reminiscing calling home during better times. Sage would answer the phone and he could feel her smile. He loved his wife from the time he noticed her walking across the campus of Maryland University. It was homecoming weekend and he couldn't help but spend the time with Sage. They were married after Sage's graduation and Brian made partnership in Kilmore Architect and Design. He was the guilty spouse. He took business trips and weekends that led to long nights of indiscretions. He blamed it on alcohol and business deals until he finally admitted he had desires outside of his marriage. Sage's voice interrupted Brian's thoughts bringing his focus to the present.

"Hello."

"Sage its Brian, how are you?"

"I've seen better days. How are you?"

Brian didn't know if he wanted to continue, her sarcasm usually led him to hang up the phone. He needed her to listen to him without any anger.

"Dionne told me you were under the weather."

"I'm better than I was. Thanks for asking."

"Dionne called me with what may become a problem."

Sage remembered what Jarad said about Dionne and Brian talking often. She became interested in what he had to say. She took a seat on her couch hoping it wasn't a problem that would affect the upcoming wedding. Brian continued, noticing Sage didn't comment.

"She told me it would be okay for me to bring a guest to her wedding. I didn't give her any indication that I would or wouldn't. Sage I wanted you to know that this was her idea not mine. I know how you feel about this and I don't want to open a can of worms."

"Your can Brian, I upheld my part of the promise. If you want to bring a guest, that's up to you. I don't think it's my place to tell you how to handle this situation."

"Sage, I wanted you to understand."

"What's your point Brian? I understood you and moved on. You didn't want anyone to know about your lovers remember. Brian, do you really think the wedding is the place to introduce a new lover."

"Sage, you know I don't want that."

"So come alone. I'm sure you can get away for a day. Are you still involved with that innocent escort service?"

"Sage, I didn't call to discuss who, or what I'm involved with. I wanted you to know that I'm on your side about this. Dionne is insisting that since we're not together I should be able to bring who I want to the wedding."

Brian wanted to hear Sage disagree with Dionne. He wondered if she still had any feelings for him. Sage's response made it clear.

"I'll have a guest there, so you're right, you should too. I mean after all we're divorced. People can't expect us not to be in new relationships by now. Bring your friend, lover, whatever. It won't bother me. I'll direct all questions to you."

Brian was stunned. He never thought about Sage dating. It was just like Sage to keep it away from Dionne. His only thought was the embarrassment he would have being at the wedding alone watching Sage and her guest. He would definitely invite someone. Brian didn't have a comment and Sage didn't allow him to think twice about responding.

"Listen, if your bringing a guest raises eyebrows, you deal with it, later Brian."

The phone went dead.

Chapter 9

S age let the phone fall on the carpeted floor. The television became suddenly louder than before and she reached for the remote to shut it off. Dionne and Brian had stirred her emotions. Sage didn't have any intentions on bringing a guest to the wedding. She didn't deal with many males on that level, even if she wanted to bring a guest. She had been offered dinner, dancing and romancing in the past seven years. She accepted the dates that ended at the restaurant or on the dance floor. She wasn't interested in the false pleasures, lies or empty promises. She was careful not to give the impression that her interest was more than being an acquaintance. She didn't want any commitments. Sage's head throbbed and she closed her eyes hoping Dionne wouldn't call. When the doorbell rang, she was beginning to drift off into a nap.

Sage stood and stretched, feeling the stiffness in her back, as the bell rang a second time. The chimes seemed to echo breaking the silence of the rooms. The temperature seemed to have changed, and she wondered if she was coming down with another fever or if the thermostat triggered her central heating system. Sage remembered Kris was sending flowers and opened her door expecting to say thank you to a stranger.

She opened the door to a beautiful floral arrangement in a large vase. She smiled as she looked for the face to speak to. "You can sit the vase here on the table."

Sage made room for the vase on a table in the hall. She noticed the man making the delivery didn't speak a word.

"Excuse me Mr. Randall where's the card."

"On the vase."

They both laughed. Sage coughed covering her mouth and fanning Kris away from her.

"I don't want you to catch this mess. Thank you for the flowers they are beautiful. You could have had the florist make the delivery."

"I could have. I wanted to see you though. Are you sure you're okay?"

"I have the flu, bronchitis. I've been taking antibiotics all week. Hopefully, I'll be back into the swing of things on Monday."

"And you wanted me to wait until Monday?"

"Mr. Randall, you're a client…" Kris stood back admiring Sage arrange the flowers in the vase. She took two steps back to view her new arrangement. Smiling she continued her sentence.

"…Clients don't usually visit the realtor's home."

"Okay, who said the visit was business?"

Sage looked at Kris, she noticed he wasn't in business attire at all. He had on a pair of jeans that fit him well. His shoes were casual and the sweater could have been worn to any sporting event and been appropriate. Again Sage thought to herself how well Kris dressed.

"Well let's not have the visit in the hall. Come in and have a seat. Can I get you anything to drink?"

"No, thank you. I didn't come here for you to wait on me. I realize you should be resting. I just wanted to talk with you for a while and let you know you were in my thoughts."

Sage picked up the phone from the floor and placed it on the table. She used the remote to cut on her stereo system and turned the music down where she could hear Kris as he spoke.

"You have a nice home."

"Thanks, I really love it. It's a lot larger inside than it looks. Are you from this neighborhood?"

"No, I live between here and Washington, D.C."

"How often do you go to D.C.?"

"Often. My business brings me here mostly."

"Really? I thought your home office was in Baltimore."

"Either office is home for me. I've been in both so long it really doesn't bother me to travel. It helps when clients come to the area and are indecisive about where they want to buy or invest."

"So, you're on the road constantly?"

"When nothing else occupies my time."

Sage smiled and began coughing. She tried to suppress it, but it got worst. She stood excusing herself. Kris gave her an understanding nod. As she exited the room Kris could hear her coughing, in the distance. He had his first opportunity to look around the room for any indication of a male companion. Sage gave him the impression that she wouldn't reveal much of her personal business, even if he asked. She was the type of woman that would present a tempting challenge. She fit into a different category. Most women would do anything to be with him. Sage wouldn't and he knew it.

The room was painted mint green with a beautiful hardwood floor. There was a grand piano in the next room that could be seen from the couch where he sat. The light from the day showed the essence of the room inviting Kris to step in. He walked to the end of the living room to find the room hosting the piano was a large sitting room. A rust chaise lounge and matching sofa gave the room comfort. Five oversized pillows, mixed in natural colors were situated in various spots on the floor around the room. Kris knew immediately that listeners would relax on the pillows as one played the piano. Kris felt an urge to sit and touch the keys as the soft jazz music played from the stereo in the other room. The French doors led to the patio in the yard. Kris could see the lawn furniture as a sense of peace came over him. As an agent for wealthy clients, Kris had been in many homes and seen a touch of elegance. Sage's home fit in with those he had longed to live in. Kris had been involved with clients who welcomed his nightly stays and unexpected visits. He wanted Sage to become a part of his personal world.

"I see you've found my sanctuary."

"Really, I can see why. I'm impressed with your taste in décor."

"I make some changes every now and then, but this room always remains the same. I don't know it just fits my need to relax."

Kris continued to scan the room as Sage described the artwork he was admiring on the walls. The room's color of antique white gave compliment to the open entrance to the living room.

"It's amazing how this room invites you in and so does the living room. Your home gives an air of comfort."

"Kris, I give the invitations here. But I'm glad you feel comfortable."

Kris took Sage's response as a step in the right direction. Sage's thoughts drifted to her conversation with Brian. *"Six months would be long enough to get to know Mr. Randall"*

"Who plays the piano?"

"I do or I did. I don't play as often now. I used to play quite a bit, back in the day."

Kris smiled. He realized the barrier was breaking down. Sage's professional demeanor as the realtor was changing to Sage the woman.

"Maybe you'll play for me some day."

"Maybe."

"So, your work is backed up in the office or what?"

They sat on the couch after standing looking out of the French doors.

"No, I'll be pretty much caught up. I may have a few calls to make up but that's it. And since you're here, that's one less call to make."

"So I won't here from you on Monday?"

"Uh, I didn't mean that. I was talking about returning calls of those I haven't talked to."

"Sage, I don't know how long I can play this little game."

"What game?"

"Listen, maybe I didn't make myself clear. I want to spend time getting to know you. I want you to get to know me."

"You said that earlier. I really don't know, I hate mixing business with pleasure. It usually leads to problems. I don't want us to have any problems."

"Good then. We'll talk over the weekend while you rest up and get better. If you need anything just tell me. I'll check on you off and on. Monday I'll talk to you about these properties and wrap up the business, so we can get to secure a friendship. If fate carries us further I'm sure you won't be mad."

Sage was surprised. Kris was almost demanding but it seemed sweet. She wasn't sure how to handle Kris. Six months would give her more than the time she needed.

Chapter 10

Karen didn't expect Sage to respond to Kris's visit the way she did. She listened as her friend talked about her surprise guest. Sage admitted that she knew Kris would make the delivery himself but welcomed his attention. Karen smiled thinking to herself that Kris Randall had charmed his way into her friend's home.

"What's that smile for Karen? I know what you're thinking. It didn't go any further than a visit."

"Okay, if you say so a girl, that man is fine. He's pushing up hard. What does he want or what's in it for him?"

"What you see something I don't? I thought he was just being nice. Karen to be honest with you, it felt good to have someone give me flowers."

"I don't know. Maybe it's all sincere, but this time I'm giving you your advice. Walk with caution."

"Always, I've got six months."

"Six months? What is going on in six months?"

"Dionne's wedding I'll need a date for the wedding."

"Since when?"

"Girl that damn Brian called. He said Dionne told him to bring a guest if he wanted to."

"Okay and what does that have to do with anything?"

"Brian wanted me to know it wasn't his idea but Karen, he didn't say he wouldn't be bringing a guest."

"Sage, I understand your feelings about Brian's cheating but c'mon girl. You know he's got somebody."

"That's what scares me."

"What?"

"I don't know Karen. I don't want to be in the midst of Brian's pick of the week."

"Sage, you've got to let that go."

Sage thought about Karen's comments. She told Karen often that she wouldn't understand how it felt to be the wife of a cheating husband. She knew Karen couldn't understand walking in on her husband and his lover in the same bed where they slept at night. Karen couldn't understand how it felt to hold on to the secret so it wouldn't destroy a father's relationship with his friends, family and his children. Sage knew Karen didn't understand because she hadn't told anyone the entire story.

"Maybe you're right. Kris seems to be nice I could proceed with caution."

"Proceed with caution indeed. I mean he can't be as bad as those jokes at that health club we went to last month."

"Or the fools on the cruise last summer."

They both laughed thinking of the misfits they had met throughout the last year and the conversation continued after they ordered pizza for their Friday night dinner.

Chapter 11

Karen left around eleven. Sage thanked her for the company and assured her friend that she would call her if she needed her over the weekend. They agreed to talk Sunday evening. Dionne hadn't called, and Sage was pleased not to have to explain what was wrong with the invitation her daughter extended to her father. Sage prepared to take a shower checking the thermostat before removing her clothes. As the water beaded on her face she allowed herself to relax in its warmth. Sage could hear Karen's voice repeating, "Let it go."

Sage completed her shower and stepped into her large master bedroom. She selected her lotion looking forward to her nightly ritual of skin care. She allowed her thoughts to drift until the nagging thought of an open invitation for Brian's guest peeped into her mind again. Sage knew she was having a difficult time dealing with Brian possibly bringing a guest. Calling Brian was not an option, but she needed to vent. She dialed Karen's number.

"Karen, are you in the bed yet?"

"I was on my way? Are you alright?"

"Yea, no, I'm mad as hell."

"Mad, about what?"

"Karen, Brian shouldn't be allowed to bring any guest to Dionne's wedding, and he knows damn well why."

Karen knew the conversation was going to be awhile. During the divorce Karen was the ear that Sage shouted into.

Karen didn't mind. Once again, she would listen as her friend explained her objection.

"Karen, I've held this shit for years. I guess it's time to do what you said."

"What I said? What did I say?"

"Let it go. I shouldn't have to hold Brian's secret. It broke up our marriage, and I held it. I'm not obligated to keep his reputation or his life in order. Damn it ruined mine. I haven't enjoyed any relationships since him. I can't trust anybody since him. You're right I need to let it go and move on."

"Does this have anything to do with Kris?"

"In a way, I shouldn't feel guilty about getting to know him. I felt awkward today when he was visiting, like he wasn't supposed to be in my home. I agreed to sell our home, so I wouldn't feel this way. Karen I didn't realize until tonight that I never invited a man to my home or cooked them a dinner here or even had sex here. I always entertained while out on a date. My kids don't live here. Why should I feel guilty about having company in my own home? Because I didn't want people thinking Brian's ex-wife was moving on. Karen, that's some warped shit. Anyway Kris wants to get to know me, and I'm hesitating because of Brian. This is… I don't even know what to say. I just need to move on."

"Sage, I think I understand, but I don't see how Brian is stopping you. I mean he's dating, I'm sure people know he has moved on."

"A couple of other friends told me they're sure he's dating but Karen, I doubt it. I mean he has his dates, but I doubt if people know anything about them and those that do have their own secrets. It's been that way for years. If I hadn't walked in on them fucking in our bed, I wouldn't have known."

Karen heard what Sage said, but as it repeated in her head, she denied hearing it each time. Sage had never told the details to anyone even her closest friend.

"In your bed? In your house? Sage, how did he? What bitch would come into your home and not know you existed? Wait! Tell me from the beginning. What did you do? How did you manage not to kill both of them? Sage, I'm so sorry I didn't know it was that serious. I mean cheating is serious in itself but in your bed, that trifling bitch."

"I can't blame anyone but his sorry ass."

"What happened?"

Karen looked at her clock noticing the time read twelve thirty. She repositioned herself in her bed and turned down the television. She was prepared to listen to Sage describe the final two years of her marriage. Sage had prepared another cup of tea thinking she would drink it and ease into sleep. She was glad Karen was willing to listen to the secret she held for eight years.

Sage began explaining the depth of her troubled marriage. She knew Karen would understand because would recognize the bits and pieces she had heard over the years. Sage told Karen there was so much she didn't know.

"Karen after those small arguments I began to think it was me. Brain let me believe I was paranoid. You know the phone calls, business meetings, over the weekend conferences. I just thought it was strange that none of it included free time, which could include me. I mean damn, there are plenty businessmen who take their wives on their business trips. You know, the wife stays at the hotel until the evening or later in the day, and they spend that time together. I didn't expect it to be every trip, but shit, he had been doing his business as usual for close to six years."

"Was it the expense? I mean, you know Brian always complained that his account for travel was too low."

"Karen, that was another excuse. And you know what, now that you mention it, he would say that shit in front of you and others, but behind closed doors he would tell me that the travel was covered. I would argue about his spending money during those trips, and he would swear he didn't have to spend any. I didn't check the accounts until I really started believing it had to be an affair. I noticed he had a change of attitude right before Trevon graduated. He stayed home during the week but on the weekends he'd leave Saturday mornings, and he'd come home Sunday morning. This went on for weeks. I decided to stop him one morning. We argued, Karen, I was tired. I loved Brian and my family, but it wasn't a marriage and I wanted to know why. Anyway I guess it was a month or maybe even a couple of weeks before Trevon's graduation when the shit hit the fan. Trevon and Dionne went to stay with my sister for the weekend. It was Trevon's gift from her. Dionne came home from school, picked up Trevon, and they met Sierra on Friday. I called Brian and told him I wouldn't be home until late. It seemed strange that he didn't ask questions but that's the way the marriage was going. He called about seven thirty, and I told him I was still dealing with clients, I can't remember the name of that group we were dealing with then. They came in from out of town looking to build near the interstate."

"I know who you're talking about. The secretary was Carol Hedding, girl I can't think of the name. I remember the week with them though." Karen smiled thinking about the successful connections they made after that deal.

"Yeah, Carol Hedding, you're right. Remember we had that long meeting and then took them for dinner and drinks? Well, he called as we were leaving the office. I know now he was time checking. He knew the house was empty, and he had brought his friend over for drinks I guess. He must have done it before because he didn't have any problems asking how long I would be and then assuring me there was nothing wrong and take my time."

"Wait, Sage. You didn't stay long. What time did you tell him?"

"That's just it. I didn't give his ass a time. I sat there at that table and the longer I sat the more my stomach turned. I wasn't getting sick I was getting mad. You know that angered stomach feeling. My nerves were flaring and for some reason, I knew it was from his call. I needed to go home, but Karen, I never asked him where he was calling from. I didn't know he was at the house. It was strange. I just knew I needed to go home."

"And you walked in on him and that bitch!"

"Listen, I drove home slowly. I didn't even know why I was taking my time. The closer I got to the house, the more my stomach churned. Brian's car was in the driveway; it was about nine thirty. It was at least two hours after he called me. There was a strange fragrance of a cologne or air freshener that hit me when I entered the living room. Two glasses were on the table but there wasn't any sign of who had been drinking with Brian. I figured he had a friend over which explained the smell, and they had left because no one was downstairs. I went into the kitchen got a glass of juice and went upstairs to go to bed. My stomach was still turning, and I really thought it was stress."

"Tell me this fool didn't hear you coming."

"Well, I guess it was getting good then and that's why they didn't hear me. My bedroom door was closed, which seemed strange. Brian knew Trevon was gone for the weekend so the house was ours. I began thinking, why would he close the door? I pushed the door open. They were fucking right in my bed. I don't know who the man was, but he was humping my man right in my bed. Brian was on his knees, his eyes were closed and his mouth was wide open. The man had mounted him and was about to nut, his eyes were closed too. Neither of them noticed me in the door and this man began to moan. I could tell this wasn't the first time, they were too comfortable with each other. It was sickening. Karen he was speeding up the rhythm when I yelled, what the fuck is this? Girl he pulled out his dick and it exploded all over Brian's back and my sheets. Brian turned over hard as hell holding his damn dick and had the nerve to ask, what was I doing home? The man stood up with sperm dripping telling me how sorry he was, and he didn't know we were still together. Some shit about Brian telling him we were going through a separation or divorce. I don't remember his exact words. Girl both of them went limp dripping fucking sperm everywhere. I was so stunned, tears just rolled from my face."

"Sage, a man? Fucking Brian?"

Karen couldn't believe her ears. Brian always seemed quiet more like the mellow man. She never would have thought of him as a bisexual. He had been with Sage for years, and she was sure they had an active sex life. Karen's thoughts went from how many times, were there others both male and female, and what about disease? She realized why Sage had gone through nights of anger, frustration and tears. Karen knew now why she hadn't let it go.

Sage laughed a little before answering.

"A good looking man too. Girl after we were divorced, I stopped questioning why Brian was with that man and started asking why a man like that wanted Brian."

Karen laughed at her comment.

"A looker, huh?"

"Girl, a looker. Brian tried to explain the shit the rest of the night. What was there to explain? In our home, our bed and a man, too much, I was done. The marriage was on the rocks 'cause Brian claimed he wasn't satisfied. Karen I had begun to question my womanhood before that night. I was confused, was it, I wasn't enough woman for him, or that he wanted a man. I felt like I couldn't satisfy his ass if I wanted to. Then I didn't know if it just about the sex or what. I mean he didn't dress as a woman or act like one, but he wanted to have sex like one? I was confused. We talked whenever I thought about it. Brian made sure of that. He didn't avoid anymore questions and tried to do anything to keep me happy. Oh, after that he was willing to travel, take off work, stay home with me, girl, he became my puppet."

"Okay, I remember you saying he changed because you caught him. Girl, I just can't believe he was with a man."

"I don't even know how many. Karen for all I know he could have been having sex with men throughout our entire marriage. I was so in love I didn't think he was cheating. Then when the thought entered my mind, I sure as hell didn't think it was a man."

"Who would?"

"But here's the burden of it all. Brian agreed finally that we needed to decide what we were going to do. Supposedly, he was willing to be the husband I wanted in and out of bed. We could move on and put this in our past. We could also separate allowing me to heal from my pain and hurt or go to counseling and take it day by day. The last decision was to separate and ultimately get a divorce. The stipulation of the divorce would be that I didn't ruin his relationships with our children, families, and friends. I couldn't see myself living the rest of my life wondering if another man was with my husband. I agreed to an immediate divorce."

"Damn, Sage, girl I don't know what to say. He wants to bring this guy to the wedding?"

"I doubt if they're still together. The relationship didn't last long after that night. He claims the man left him after he found out he was still with me. I accused him for at least a year after that night of going out to meet Mr. Drip."

"You never found out his name or where he was from."

"I should have. No, just joking. He claimed he met most of the men he dealt with through this escort place. I never heard of males having male escorts but I guess it's possible. Brian claimed they were totally discreet and signed papers to keep everything on the DL. Karen, it was pathetic. All I could think of was how many women didn't know their man was seeing these escorts behind their backs."

"Have you ever tried calling the place?"

"No, I thought about it a few times, but I didn't want to know who they were or who the clients were. Brian claimed a lot of them did it for the money, but I just didn't believe any man would escort another man anywhere for money."

"Shit, I need to hit that spot."

"Karen, they might be gay. Stay away from it."

They both laughed.

"So, who is he talking about bringing?"

"He said it wasn't his idea. I know he didn't argue when Dionne told him. He knows how I feel about this. Brian can't possibly use that day to come out. He'll ruin Dionne's day. Dionne and Trevon don't know, and I don't want her wedding day to be the topic of gossip for years. So I need to be ready for his ass. He doesn't think I'm dealing with anyone. He thinks it's because I can't get over him or so that's what Dionne tells him. It's not that Karen and I guess that eats at me too. I need to make him understand that I don't trust him, and I do date off and on. I have moved on and I'm content with the way things are."

"And frustrated, Sage, letting it go means just that. Every man ain't Brian. Allow yourself to get to know them and if your personalities don't match move on."

"Karen, I don't want to wonder whether or not they get with men? I mean what do I do? One night over dinner just say, 'By the way, do you have sex with men'? That's a problem."

"The chances we take."

"I don't know. But I know Brian damn near sent me over the edge, and I won't let him get me again."

"Let go, girl. Date Kris for a minute by June you'll know whether or not he's on the DL. Take him to the wedding or flaunt him as your man before then and let the news get to Brian. If Kris is what we think, girl, he's a good catch."

"I was thinking about that. He is nice and he is packing. I don't know though Karen, I really need that question answered up front."

"So ask him. And how do you know he's packing?"

"Karen, don't try it, I can't ask that man that, and you looked him over too. The brother is holding."

"So you better work quickly. I may size him up."

Sage shook her head.

"Karen you won't get the chance. I'm letting go."

Chapter 12

The months passed quickly and Sage began working with Dionne on finalizing the guest list. It was agreed that the parents would get invitations for keepsakes and wouldn't be expected to send a response. Sage told her they would need to know if Brian was bringing a guest for the count to be accurate. Dionne didn't question Sage about her bringing a guest assuming she didn't have a date for the day. Jarad's father was still battling sickness, but it was certain he would probably be able to attend the wedding, which was now three months away. Dionne noticed a change in her mother's attitude and her schedule. Sage wasn't home as often, and they spoke more on the cell phone than she had in the past years. Whenever Dionne would ask her mother what was new, Sage would reply she was finally learning to let go.

Sage didn't bother to introduce Kris to Dionne, just as she hadn't introduced any of her male friends since the divorce. Sage wanted to be sure Kris would be around awhile. Kris was one of the few men that she could talk with and enjoy his company without the thought of him pushing her toward the bed. She had been tempted to ask him about his sexual preferences to ease her mind, but there was a part of her that was scared to hear the answer.

She hadn't mentioned her daughter's wedding to Kris, but she did decide to talk to Dionne about him.

Dionne was on her way to her mother's house. They had to finalize the plans with the florist, bridal shop, and the reception hall. The coordinator would take over once the plans were finalized.

Karen and Sage were waiting for Dionne having breakfast and coffee. They stayed up late going over monthly figures for the Berger Group. Sage invited Karen to tag along with her and Dionne. She would be her support when she told Dionne about Kris. They both agreed Dionne might not take the news of Kris and Sage's dating well.

The weather was slowly changing. It was late April and the temperature had hit the high sixties without the normal April showers. The first appointment was at ten o'clock and Dionne told her mother she would be at the house by nine. Karen and Sage rushed to shower and get ready but slowed down to eat when they found out Dionne had overslept and would be there between nine thirty and nine forty five. "That girl is gonna be a nervous wreck by June. Karen do you want another cup of coffee?"

"Yea, thanks. I thought the coordinator would be more helpful."

"Karen, Dionne wants to do everything. The coordinator gave her a time line. She was so busy doing things the way she wanted now what should have been done isn't. All of these decisions are last minute. She could have taken care of this when she was telling Brian he could invite a guest. Now the guest list is done and she already mailed the invitations three months before the wedding. You know damn well some people are gonna forget to mail those things back. Ms. Dionne jumped the gun but she didn't finalize all this other stuff so that girl could do her job."

"Well, I guess it's just the bridal jitters Sage. I mean you know that Dionne is a perfectionist. If something goes wrong she doesn't want to think she could have prevented it."

"That's just it. Something always goes wrong at weddings, funerals, any event like that. That's why you put people in place to help you handle it. When your emotions are involved you forget things, and don't think straight. Dionne should have followed those guidelines. The only thing she should still be doing is fittings. That's it. But she's hard headed Karen."

"Have you heard from Trevon?"

Karen agreed with Sage but preferred to change the subject before Sage would be too angry to help Dionne get through the day.

"Yea, they're fine. He'll be here the week before. I think he took off two weeks. That way Lynn can visit her family with the kids while they're up this way?"

"Where do her parents live now?"

"In D.C., I think. Yea, D.C. they own a nice home there."

"So Ms. Thing, how's it going with Mr. Randall?"

"Girl, too good, I really thought things would die down after the closing of the strip properties. I really thought he was playing that game, and I played it too. The calls slowed down for about a week, but he said he went to D.C. to handle some family business. He still called though. We talked about our past jobs and touched a conversation or two about past relationships and our families. He knows now that I'm divorced and have two children. He's been close to the altar and doesn't have any children."

"How old is he?"

"He's forty five."

"Forty five, and no kids?"

"I know girl, you know I threw up the red flag. He said no kids without marriage. I guess he intends on marrying some young girl 'cause, I don't know any woman our age who wants to get married and have babies."

"Yea, you're right. They may want to get married but having babies and reaching fifty at the same time is a bit much."

"Anyway, he has three nephews and a niece. His parents are still living but his sister and brother-n-law died in an accident five years ago. His parents are raising the children."

"Wow. I guess he doesn't want kids. How old are the children?"

"I don't remember if the girl is the youngest but the youngest is seven. I think the oldest is thirteen."

"Yeah, he probably has his hands full from time to time. Where do they live?"

"D.C. that's where they live now. He said his parents were moving to Virginia this year. He wanted us to go and look at a couple of spots for them next month. They probably won't move until the end of the school year. He's a family man in the sense of the word but so was Brian."

"Girl there you go, making comparisons. Let it go."

"Let what go? Mom you've been saying that a lot lately."

Dionne had walked into the kitchen without Sage and Karen noticing the front door opening or closing. They gave each other the look knowing the conversation was gonna touch Brian's secret in the next sentence or two. Sage smiled and hugged her daughter as she put the dishes in the sink. Dionne turned from her mother and kissed Karen on the cheek.

"I made you a little breakfast. I know we have to be there by ten so you can make a bacon and egg sandwich and take it with us if you want."

"No mom that's okay. I'll eat it here. The bridal shop is opening at eleven. The lady called to say someone broke the key in their lock. They're waiting for a locksmith. She'll call if they can't get in by eleven."

"Are your girls meeting you there too?"

"Only three of them, I think the others went there yesterday. Aunt Karen did Melissa get her shoes yet?"

"Girl, Melissa got everything you asked her to get. She's done. I don't think we'll have to worry about her gaining any weight."

They all laughed. Melissa, Karen's daughter was weightless. She was so excited about being in the wedding she couldn't wait for the first fitting. Of all the bridesmaids Melissa didn't need to go back for another fitting. The seamstress pinned her dress at the first fitting and told her to come for the final fitting in May. Dionne told them the men had it easy. Jarad hadn't run around as much as she had and didn't volunteer to run with her.

"Dionne the men show up that's it. Tell her Sage, half of the time they're recovering from hangovers the morning of the wedding."

"That's right, that's when the drama begins. As the wife you won't hear about it until the ceremony is over but those men party hard before the wedding. They look at it as the last hurrah."

"Dionne, that's the bull too. They go out regularly with their boys after they get married."

"Aunt Karen, why didn't you get married?"

"Who knows, I was never asked. Melissa's father can't slow down long enough to settle down, and I never thought about marrying anyone else."

"Karen, you're joking right?"

"Girl, you know we always have that love we never get over. I guess he was it."

Dionne and Sage smiled as they said together. "Let it go." Karen paused in thought and joined the laughter. They left the house and began their day of appointments talking about relationships.

"Kris Randall?"

Dionne repeated the name, as though she heard it before. Sage felt a twinge hoping her daughter didn't know something about the man she was dating. Karen had the same thought. *"Could Dionne know Kris?"* Neither Sage nor Karen interrupted Dionne's thoughts. She repeated the name again saying it slightly above a whisper. Sage couldn't hold her question any longer.

"Dionne do you recognize his name?"

"I don't remember where. I don't know it might be a coincidence. So where did you guys meet."

Sage gave her a quick update of the past three months leaving out the conversation with Brian that ignited her reasons for dating Kris. They had been to dinner, a couple of shows, the movies and lunch. Sage didn't give details about their conversations and was vague about any mention of her feelings.

"So is he the man in your life now?"

"Dionne what does that mean? He's a friend. Someone I can talk to, and enjoy on a personal level."

Karen knew the questions were going to get deeper. She hoped it wouldn't lead to an argument. She realized now why Sage invited her as a buffer.

"Enjoy on a personal level, that's a good way to put it. So you've found someone you relate to. I guess it's about time to as you say, let go. Did you tell daddy?"

"Tell him what?"

"That you've got a friend that you can enjoy on a personal level."

"Dionne your father and I are divorced. He didn't call me to tell me who he was enjoying even when he was married to me. Your father cheated on me. I don't need his approval to date or enjoy anyone."

Karen needed to ask Sage had she and Kris got busy. The way the conversation was going it sounded as though Dionne thought they had.

"Let's drop the subject. It's not my business anyway. You're grown. Let go if you want."

"Listen Dionne, your father lives his life, and you embrace it including his friends. You even told him to feel free to bring a guest to the wedding. I tell you I have begun to date, and you sound disgusted. I don't understand you."

Sage was getting upset and Karen didn't know when to cut in. Dionne didn't respond to her mother's comment. Sage was right she wasn't upset about her father but hearing her mother was actively dating made the divorce a reality for her. Throughout the years that her parents had been apart Dionne never thought of them as divorced. She pulled into the parking lot of Elegant Bridals and hoped the conversation hadn't ruined their day.

Chapter 13

Kris had phone calls to return. Staying in D.C. for two weeks made it difficult to handle his clients in Baltimore. His work with investors was increasing rapidly since the strip mall deal was finalized. The Berger Group helped Kris secure his position with his top investors. He began his business as a Real Estate Investment Liaison three years after the death of his sister. He used monies left to him from his sister's insurance to start his office in Washington, D.C. Business was slow in the beginning but picked up as the real estate market opened in the surrounding areas. The property values in Baltimore fit the margins for most of his clients and Kris looked into opening his second office. The problem was his profits weren't quite enough to pay staff, hire new staff and start another office. Kris spent a lot of time treating investors to dinner, lunch and taking business trips to meet those who were out of state prospects. His close friend, Greg told him there was a way to make the money to open the second office doing what he already did.

Kris reviewed his messages and the number of Tempting Escorts came across the screen four times. Greg had been right. The money Kris made through the escort service filled the gaps and within eighteen months he had made enough to start his office in Baltimore and get a second condo close by. He owned a BMW and a Durango and kept a vehicle at both homes. His profits from the last month proved he could quit his job at the escort service. The thought crossed his mind after he began dating Sage. He didn't want her finding out what his part time employment was. The explanation wasn't simple. Most women found it unusual for a man to want a serious relationship if they worked as an escort at night.

Greg's number was on his machine and he needed to talk to his friend about his decision. It was close to twelve. Greg would be at the gym. He would meet him there. As he grabbed his keys from the kitchen counter the phone rang. Kris picked up the receiver without looking at the name on the neon lit panel.

"Hello?"

"Hello. How are you Kris?"

"Oh, hey. I'm on my way out can I call you from my car?"

"Listen, is it something I said. I mean me wanting to see you more can't scare you that much. We've gone out a few times, and I thought we kicked it pretty well."

"It was business. I was merely an escort, nothing more."

"You gave me your home number and your cell number. That had to mean something."

"I believe I gave you the number when I was coming in from D.C. You claimed it was too late to get someone else. They called me, I accepted, but I was stuck in traffic. The numbers were for us to coordinate times. That's how I remember it, no more, no less. I told you escorting is purely business for me, no relationships, no foreplay, no overnights."

"Your business charges enough for it to cover it all."

"That's up to them. I get my cut. Listen you can call back and get someone who will fulfill your fantasies. I'm sorry it won't be me."

"So that's why it's called tempting. They get brothers like you to bait us in and then drop us onto someone else."

Kris sighed and shook his head. He knew the first time he wrote his information on the form, prior to being hired, this type of conversation would happen with a client. He had broken the rule. He gave the client his contact information. It wasn't forbidden, but it was one of the warnings he got from Greg. Usually Greg would take on clients that Kris refused to get personal with. Greg wouldn't touch this one.

"Listen we need to talk. They're a few investors that I met that know you. I don't think they know you're an escort. Let's just say they don't know yet. Don't say no to me yet Kris. I could steal gold from the gold mine you've built for yourself. Anyway I don't want much. You to be my escort, get to know me better, and if I decide it's not working you'll be on your way. I'm just asking for a chance with you. Not much to ask considering what you could lose. I don't know too many investors that would understand why you're in the escorting business, unless you fulfill some of your own pleasures. I think that's what you're scared of, me fulfilling your pleasures, and you fulfilling mine. It could be fun. What time should we meet? Say five?"

"Five is fine. You're right we need to meet and get this straight. You're not going to blackmail me. As far as what I do to fulfill my pleasures, you'll never know."

"Kris let's just say if I don't find out, your investors will know."

The phone went dead. Kris hated adult games, especially when his livelihood was at risk.

Chapter 14

Greg grabbed his gym bag and met Kris in the parking lot. They shook hands while walking to the car. Greg got into Kris's car on the passenger side, pushing the seat back to accommodate his long legs. Kris let both windows down and began talking about the phone call he received. He explained that the profits were more than enough to maintain the two offices, and he should have gotten out before receiving this call from a lonely client. Greg didn't make any comments. Kris told him when he moved to Baltimore, he would work for the escort service until he could run both offices without the extra funds. Greg didn't want to lose an escort, but he knew Kris was a temporary hire. Greg owned the escort service and had been in business for more than ten years. The money had increased rapidly with the growth of his clientele in both the Baltimore and D.C. area. Occasionally, Greg would escort the clients for his own entertainment. He employed both male and female escorts and the money was paid to the service prior to the date.

"I don't want any problems with my business or my personal life. Greg I'll deal with this guy today but when can I fill out the papers to quit?"

"They're no papers to fill out man. I'll talk to Lamont or Sharonda tonight. They'll pull your name from the computer and file your profile. If you want to come back you update it and they reload your information into the computer. It's simple shit. I hate to see you leave us though. We made good money off your ass."

"That's the problem. Clients think they pay for my ass. At least this one does."

"Who is it? Tell me it's that damn Tracy. She asks for me all the time to talk about you. I'm surprised that in the heat of the moment that she doesn't call your name. It's the shit that these clients fantasize about that keeps them coming back though. Look at it this way, you're a great fantasy."

"Shit, give me Tracy then. You're bisexual, you take this damn nut off my hands."

"I asked you who is it?"

"Brian Drakeford, that brother that Simone tried to talk to. Simone said they usually meet after I drop his ass off, and she does her thing but that's not what he implied was his cup of tea today. He wants to get to know me. Greg man I do many things but not with a man between, on or under the sheets."

Greg smiled. Kris had told him the same thing when he found out the escort service was available for both men and women. It was the choice of the client who their escorts would be and according to the profile the escorts were selected. There were times that the clients would call making requests for who they wanted. After three months Kris Randall was on the top-ten request list for both male and female clients. The basic fee for males escorting males or females escorting females was a higher rate. Fees for the after hours were purely up to the escort and had nothing to do with the agency. Kris didn't go beyond being the escort for dinner, business functions, corporate dances, etc. even when the client was a female.

"So what do you think this guy wants?"

"I'll see at five. I don't want to lose my relationship with Sage. I have a business base that is growing, and now I have this gay ass client who thinks I want to be his boy toy. Greg, c'mon why not date this guy for me. Give him a lesson in after hour treats."

Greg and Kris had been friends for more than ten years. Greg knew Kris was straight. He had no interest in men. Greg bailed him out many nights when male clients wanted to test his obvious resistance to staying with them over night. Greg had his choice when the appointment request came through.

"You know my rule. I don't touch pushy men. They think they're the shit. I wish I knew your secret. You don't touch them, and they flock to you. What type of shit is that?"

"I don't know I'll find out at five."

"Kris the more I think about it, the more I'm wondering what other problems this may bring. Tempting Escorts could catch some heat behind Brian and his bullshit. We keep all personal business confidential, if clients or the escorts feel their personal business is not protected we lose. I can't afford for that to happen. He's talking about going to your investors, and some of them are clients. This shit could get ugly. Let me do some research. A little heat under his tight ass may stop his mouth from flapping."

"I'm lost Greg. What are you talking about?"

"He's threatening to expose you like you're hiding something. Well, your part in this can be explained, you escort the clients referred to you. But that brother has secrets too. I mean think about it, he calls often, which means he's probably not in a relationship and probably not openly gay. His file can tell me more, and then I'll do some probing. Do me a favor let this linger a few days? Put him off a minute while I check his ass out. Once you can throw his shit in his face he may change his mind about talking to anyone."

"I guess you're right if he knows the investors, I know it's on a business level. Alright I'll give you a couple of days, but I don't want this guy thinking I'm on the DL or interested in his ass at all.

Greg I think I better talk to Sage about this shit too. She's a realtor. Suppose she knows this asshole or someone he deals with. I don't want her to be shocked if she hears about this."

"Yea, that's a good idea. That's one person that he won't be able to use against you if you tell her what's going on. Make this left man, I need to stop at the store."

"How'd you get to the gym?"

"Doug dropped me off. I'm sick of his ass. I told him before that I ain't into swapping or the swing thing. His ass got mad 'cause I didn't show up at that party Tasha threw."

"That's what was going on at the party?"

"Everything was going on at the party. I love her parties but Doug can't expect me to watch him roll his tight ass around with every swinging dick there."

"Damn, I missed that one."

"You wouldn't have liked it. You're straight it was for gays and bisexuals. They play games and you deal with one sex or the other. Kris we both know you don't like the other."

"Tell that to Brian. Is that the only kind of parties she gives? I heard about a few, but they didn't mention swinging."

"She gives them all, twice a month. She makes good money throwing them. There's entertainment, sometimes a dinner, and sometimes it last for the weekend."

"Hmmn ... I think my days for that kind of shit is over. Plus it's too open. A smaller group may be fun but then even that can bring problems."

"You're right I go once in a blue moon. But that damn Doug is addicted. He goes once a month faithfully. It's okay with me, I just ain't watching his ass on everyone."

"You should go once and let him watch your ass."

"Only if it was with you, my friend."

"Fuck you Greg."

"Please do."

They both laughed. Greg met Kris at a party where they both disliked the crowd. They left and went to another club nearby talking and drinking for more than half the night before Greg told Kris he was interested in both men and women. Greg teased Kris often but understood his friend had no desire to be romantically involved with men. They remained close friends over the years sharing problems and celebrations. Kris parked in the plaza where Greg got out the car to go to the store.

"Thanks man. Look, call me after you meet Mr. Drakeford. I'll call the office and have the file pulled. By the middle of next week, I should have enough to shut his damn mouth. Just stall for a week, duck him or date him find out about him while he's peeping you."

"Greg man I don't want to date his punk ass. And I don't know how long I can stall him. Do what you got to do. I'll call you and tell you how this so called meeting goes."

"Alright, call me."

"Gotcha, later man."

Chapter 15

Kris didn't bother to change clothes for the meeting with Brian. He wasn't trying to impress a client or get paid. Brian Drakeford wasn't meeting an escort he paid for in advance. He was meeting a man that didn't want to be involved with another man. The light at the corner of Main Street gave Kris a reason to slow down and think about what Greg was asking him to do. He realized waiting for Greg to get information about Brian may take a while. He shook his head at the thought of how the conversation with Sage would go. Kris and Sage had begun to get close. Neither of them mentioned a "relationship" but they did enjoy each other's company. Kris felt a lot different about Sage then he had with other women. Sage attracted Kris's attention by allowing him to win her over. She didn't go out of her way to impress him. He didn't expect her to act different if they dated for months or years. Sage had been real with him, since they met. Lately, she was more relaxed, but she still was all woman; sexy and professional, bold and beautiful and if necessary stern but not rude. The light turned green as Kris dialed Sage's number on his cell.

"Hey Ms. Lady."

"Mr. Randall, how are you today?"

"I'm okay. What are you doing later? I know you said you had a full day but can I occupy some of your time this evening. Before you say no I really could use a friend to talk to."

"Can I call you back when I'm free? I can't give you a time yet."

"Just say you'll save me an hour or two. I don't care about the time."

"Kris, are you okay?"

"Yea, I'm fine but I need to talk with you about something serious."

"Oh, uh, okay, I'll call you when I'm on my way home."

"Thanks. Listen, don't let this ruin the rest of your day. It's nothing devastating, I just need an ear and yours are beautiful."

"Yea, now you've got me wondering what's up."

"Sage, trust me. I just want to talk. I need you to know something, and I don't want it to come from someone else. It's nothing about me that … well let's just say if you listen to me, you'll see it doesn't affect us at all. It's just a precaution."

"I'll be sure to call you then. Other than that how was your trip to D.C."

"Other than that it was uneventful. The kids are fine; my parents are good. I didn't get time to handle any business deals. So I guess it was a vacation."

"You stayed with your parents?"

"No, the kids stayed with me while my parents handled some legal matters; something to do with my brother-n-law's family. I don't get too involved with that."

"But everything's okay right?"

"Yea, as far as I know. Listen, I've got to see a client, and then I'll be home. I'll wait for your call."

"You're working today?"

"No, that's the problem, pushy clients. We'll talk about it, though I need your input. Anyway I see them coming this way. I'll talk to you later."

Kris hung up after Sage told him goodbye. Brian was walking toward his car and for the first time in years Kris felt like fighting.

Chapter 16

Karen watched Sage's attitude change again. Dionne had grabbed her emotions earlier and now a phone call that caused her to respond with a smile ended with in serious mood change. Karen waited for Sage to say what the problem was. The appointments were met and despite the difference of opinions about Sage's dating, the three women had a productive day. Dionne talked about the problems with the bridesmaid's dresses hoping they all would be handled in time for the final fitting. The shoes were another disaster. Two of the girls couldn't find their sizes. The cake was the easiest of all the appointments until they found out the delivery would have to be earlier than expected. They went to the reception hall to finalize the menu and spoke with an assistant who couldn't find the couple's initial request form. Dionne settled the matter by putting in a new form. In the confusion, she forgot to tell them about the cake and decided to let the coordinator handle that problem.

Sage told Dionne something came up, and she needed to go home and check the paperwork for a client. Karen not realizing it was an excuse prodded Sage the entire ride to her house asking what the problem was. Sage and Karen got out of Dionne's car while promising to call her later.

After entering the house, Sage got two glasses and filled them with wine. She handed Karen a glass and went to the living room with Karen close behind her.

"Sage, what the hell is going on?"

"Kris called. He said he needed a friend to talk to. Something he didn't want me to hear from someone else; something that if I listened wouldn't affect us. Karen I don't have time for that surprise, "I got baby mama drama"; or "My ex just doesn't understand" or one better, "I'm gay". Girl, I can't stand for another round of guess what I am."

"Sage, what makes you think that's what it is?"

"Why would he say I need to listen and for it not to affect us? That's the bullshit right there Karen, that's the bull!"

"Sage, you're getting mad over something you don't even know for sure. That's what I'm talking about. You can't compare every-thing to the past. It may not be anything like that. Kris may just need to talk about what's going on with his mother and the kids. Maybe he's getting the kids."

"I hadn't thought about that Karen. He did mention his par-ents took care of some legal matters with his brother-n-law. Okay, I see your point. He told me to call him. But wait no, he mentioned a client too. Something about this pushy client he had to meet."

"See you jumped to conclusions. That doesn't sound like kids or another woman."

"I don't know. Karen, I just don't want a relationship with secrets hiding in the closet."

"Brian was in the closet. I don't think Kris is the closet type."

Chapter 17

Brian suggested they talk at the diner on the Boulevard. There always were plenty of people there, and he knew Kris didn't want to be alone with him. He would wait to hear Kris's reasons for not pursuing a relationship before he would make his threat clearer. Kris drove to the diner with little to say and turned the radio up letting Brian know he didn't want to hold a conversation. He parked his BMW in the parking lot and didn't hesitate to get out of the car. Two females were walking to a nearby car and smiled at Kris as they passed him. Kris acknowledged them with a nod and a soft hello as Brian walked past giving the women a stern look. The women quickly moved on shaking their heads at Kris. Kris realized they thought he was Brian's date.

"Brian, cut the shit or there won't be a discussion."

"What? I called the meeting and just remember that. You're not here to pick up anybody. If this is too open, we could go to my place."

"That won't happen."

Kris opened the door and let it go causing Brian to catch the door or be hit by it. Brian realized Kris would have to be convinced the relationship had its benefits including his maintaining his investor's accounts. The hostess gave them a table near the window where they could watch the traffic on the Boulevard drive by. Kris was pleased with the seating. It gave him another direction to look while talking with Brian.

"Can I get your drinks before you order?"

"Yes, I'll have a Corona with lime."

Brian looked at Kris, as though he had done something wrong.

"I'll have a Pepsi."

"I'll bring your drinks would you like me to take your order now?"

"Thank you. We'll order now can you tell me your specials?"

Kris shook his head and looked out the window as the waitress went down the memorized list of specials for the day. Kris had no intention on ordering a meal. He couldn't deal with Brian for an entire week. That would cause a problem. He would tell Greg forget his plan if it was going to take any longer than the next few days.

"Sir would you like to order?"

"No, the Corona will be all for me."

The waitress left the table taking the menus and promising to bring the drinks.

"Kris, you've got to be kidding. You loved the steak here, you said so yourself. You should have ordered it."

Kris leaned forward toward Brian hoping not to be too loud with his response.

"Brian, I'm not for your fucking games. I will not be eating a meal with you like we're on some damn date. I am not your friend, associate or acquaintance. That's the first thing you need to understand. Secondly, I no longer work for Tempting Escorts, so I won't be your escort to your faggot affairs either."

"Kris, this is not about Tempting Escorts. I want to be at least an acquaintance. You'll want me to be yours too. I mean if we can't start there you'll find some problems with your business relationships."

"Brian, are you so hard up that you want someone who doesn't want you?"

"You want me or someone like me. You're one I call border line. You haven't decided yet but you're more than curious. Think about it why would you, a fine strapped man like yourself escort men if you weren't interested in them in some way?"

"I told Greg this shit wouldn't work. I don't like men. I love the money you fucking punks pay and that's it. I love women. I date women and I fuck women. You've got me wrong sweets. There's no room in my business or my life for you or the life you live."

"I think you'll change your mind. Kris, I'm just asking you to try it. We get along fine. It's like any other relationship, we just need time to get to know each other."

"I don't like women who chase me. I like to do the chasing. So even if I had an interest just you begging would turn me off. So what is this ultimatum you keep throwing at me? You'll tell who? Who do you know?"

"There's a few of your investors that are gay my friend. You don't like gays and you're animate about it. They may want to know about your "faggot campaign"."

"I don't dislike gays. I am heterosexual. I don't want a man chasing me for a relationship outside of friendship or business. You're not my type, I wouldn't want you as a friend. And yes I do have gays that are my friends. I am secure in my sexuality, and I don't invade anyone's rights to choose who they want to be with. But you my man have chosen the wrong one."

Brian waited until the waitress left the table. She brought his salad and their drink. Brian put his napkin in his lap and smiled. Kris shook his head in disgust and looked out of the window.

"Give me one more date. Escort me to bed; sleep with me Kris. You're curious. I know you are. Let me answer your questions. I'll pay you; if you can walk away afterward, I won't say a thing."

Kris stood up. Brian stopped eating and waited for Kris to speak. Kris downed the rest of his beer and left the table. Brian laughed to himself as he watched Kris exit the diner to the parking lot. The waitress returned to the table bringing Brian's meal.

"Would your friend like another beer?"

"No baby, something came up. He had to leave."

Chapter 18

reg phoned Sharonda. He told her the file for Brian Drakeford was to be put on hold until further notice. This hold
would eliminate him from requesting any escorts including Kris. It was a formality Greg developed when escorts or the
agency had problems with clients. Once the problem was handled
the file would be released. Greg had decided Brian's file would be
removed permanently. Sharonda listened as Greg explained what
the problem was and that he would need her to call a few friends
that loved to do background investigations. Sharonda agreed the
matter was urgent. She promised to call him later with baseline
information. Greg knew Sharonda would be calling a few of the
clients that were detectives or officers. They would agree that a client that was willing to blackmail the escorts for whatever reason
was a risk to everyone.

A lot of the male clients were still on the DL. The clients were
in various professions ranging from ministers, doctors, and police
to sanitation workers and the men from the nearby military base.
Tempting Escorts had never had a problem with any client's information being kept confidential and Greg understood Brian's threat
could ruin his business. Before Greg ended his call with Sharonda
he asked for Brian's contact number.

Greg looked at his watch and thought twice about dialing Brian's cell phone number. It had only been two hours since Kris was to meet Brian. He needed to wait for Kris to call him but he was becoming impatient. Greg put his bags in the kitchen on the counter when he got home and decided to past the time now by unpacking them. The light on his phone was flashing, an indication he had messages.

Greg pushed the button to listen to the messages and continued to unpack the bags.

" Greg, call me man. I almost lost it. That punk ass faggot almost caused me to go to jail. I'm not waiting for you to find information on this guy. I don't care what he tells or who he tells it to. If they don't want to do business with me after talking to his ignorant ass then I don't need their business. He's fucking crazy man. Call me!"

Greg stopped unpacking his groceries and played the message again. He dialed Kris's cell phone.

"Yeah, man listen, I don't need this bullshit man."

"Kris, what happened?"

Kris told Greg about the short meeting between himself and Brian. He repeated their conversation verbatim. When he finished he waited for Greg to respond.

"Whew, he is direct huh?"

"I got his direct. I'm telling you Greg, I don't know what I'll do to his gay ass if he even suggests that shit to me again."

"Look, this is one guy, one ass who thinks he can use his situation to control someone. He probably can't keep his love life in order because he wants control."

"I don't give two shits what he wants. It better not include me and he tells me about it. Shit. Whatever happened to "you can't have everything you want"? I told him I wasn't down with that. I tried to explain I was straight. That should have been enough. Most guys respect that. If they continue to be an associate we speak and nothing else is said. I walked out in time, cause I could tell he wanted to continue to push himself on me. Greg, that can get ugly. What's your plan? How long is it gonna take to get something on this man?"

"I just got off the phone setting things up. I talked to Sharonda about contacting our people who do the investigations."

"You investigate all your clients?"

"No, only if they become a problem. Don't pay their bill or problems that might be reported by the escorts."

"If he calls me whatever you got on him is it. I'm not waiting for a complete file to be done on his ass. I don't want to go to jail for killing this dude."

"Give me a day or two. It shouldn't take long."

"Call me when you find out something."

"I gotcha covered. I'll talk to you later."

Kris didn't feel any better. The problem needed to be solved.

Chapter 19

Sage called Karen to tell her to stay by her phone after she received Kris's call asking could he come by. Karen left Sage's house about eight o'clock and was watching a movie when her friend called.

"Girl you'll see, the problem will be small."

"I thought about it when you left, Karen it still could be an old flame. She could be the client. Who knows it could be one of the investors. There's still possibilities with problems."

"Sage, stop. He'll be there shortly just wait; you're killing yourself with those so-called possibilities. He'll talk, you listen and then…Well, then you make your decision."

"Girl, I'm not feeling this. It almost feels like that night with Brian."

"Stop comparing. Let it go. Have an ear for listening."

"Karen, I really like him. You know me, if I didn't like him I wouldn't care what he had to tell me. But Karen he is good looking, an achiever, responsible and girl I don't know what else. I was just getting to know him."

"Speaking of that, did you, and him get busy yet?"

"No, why?"

"The conversation with Dionne about a personal level; for a minute I thought you had. I think Dionne thought so too."

"No, and we've been talking for over two months. Not once Karen, he hasn't made an attempt. Shit girl here I go again. Why hasn't he made an attempt?"

"I don't know. Two months? Shit why didn't you make an attempt?"

"He could have tried something."

"Maybe you're not catching the hints."

"Karen, either you make a move, or you don't. We're not school kids."

"You've gotten to the passionate kissing right?"

"No not really. Maybe this is the "I'm not what you think" conversation.

"I don't think so. I see him as a man who is cautious. Maybe he wants to be sure on his part and yours."

"Do men do that? I mean, I remember dating and sex was the reason for the date."

"If he had attempted to lure you into the bedroom would you have gone?"

"Girl I would have turned down the sheets!"

The bell rang and Sage left the couch laughing and continuing her conversation as she went to open the door. She didn't tell Karen goodbye until she opened the door and saw Kris's face.

"Good evening Lady."

"Sir."

"I'm glad to see you."

"Hmmm."

Sage's reply caused Kris to take notice of her tone of voice. He hoped she wasn't in a bad mood. He had no idea that Sage's wall of protection was rebuilt. They walked into the living room where they both sat on the couch and Sage cut off the television. Kris attempted to smile, hoping to get a smile in return. Instead Sage sat back preparing herself to listen to Kris's problem.

"Kris, before you tell me about your situation, I think you should know something."

Kris realized Sage's attitude was her reaction to their conversation earlier. Brian Drakeford had begun to cause problems for Kris already.

"There are some things in my past that I have had a hard time accepting. I don't want to offend you, but I'm not ready to deal with a lot of drama in a relationship."

"Sage, I don't know what you're expecting me to tell you, but I can guarantee if you listen without judging me in all this, we won't have drama."

"I can't promise that I won't be judgmental. Kris, just tell me."

"To put it in simple terms, I have a client or ex-client who is trying to blackmail me."

"Blackmail, an investor?"

"No not quite. Let me start at the beginning so you'll understand fully. Whenever I came to Baltimore it was to visit a friend. I had my business in D.C. and really had no thoughts of expansion. I really couldn't afford to run two locations. My friend and I discussed it, and he showed me a few ways it could be done. One was to work part time in his business to generate the money needed. I agreed and it's been beneficial. I opened my second office here, and I decided last month I no longer needed to work for his agency. Sage, it's an escort service."

Sage moved shaking her head no and sighing. Kris stopped talking waiting for her to respond.

"Go ahead, I'm listening."

Sage was trying not to be judgmental, but it was hard not to think what Kris's evening entertainment included or what the client could use to blackmail him.

"The service is Tempting Escorts here in Baltimore City and the service is extended to both males and females. It is an elite group for business escorts, not a dating service. Someone calls for an escort for special events like conferences, programs, and dinners. Anywhere they wanted to be seen with someone on their arm. If the escort and client decide to take it further it's totally on them. It's not promoted by the agency, but it is not prohibited. Some escorts become the clients lovers go on business trips with them, you know start relationships. Anyway I worked there for close to two years when I was asked about escorting males."

"Males?"

" Yeah it goes both ways. I don't but the agency does. A male escorting a male or a female escorting a female can make twice as much. I figured I could do that and secure the second office with a financial cushion quicker. Like I said last month I decided I didn't need the extra finance any longer. My investment clientele is bringing in enough to fund both offices and my staff."

"So you escort both males and females, and you're not dating these people? I thought that was the reason for an escort service."

"The service Greg set up is a little different than I guess what you would consider the norm. A lot of politicians, people of various professions, look for people to give the public the appearance they have a well rounded social life. That includes who they come and go to events with. The escort fills out a profile form and the agency matches that with the client's specifications. My profile has quite a few "I don'ts". For example; I don't go beyond the escort. In other words, if we're going to your company's dinner, after the dinner you're escorted home, or wherever you choose but our night is over. That's for both male and female. I don't do dates outside of the escort, which is set with the agency. I don't kiss, touch or buy gifts. The exception is a female who may need an escort to a dance; I will buy a corsage or a bouquet of flowers. I don't go to dinner dances with males, and I don't pretend we're a couple."

"I'm surprised you were picked by the clients or the agency."

"I don't think I could have made those stipulations with anyone except Greg. He knows me well. I can deal with a person's sexual preferences as long as I am not the choice."

"You just lost me."

Sage realized the answer to her question was about to be explained. The question of Kris being gay could stop haunting her.

"I am strictly a woman's man, but I don't want a woman who pushes themselves on me. I don't deal with men at all on that level. So while escorting the men it was simply two friends at a business event. Although other requests were made, I would turn them down."

"And a client from this agency is trying to blackmail you?"

"Yeah, he wants a relationship, or he'll tell some of the investors that I work with that I am gay or against gays or some bull that will cause me to lose their business. Sage, I don't know what his plans are, but I can't let him think he can control who I deal with or ruin my business. So I met with this fool to tell him I am a heterosexual. He tried to tell me I was in denial and give him a chance to prove it to me."

"How would he be able to prove that?"

"Sage, excuse my language, but that ass told me to have sex with him. I almost beat the shit out of him."

"Whew, what gave him the impression that you would sleep with him? I mean, he's a client of the service. Where did you go with him?"

"A conference in Washington, it was a luncheon and dinner for architects in the region. We went to the dinner. I met him there. We went to the dinner and left. I didn't think much of it. I also went to a couple of basketball games with him, guys from his job and their clients. It was a public forum and I left right after the game. I picked him up for the games but the conversations never got personal. One mistake I made was giving him my cell and home number. I was running into traffic one night when we were going to a structural presentation for a proposed building downtown and we needed to coordinate times. I regret I did that now because for some strange reason he thought that was me taking the lead."

"You're joking right. I mean Kris you take these guys out, and you can't tell they're interested in you for more?"

"Sage I never even considered it but my eyes are wide open now. I mean I don't want to lose you or my business, but I definitely don't want my manhood questioned. "

"Kris, why haven't you made any attempts to be with me sexually?"

"I didn't want my physical desire to cloud my opinion of who you really are. I could have done that within the first few weeks of being with you. But I wanted to know if we had something outside of the bedroom. I'm sure we will please each other in bed. Sage, I guess I'm different when it comes to who I have sex with but baby it will never and has never been a man."

"So, what are you going to do?"

"I've started already. I didn't want it to get to you, and you not know the full story. I don't know what he plans on doing. I don't think me walking out of the diner and leaving him without a ride went over well. So, I can expect phone calls from a few of the investors. Greg said they're probably clients too. In the meantime, there's someone going into his background. I'm sure he has a few secrets that he doesn't want revealed."

"How did you think I would find out?"

"Gossip in the field. He's an architect, they talk to investors, realtors who know who is in his circle."

"Yeah, I guess you're right."

"I just feel better telling you."

Sage felt better too. Kris was right. It helped not to judge him while he was explaining. She didn't understand the concept of an escort service, but it seemed logical that they didn't have to be dates, unless it was agreed between the client and escort. She believed Kris. He had no reason to lie because the truth would surface. Sage respected him; he could have kept her in the dark about the situation. Kris's cell phone rang. He answered that it was Greg. He excused himself from his seat and moved into the hall. Sage took the opportunity to go into the kitchen and bring glasses for wine and ice. Over the past two months, they had many discussions about their likes and dislikes, Sage understood more about Kris being an escort than she had about Brian being on the DL. As she walked back into the living room, she could hear Kris talking.

"Double check that Greg. Her last name, yeah. This is … yeah … okay call me back."

Kris returned to his seat and looked at Sage with his own questions written on his face.

"What's wrong?'

"Sage, you said you don't want drama. Baby, there's gonna be drama if what Greg says is true."

"Drama? What, I don't understand, is there something else I should know?"

"Yeah, the client is Brian Drakeford."

Kris waited for Sage to reply. He knew she would be too shocked to respond right away. Kris didn't know if she was aware that Brian was dealing with an escort service, or that he dealt with men. Greg had told him Brian was married and divorced. His ex-wife was Sage Monroe the owner of the Berger Group.

Chapter 20

While Sage tried to collect her thoughts, Kris excused himself and went to the bathroom. Sage sat staring wondering why this was happening to her. For the past eight years, she prayed for her life to be fulfilled again with love. Over the years after her divorce, she missed that feeling the most. Sage lost her love for Brian long before she knew it. Kissing hello and goodbye had become routine; his travel and weekend outings without her had become routine; and when they did have sex it was routine. After the divorce Sage missed having a relationship with a man. She missed the warmth of a man's touch at night and knowing that he truly loved her. Kris made her twinge. Like a school girl, she blushed inside when she was around him. Sage felt she found what she had been missing. Although she wasn't quick to show her emotions, Kris was fulfilling the gap in Sage's life. She agreed this was a problem. She wished it was an ex-girlfriend. She could have dealt with that. Kris returned from the bathroom and grabbed the ice bucket to fill it with more ice.

"Lady, do you want anything from the kitchen."

"Kris, are we going to talk about this?"

"Yeah, babe, I'm going to get more ice for the wine and get myself a beer. Is there still beer there?"

"You bought beer before you left for D.C. I don't drink it so it should be there. Was that a test?"

"That's why I left it."

Kris chuckled to himself and walked into the kitchen leaving Sage to continue thinking. He had revealed his problem without keeping anything secret. Again Brian would be hoping Sage wouldn't say anything. If she didn't tell Kris what happened, he would only assume. Brian's secret was getting harder to keep. Kris returned with the ice and beer and sat next to Sage. She helped him arrange the bucket on the table with the glasses, beer and wine. Kris leaned in toward Sage and kissed her cheek. She turned to his face allowing their lips to touch. They kissed and sat back on the couch finishing a kiss that should have led them to the bedroom. As they parted Kris shook his head.

"Girl, we've got business to discuss."

Sage smiled thinking of how she reminded him in the beginning of their relationship, he was a client, and she didn't deal with her clients.

"Yeah, that business can wait a minute."

"Really, I thought it was business first with you."

"Oh, no, I mean … never mind. You're right we do need to handle this now. The other business will take some time I hope."

"Oh that business, believe me, I plan on taking my time. Now tell me about Mr. Drakeford. I don't think Greg will be able to help me as much as you can. I didn't tell Greg I was seeing you, but he does know I've done business with the Berger Group."

"So what else does Greg think is in Brian's background?"

"I don't know, he said he would call me back. Is there something else about him, we should know? Was he using the service when he was with you?"

"I don't know if it was that service. He mentioned that was where he met the men he dated. How many of them became his lovers is the question. I only knew of one."

"The one that caused your marriage to end."

"Kris it was over before I knew about it. But that's not important now. Yes, I caught him where we lived in the bed with the guy."

"Damn, he is bold, in your bed, in your house?"

"Yea, anyway, we separated and got divorced. The stipulation was that I didn't reveal who he cheated with. Most people think it was a woman. I say most because I believe some of his associates knew. I never knew many of his business associates or clients and only a few of his friends, but if they knew they didn't tell."

"So he dates through this escort service. I wonder why he didn't use a dating service?"

"Secrets, he needed it to remain secret. If it was an escort service like the one your friend has the chance of it getting out was slim."

"Unless he tells, do you know the name of the guy he was with?"

"No, I used to call him Mr. Drip."

"Mr. Drip?"

"Long story but his ass was dripping when he left."

Kris shook his head and laughed. He pictured the scene in the bedroom and knew the name Mr. Drip had to do with the position, she found her husband in.

"Sage, I don't want to pry but did you try to deal with your husband and his desires for men after you found out?"

"No, I thought seriously about it, I couldn't. We waited until my son graduated and a few weeks later he left.

"How did your children take the divorce?"

"My son rebelled. He wouldn't speak to Brian. He barely speaks to him now. I think it has to do with respect. Anyway he joined the service, and he calls me twice a week but I don't even ask if he's talked to his father. When he comes home, he tells his sister, and she calls Brian to let him know. His children love to see their grandfather and Dionne will pick them up and make sure they visit him. Now Dionne is his liaison. She will make sure he is in the loop for all family functions. It's because she doesn't know. I won't tell them the truth. If they find out…oh well it's his secret."

Sage thought about Dionne's wedding. Brian wouldn't be bringing Kris to the wedding, she would see to that. Brian had hurt Sage and she still felt the pain, whenever she thought about it. Brian was now attempting to hurt someone deeply again. His feelings hadn't been touched. Whatever they decided to do it needed to have a lasting effect on Brian's emotions.

"I haven't spent any time with him on a personal level, and I don't know how to deal with a man that way. Sage I don't want to lead this man on. Greg seems to think that if he finds out, he can't deal with me on that level he'll disappear. I don't agree. First of all, suppose he does like me resisting him. Secondly, what's to stop him from telling the investors, even if I do deal with him? I don't trust him."

"You're right. I don't trust him either. It's just something about someone who sneaks around instead of saying hey accept who I am. I would have felt better if he

came to me and said listen I love you, my children and my family, but I can't satisfy my pleasures pretending I don't want to be with a man. I don't know if that would have kept us together, but I would have respected and trusted him more after that."

"I'm glad he didn't tell you. It left room for me to get to know you, start a beautiful relationship with you, fall in love with you and whatever else the Lord has in store for us."

Sage heard his words and melted. He handed her the wine glass, and she sipped from it with a smile.

"Kris, listen to this. Can you string him along for another month or more?"

"What? Woman please, no, I don't want to be around that man."

"No listen, I think a dose of his own medicine, is in order. Dionne is getting married in June. Get him to invite you. I'll tell

Dionne I'm definitely bringing a guest. She got upset when I told her I was dating again so I know she'll disgust it with her father. He'll feel compelled to bring a guest, why not let it be you."

"What about your daughter telling him who you're bringing?"

"I'll tell her that I would feel bad if she repeated my personal business to him. Dionne will tell him I'm bringing a guest and that's it."

"I don't know Sage, he was your husband, and maybe you know how this would turn out. Let me tell you what I see; me pretending to be okay with his calling me, us going out occasionally and at times being alone with him. Now I'm trying to run a business and keep my love for you living, but my time is limited. I can't make dinners with you because I have business appointments. I'm entertaining this fool one night and a client has me tied up the following afternoon. No, I won't have you wondering who I'm with, or if I'm spending more time with Brian then I have told you. No, that's why I've never cheated. Once the woman you have feelings for knows about it, she's always wondering no matter how much she trusts you. That's why I came to you with this problem. I don't care about him and his mixed up desires and emotions. I care about us."

Sage listened to Kris talk about his love for her and his desire for a relationship. She didn't realize he felt that way about her before their conversation.

"I guess you have a point, but I still want you to escort me to my daughter's wedding."

"No, I won't do that either. I'll go with you but I don't date people I escort. And I told you I quit escorting as of today."

"Okay, but what about this thing with Brian. What are your plans?"

"I just think that if Brian was bold enough to bring that man to your house and ask me to sleep with him like that, he's had someone who is receptive to him being that way. I'll wait the day or two like Greg said and come back with something. I don't want to lead him on though. That's the problem. Gay guys are as bad as an outraged woman when they can't get what they want."

"I wouldn't know about that, but I believe you. So what about your clients?"

"Lady, I don't know. My personal life shouldn't reflect on my business, but if they believe whatever rumors Brian creates, I don't need their money. Sage if I pretend to be with Brian, I can't deny the rumors that follow."

"Kris, not to change the subject but why do you call me Lady?"

"It just stuck. For a while when I would call your office, I would describe you as the lady, who had the office to the left. I don't know you were so professional it turned me on. Lady just fits your personality. Does it bother you?"

"No, I just didn't know why. Anyway you said Greg would call you later?"

"Yeah, but enough time has been spent on Mr. Drakeford. What about that other business we wanted to attend to?"

Sage smiled. They picked up the wine and glasses as Sage led Kris to the bedroom.

Chapter 21

Lamont and Sharonda pulled the folders needed to stop Brian Drakeford from threatening Kris or anyone else at Tempting Escorts. Greg explained the damage could cause the decline of business and eventually its closing. The trio would meet at the office after the last appointment. Ten o'clock the lines went down with any emergency calls going to the twenty-four hour service. Greg provided the emergency call line for clients as well as employees.

Lamont was employed as the office manager and Sharonda handled the accounts and appointments. The two handled business differently, but they worked well together.

Sharonda mentioned her findings in the folders and Lamont remembered Brian Drakeford immediately.

"That man was trouble from the beginning."

"Lamont, I don't remember you saying he was trouble. You usually talk about problems before they start. How did he get past you?"

"He didn't. I told Greg about him. Look at his file. He was asked in the folder did he have a sexual preference for his escorts. Do you see it checked? No, he didn't check yes or no. Confused, girl, confused. Everyone who knows what they want clearly checks it."

"I didn't pay any attention to that."

"Figures, neither did Greg. Another thing, look at the appointments. Most of them are male. Let me see…..yeah, look. No females unless it was near the holidays. Family, friends you know festivities. Girl he's on the DL. But we don't discriminate, so he's a client. But he's definitely confused."

"Okay, why did you tell me to pull these other folders?"

"Give me one. Okay, let's look at this one. Carla Meadows, she was an escort. Sweet girl too, she quit shortly after she dated this confused bitch."

"Lamont who?"

"Brian Drakeford, did you at least look at the files?"

"I didn't know what I was looking for."

"Hmmmm, stick to the phones and the books. You don't know nothing about reading people. Now look. She escorted him twice and refused four times after. He probably was an ass. Anyway, the last time he called for her, it was for a private party, but he also called for…. Let me see, if I'm not mistaking that folder there."

Sharonda handed Lamont the folder she had in her hand.

"Yes, Demarest Graves. I always wondered about that name. Anyway, he was called by Brian the same night for the same party. So, you do know what type of party it was or do I have to spell it out for you."

"Two of them on the same escort?"

"Girl, where have you been? The after hours is what makes the escort."

"Greg should be here shortly. Does he know this went on?"

"What?"

"Two escorts on the same date, Lamont that can't be protocol."

"Sharonda, there's a lot about our service that isn't following the norm. Or haven't you noticed. Did you pull Kris Randall's file?"

"Yes, here it is. Did he call for him too?"

"Yea, but Kris won't do the after hour thing. Didn't Greg fill you in?"

"You confused me though with two escorts with one client. I don't understand how they fit in."

"You will girlfriend. You will."

Greg walked in the office with three sandwiches from the nearby deli. Sharonda and Lamont knew it meant the work on the files would be longer than they had expected.

"I didn't bring sodas, I filled the fridge the other day with sodas. They're still there, right?"

"What kind of sandwich did you get me? You know I don't like their roast beef. I love the..."

"Lamont, I got you the turkey breast."

"That's it sugar you got it. You're a man after my own heart."

"Don't get it twisted. I am not after your heart."

"I don't know why. You won't find another like me boo."

"The two of you are ridiculous. Let me get the plates and sodas. We can eat and look at the files."

"Just don't get the files greasy. Watch your fingers Greg. Let me pull the paperwork out, you'll make a mess."

Lamont pulled out the paperwork explaining as much as he had with Sharonda to Greg.

"The three of them went to this party and all hell broke loose. Apparently, neither of them knew the other was coming to the party. Brian had been seeing each of them after hours which of course we don't have records of. Anyway I've called Carla and Demarest, and they have agreed to talk to us about what happened."

"So, tell me what does this prove? How is it gonna help Kris?"

"Greg, they're gonna reveal his dirt."

Lamont put the paperwork back in the folders content with his findings. Sharonda and Greg looked at each other confused. They both knew Lamont knew more than he was saying.

"Lamont, what did they tell you?"

"Sharonda, you better hold your ears. You're so naïve about this it might hurt."

"Shut up Lamont. Go ahead and tell us."

"Alright."

Lamont went to the kitchen leaving Greg and Sharonda at the conference table shaking their heads. Lamont was babbling about the mustard being low and him being the only one who shopped for the office. He kept going on complaining until both Sharonda and Greg yelled from the table.

"Shut up Lamont and c'mon."

"Bring your gay ass on now."

"Lamont, keep talking about my ass, and I'll think you what a piece of it."

"You're too gay for me Lamont."

"What's too gay Greg?"

"Fellas, the files?"

"Yea, listen. Demarest said he was in love with this confused ass Drakeford. But he was abusive in the bedroom. You know, rough sex. Anyway, he was dealing with it and thought it was getting better. They had been seeing each other for more than six months. He called him for this escort to a swinger's party. Demarest didn't like the idea but didn't want Brian to go by himself. Brian agreed not to swing if he could bring another person from the escort service. Carla Meadows was his choice. Carla had been seeing Brian for about four months at the time. Demarest didn't know about their relationship. He met her at the party and the night went well until they went into one of the bedrooms. What he thought would be a simple threesome turned into mental torment. Demarest watched while Brian made passionate love to Carla. There was no sign of violence or rough sex. Demarest thought it would be the first night for his love to be appreciated. Brian rolled over to Demarest's side of the bed and began smacking his ass and treating him the same as usual. The humiliation caused him to run out of the room and the party hysterical. Brian called him for more than a week, Demarest wouldn't answer his calls. He called Demarest drunk and threatened to ruin his reputation at the job if he didn't return his call. Demarest had landed a job at Kilmore Architect and Designs with a reference from Brian. Demarest was at Brian's beckon call for weeks to follow until he got a call from Carla. She told him to file a harassment complaint against Brian. The abuse didn't stop it got worst. Demarest finally told Brian he would file a complaint. It was kept undercover over the years. The agreement was paid monthly. Demarest bought a home in Virginia and left his job."

"Damn, he's got some shit with him. Why didn't Brian stop paying him after Demarest left the job?"

"Cause Sharonda, girl where there's the smell of shit there is shit. Carla was calling Demarest because Brian wouldn't return her calls. She found out she was pregnant. Brian wasn't interested in her at all. That confused ass would call her when he thought he missed being a man. She said he would say it all the time. Some shit. Anyway, he was only with her that night to get Demarest mad. Carla told Demarest she was keeping the baby. Nine months later a baby boy was born and Demarest stood in as the Godfather. So your boy, Mr. Brian Drakeford has a child that he knows nothing about and is paying money to Demarest for years. Demarest and Carla live together in the home. Girl, living off that assholes money, I think it was more to his relationship with Demarest. I mean, why would he still be paying him?"

Greg was hoping Lamont had the information right. "How old is the child?"

"Shit Greg, I 'm not sure. Carla will tell us though."

Lamont went to the refrigerator. Sharonda gestured for the soda as she made her comment.

"He would have to be about eleven or twelve for it to really effect his reputation. I mean he's been divorced seven years. The child needs to be old enough so that it shows he was born while he was married."

"Sharonda's right, when will Carla and Demarest be ready to talk to us? I think Brian may know she was pregnant, he's paying them to keep quiet."

"They'll be waiting for your call. They would know the answers to that question. What about Mr. Drakeford?"

"Greg, what are we offering them for the information?"

"Sharonda, they just want Brian to feel the way they felt that night. Carla said she thought about child support, but since he wasn't married anymore it wouldn't have the same sting. This would and they're willing to help."

Greg smiled. He knew they had enough information to cripple Brian Drakeford. He needed to know if Sage knew about the child before the divorce. Greg knew he would be talking to Mr. Drakeford eventually. He imagined the conversation as he told Brian about his personal information. Information he wouldn't want his family and business associates to know about. Greg dialed Kris's number laughing. Sharonda gestured to Lamont and pointed at Greg. Lamont began to laugh.

"People in glass houses shouldn't throw stones."

Chapter 22

Sage couldn't believe the battle she was having with herself. She looked in her bathroom mirror and splashed water over her face. Kris laid in her king size bed waiting for her. It would be their first sexual dance together. Sage had not been intimate with a man in years. Until now she hadn't thought much about it. It was as she told Karen she felt she was still in a commitment, as though she was still married. Mentally, Sage was still bond in the bedroom to her husband. Although she knew they were divorced, and he no longer desired her, she didn't quite understand her commitment to their vows. Sage adjusted her robe and tied it wrapping her naked body. The thought of proving to Brian and Dionne, she had moved on with her life led her to dating Kris. Now she didn't know how to explain what led her to the bedroom.

Kris had been the perfect gentleman. He allowed Sage to be the lead, pacing the relationship as they learned each other's personalities. They had grown to have an understanding over the past few months and now Sage was confused. Her heart told her she was in love, her thoughts told her to wait. She pulled her hair back behind her ears and cut off the bathroom light.

Kris was sitting on the edge of the bed talking on his cell phone when Sage came out of the bathroom. She looked at his naked body and knew she wanted to make love to this man, even if the relationship ended in the morning. His physique was sculpted with a sexy softness, and dark chocolate in color. Sage sighed at the sight of his beautiful skin. There were no blemishes from his bald head to his feet. His thighs showed the definition he obviously worked for at the gym. Sage's desires were beginning to take over her emotional confusion. Kris hung up the phone and watched Sage as she approached the bed. He stood to his feet meeting her at the end of the bed. It was as though he understood he had to be patient with a woman whose confidence in the bedroom had been questioned by a man who desired another man in bed. As he touched her shoulders, he removed her robe and kissed her gently on her forehead and down her neck.

Sage felt as though she was falling under a spell. Kris kissed her shoulders and pulled her gently to the bed where he laid her down. As they kissed and adjusted their bodies, Kris massaged her breast until her nipples responded. He continued kissing her breast, and then he stopped and raised himself on his elbow to look into her eyes.

"Baby we need to talk a minute."

Sage couldn't believe her ears. Her body was tingling and she had finally blocked her thoughts of guilt. She was ready to make the night a lasting memory. Sage's thoughts returned to Brian and his attempts to please her months after he got caught. He would always start with *"Baby, we need to talk about this, so we can move on."*

"Look, I don't want you to do anything you're not ready for. Really, I think I can understand your feelings about this. Or am I reading your body language wrong."

Kris was right. She was tense, her body was responding to him, but she had feelings of confusion, guilt and fear. Sage wanted to lie. She wanted to tell him she was fine and had overcome her bedroom fears years ago. She wanted to tell him that she had put all her thoughts about that night, seeing Brian with another man, had not affected her desire for sex. Tears rolled down her face.

Kris lay down and pulled Sage closer to him. Her head rested on his chest. Sage cried silently as he stroked her hair.

It was two o'clock in the morning when Sage lifted her head and realized she had cried herself to sleep. She looked into Kris's face, and he smiled without opening his eyes.

"I'm sorry. You must think I'm unstable."

Kris answered keeping his eyes closed.

"I would have left if I thought that. What's wrong? Do you need me to leave so you can relax?"

"No, no I'm fine with you here. Actually, I like you being here. It's just; well, it's been a while."

"Understood, there's no rush baby, when you're ready."

Sage stretched repositioning herself catching a glance at the rise in the sheets. Her body told her she needed the satisfaction of a man. As she pulled up the sheets, she put her thigh across Kris's legs. He smiled still not opening his eyes. Sage watched his expression as she kissed his shoulder and chest. Kris opened one eye but didn't move. Sage kissed his chin and touched his lips with her finger. Kris kissed her finger acknowledging her touch. Sage realized he was leaving it totally up to her to start their physical engagement. She needed to prove to herself that she had not lost her womanhood when she lost her husband.

Sage rolled on top of Kris, he smiled, but his eyes remained closed. She kissed him on his face, neck and lips. Sage could feel his manhood pressed against her stomach. He was larger than she thought. She smiled thinking to herself that she indeed had a prize. He opened his eyes as his penis reacted to her body's motions. He gave her a passionate kiss and their lovemaking began.

Kris rolled over kissing Sage from her neck to her navel. He held her hips in his hands kissing her across her panty line. Sage felt herself drifting as she had earlier and prayed he would continue.

Kris lifted his head, as though he wanted her approval to continue kissing her below her waist. Sage's body tingled and he felt the tremor in her legs. Kris lifted himself attempting to move toward her head. Sage gently placed her hand on his head leading him toward her vagina. He smiled to himself knowing he had broken down her walls totally. Kris continued kissing the lips of her vagina as she moved fulfilling her need for sexual satisfaction. Sage began moaning and Kris reached for the condom he had on the nightstand. Sage put her hand across his and whispered, "Let me."

Kris continued licking her clitoris until it was erect and Sage quickened her pace. Kris turned his body allowing his penis to fall in Sage's breast. Sage had a full view of his works and was amazed at its perfection in color and size. He could have been a model from head to toe in the nude; there were no imperfections. Sage took his penis in her hand as her body cried for its entry. Kris went deeper with his tongue as she released her juices with an emotional outcry.

"Kris, please give it to me."

Sage felt Kris's penis enlarge in her hand. She put her mouth on its head and began to return the pleasure he had given her. She could feel the veins pulsating as Kris began to breathe harder. She opened the condom packet and put it on the head of his penis with her hand. She completed putting it on with her mouth and Kris let her know she had given him a new arousal. He turned his body to mount her in the heat of the moment. They held each other as Kris led the lovemaking dance. Sage couldn't believe she was willing to miss this pleasure thinking about her past. His pace was increasing and Sage could feel the warmth of her body elevating. As she reached her first orgasm, she realized how passionate he was. His penis remained hard as she tingled again and again.

Kris rolled over on his back allowing Sage to sit on him as he continued to move slowly in and out of her warm cove. Sage was woman enough to fulfill his sexual needs. He kissed her breast as he quickened the pace again causing Sage to moan in ecstasy. Sage sat straight up and reached behind her to massage his sacs. They were large and filled. The more she massage the more Kris responded.

"Aw, shit. Lady, Lady, aw…"

Sage was pleased. She rolled over on her back knowing that the next steps in their dance would lead Kris to his fulfillment. Kris raised up prepared to change the condom he had on. Sage pulled him to her and he entered her bareback. The touch of his penis, feeling its heat caused another orgasm. She was pleased. She moved in ways she hadn't in years. Her juices flowed and Kris exploded. Sage could feel the warmth of his sperm as it united with her fluids. Kris continued to move in and out exploding until his body trembled. Sage knew it had been a while for him too. Kris rolled over on his back. His penis was dripping with his sperm and covered with her juices. Kris's hand found a place to rest touching her clitoris softly. Sage opened her legs allowing him to massage her as she had done over the years. His finger penetrated her and her body responded. Sage reached to hold his moist penis. He had been pleased, as it now was limp but still pulsating. Sage's clitoris was rising again and her body tingled for Kris. She began to move slowly. Kris kissed her and rolled onto his knees. He kissed her vagina passionately. Sage couldn't count the orgasms she had that night but again she reached a climax and trembled as his tongue went across the tip of her clitoris. Sage moaned in pleasure as Kris rose to his feet. He held his penis in his hand as he walked toward the bathroom. She hoped their next dance would be soon.

Chapter 23

It was after three o'clock when Brian Drakeford decided to call Tempting Escorts for Kris Randall. Kris hadn't returned any of his calls for over two weeks. It was Friday, and there was a dinner the next night that Brian had booked with another escort. He had hoped by now that he and Kris would have been together, and he wouldn't need the escort. He canceled the escort and told them to apply the fee to his account. Tempting Escorts called leaving a message for him to call them regarding his booking. Brian returned the call and tried to book Kris for the evening. If he wouldn't answer the calls, he would talk to him while he worked. He was told by Sharonda that Kris no longer worked for the service. When his questions about Kris continued Sharonda told him to call back regarding his account and speak to Greg Tempts.

Brian didn't believe Kris quit the service, or that he wasn't a bisexual. He did believe Kris was upset and confused, and he gave him time to think about what he said to him in the diner. If Kris didn't respond after today Brian was ready to talk to a few of the investors and find out what they knew about their liaison. Brian checked Kris's background for a wife, family and romantic ties in his business. Nothing was found. Kris was free to love anyone he wanted to. Brian wanted it to be him.

Brian could imagine what their lovemaking would be like. He wouldn't have to be dominant, they could exchange positions, and he would get the fulfillment he found with

Zach. Although their relationship ended when Sage walked into the bedroom on them, they still met occasionally for lunch and an afternoon roll in the bed. Zach wouldn't be involved with Brian as his lover after he found out the lie he lived with his wife. Zach knew about his prior love Demarest, and his encounters with Carla but Brian never mentioned his wife. Kris reminded Brian of Zach. Zach resisted Brian's approach too. Brian wanted Kris, he needed him to fill the void.

Brian hoped Sharonda answered the phone, but as he looked at the clock he remembered she worked until one on Friday's.

"Hello, this is Brian Drakeford. I am returning a call I received earlier. The message was for me to call back and speak to Mr. Greg Tempts."

Lamont stood at the phone listening and rolling his eyes. Greg walked by with a confused look and whispered,

"What's wrong?"

"It's Mr. Drakeford for you Greg."

Greg knew Lamont was announcing the call in a deliberate tone for Brian to hear. Greg shook his head and pointed to his office. Lamont transferred the call.

"Good afternoon Mr. Drakeford."

"Hello. I'm returning your call, but if this is about my cancellation for tomorrow night I've decided to go with an escort anyway. Is Mr. Kris Randall available?"

"Mr. Randall no longer works here. The reason for my call is just that sir. You indicated to Mr. Randall that you would ruin him in his business matters by letting his clients know about his escorting through our agency. I don't understand your reason for divulging any of his information. We run a legal business and do not want any negative feedbacks. Were you dissatisfied with him during any of his escorts? I see here from reviewing your requests you asked for him often, as you did today."

"Mr. Tempts, what I do in my personal time is none of your company's concern."

"I beg to differ, Mr. Drakeford. It is your business if it doesn't affect my business. You see, just as your personal information that is filed on your profile with us is protected so are the escorts that work for me. If my clients and escorts thought their personal likes, dislikes and in some cases just the fact that they are involved with an escort agency, was information that would be shared, I could lose business. I could be subjected to law suits."

"So your concern is your business?"

"Yes sir. I wouldn't allow anyone to divulge to your wife or business associates that you were involved with an escort service. The fact that as a married man you are escorted by males and females is solely your business to tell. I am sure we have kept our word to you by not letting your business or home life become disrupted because of any information we have about your escapades."

"Escapades? Mr. Tempts you know nothing about my so called escapades to tell." Greg had baited him, and now he was going to reel him in.

"Mr. Drakeford, I've been in business a long time sir. I have been subjected to investigations for divorces, separations, people being fired and even murders. This business carries secrets. Your indiscretions were not revealed through our agency. Your wife had no idea you were into men. We could have told her before she walked in on you in your bedroom at home. Your secrets are your secrets. And by the way, Mr. Drakeford, your job and business associates, those who aren't close to you, still don't know. They don't know you harassed Demarest Blanding, or that you are currently trying to blackmail Kris Randall. So you see we value professionalism and the confidentiality of our client's information."

The phone was silent. Brian didn't know what to say. He had no idea how Greg Tempts got his information. Brian didn't understand why Kris had gone to the owner of Tempting Escorts and told him about their meeting. He needed to talk with Kris. No, he needed to ruin him. Brian couldn't lose his wife or his business associates. He was already divorced and he had been transferred to a different department after Demarest threatened to file harassment. His association with clients at the job was little to none. He handled their architectural designs and prepared the presentations. The members of the escort service that worked with him were his associates; there were only a few that worked at Kilmore.

"I don't know what Mr. Randall has told you. Is that why he quit?"

"No, there is a policy agreement that you signed when you became a client. You have violated that agreement. We will no longer be servicing your escorting needs."

"What? That's the stupidest shit I've ever heard of. Randall's bitch ass complaint and I lose my service?"

"Sir, you signed an agreement that was clearly explained when you filled out your profile forms. I can't have a client threatening the escorts by divulging information about them. The truth or not, it doesn't matter. Understand my position. I am protecting you and Mr. Randall."

"Protecting me?"

"Yes, I don't know how Mr. Randall would retaliate. He could approach your business associates, family or friends. This could get ugly. Mr. Randall is no longer an escort, and you are no longer a client. It takes Tempting Escorts out of the picture entirely. Now if you wish to pursue the matter with Mr. Randall, feel free to do so. But Mr. Drakeford, what goes around comes around and from looking at this file you're not squeaky clean."

"Again, my personal life is my own. Do you have a number where Mr. Randall can be reached?"

"No, and if I did my policy states I couldn't give it to you. Mr. Drakeford these things are in place for times like this. From what I was told you don't take the word "no" well. I suggest you do, for your own sake. Mr. Randall is not the average escort. He won't file a harassment complaint and wait on a financial settlement."

"How much information do you think you know about me?"

"Just know, that I know. Have a good day Mr. Drakeford."

Chapter 24

Greg hung up the phone and immediately dialed Kris's number. Lamont came into his office and took a seat knowing Greg had what Kris needed to stop Brian's attempt to ruin him. Lamont sat back and crossed his legs waiting to hear their conversation.

"Kris', Greg. What's up man?"

"Nothing, I'm getting ready to go to Virginia."

"Virginia? For what?"

Greg told Kris about Carla and Demarest. They agreed there was no need to push the matter if Brian didn't bother Kris anymore. Kris didn't answer Brian's calls and didn't think much of it. Greg thought Kris was taking matters into his own hands.

"My parents are looking to relocate. Sage and I are going to look at the properties they picked on the computer. You know, narrow the list and hopefully find a place for them. We'll be gone for a few days. I was going to call you before I left."

"Man, listen. Brian Drakeford called. Shot out brother. Anyway, he's pissed. I baited him. I let him know that I knew about Lamont, the harassment and the reason for his divorce. Hopefully, it will put an end to the calls. But this is what we need; if he calls you answer the phone and see what he wants. Shit, maybe he'll back up if he knows you're working with Sage."

"Greg, we're intimate. I've been dating her for a few months now. I didn't know she was married to him until you called and told me. She goes by her maiden name, Monroe. I told her about that shit with Brian because I didn't want it to ruin our personal relationship."

"Damn, what did she say?"

"She listened and I guess she feels like Demarest and that female, what's her name?"

"Carla."

"Yeah, man that's got to hurt in more ways than one. We're working through things though. I really like her a lot. I don't want Brian involved in our relationship anymore than he needs to be. Their children are grown and he has no contact with Sage. So, family events, holidays that's it."

"Listen, I really think that would stop him. I think that when a man sees his wife has moved on it stops his madness."

"Greg, you're forgetting. This man wasn't into his wife. Why would he care now?"

"It's embarrassing. Listen, everyone thinks he cheated and his wife has suffered. He wouldn't want anyone to know the truth, and he wouldn't want her to know about how he feels for you. He'll back up."

"So, we invite him to dinner?"

"No, Kris he's not stupid. He knows you know about Demarest and his wife. What he doesn't know is that you're dealing with her, and you know about Carla. Talk to him see if he's backing up; if so it's a done deal if not … well we've got to find a way for him to see what's going on."

"Listen, Sage invited me to their daughter's wedding. He has to be there."

"Ask Sage about two other guest; they don't have to be at the reception. They could greet Sage and you talk a bit and that's it. He only needs to see Sage with you, Demarest and Carla. The rest of his family will never know. You still have an ace in the hole. If he continues to threaten you, introduce his children to his child."

"Whew, but that means Sage would have to know the relationship he had with Demarest and Carla."

"Yeah, but if she found out that you knew about this child, and you didn't tell her..."

"You're right. I'll talk to her about it and call you. Didn't you say they lived in Virginia?"

"You could meet them if you'd like. They seem to be okay with this. They both worked with me, and they'll be willing to help you."

"Well, let me talk with Sage. I'll let you know if Brian calls, and what we're gonna do. You're right though, she needs to know."

Greg hung up the phone and smiled at Lamont.

"That damn Brian Drakeford is still trying to get at Kris?"

"I think he'll stop after the phone call I just had."

"The call with him or the call with Kris, he's a persistent ass."

"Lamont, it's okay we've got enough information to bury his ass if he doesn't care about his life being ruined."

"Greg that's just it; he doesn't care. I think after his marriage went under, he lost it. I mean he didn't care about anything else. You know a lot of these people we deal with don't have a life. I mean they can't even meet people that they would invite to an event, so they use our escorts. Most of them have insecurities."

Greg laughed. He knew what Lamont meant, but it sounded funny.

"You know people would say the same about us. You being a homosexual and me being bisexual; they say we have insecurities."

"Talk about your damn self. I'm secure with who I am, and I don't need no damn escort to got out. If it gets that bad sugar, I'll go out by my damn self."

"Anyway, Kris is gonna talk to Sage. I don't think she knows about this other child. Kris is involved with her, and he wants to keep everything on the table."

"So she hooks up with Kris, and he knows more about her husband than she does. I'm thinking like Demarest now. It's about time Brian Drakeford realizes how he has hurt the people who loved him."

Chapter 25

Karen looked at the clock in her office and decided five o'clock would be her quitting time for the day. The few clients that came in were scheduled for viewings and there were no other appointments set for the afternoon. Karen closed the file on her desk and decided to pour herself one last cup of coffee. She walked out of her office as Dionne came in the front door.

"Hey girl."

"Hey Aunt Karen; is my mother here?"

"No she left early today. She's going to look at properties in Virginia, so she'll be leaving sometime this afternoon. You better call her to catch her if it's important."

"Is she going for the weekend?"

"No, I don't think she'll be back until Tuesday or Wednesday."

"I haven't been able to catch her."

"Have you called her?"

"No, just stopping by the house or here."

"Why didn't you call her Dionne?"

Karen listened as Dionne's excuses for not calling Sage sounded as though she really didn't have one. Dionne wanted to see her mother, but she wouldn't say why.

"My mother is never home, and she's barely here; where is she spending her time, and with who?"

Karen smiled. Dionne wanted to see who Kris was. She wanted to meet him without a formal introduction.

"Let's call your mom. She's packing and picking up last minute items. If we call her cell, she'll answer. But I know you knew that."

Karen dialed Sage's number on the receptionist's phone.

"Sage, hey, Dionne's here at the office looking for you. Hold on."

"Mom, I was in the area and stopped by. Will you be home I need to talk to you?"

Dionne listened to her mother's response and hung up the phone.

"Thanks Aunt Karen. I'll see you later."

Dionne left the office and Karen dialed Sage's number again.

"Yea girl, what's up with Dionne?"

"Karen, your guess is as good as mine. I talked with her twice since we went out that day and both times she wanted to know if I was still bringing a guest to the wedding. I told her yes and she never asked anything else. I think she's having a real issue with me having another man in my life."

"She did act funny when you said Kris's name. Maybe she knows him."

"I showed pictures of Trevon and Dionne to Kris. He would have said he knew her. I don't think that's it. Anyway, we're leaving tonight, that will give me time to talk to her."

"Maybe it's something else. She only has two months before the wedding, maybe she's nervous."

"Karen, nothing would surprise me. I've been shocked so much lately Dionne couldn't tell me anything that would rattle my world."

"Okay, call me after she leaves."

Chapter 26

Brian left his office and went to the gym as he often did on Friday's. During his workout he thought about the conversation he had with Mr. Tempts. His social life was becoming complex. He wanted to be with Zach and if not Kris; neither seemed to be interested in a relationship with him. Starting a new relationship took time and patience. Kris had presented a challenge, and though he could dismiss it, he needed to know how much Kris knew. One group of investors that Kris worked for had bought plaza property from the Berger Group, which meant Kris had done business with Sage or Karen, maybe both. Brian didn't want Sage to know anymore about his past or present relationships. Brian didn't want to call Sage and ask her about Kris. He would definitely ask Kris about his business with Sage.

Brian went through his exercises and still felt tense. He would call Zach to see if they could get together. Brian went to shower and spotted Zach coming out of the sauna.

"Brian, what's up?"

"I was thinking about you."

"Sure listen, are you going to the LMN Groups dinner tomorrow night?"

"I have tickets but I haven't decided to go. Why?"

"There's a possibility of you settling in with their planning department. I threw your name out there for consideration. They work out of Washington, D.C. though."

"So, are you going to the dinner?"

"Yea, I was invited by the Chairman of the Planning Board."

Brian looked away hoping Zach couldn't read the look of disappointment in his face.

"The man is coming there with his wife Brian. Look I want you to go with me. It could be good for you and me. After a night of business we could share a night of pleasure."

"Sounds good, I'll call you later."

Zach winked and walked off. Brian hoped there was an empty stall in the bathroom. He needed to relieve his stress.

Chapter 27

Sage was excited. It was her first getaway in months and the first in years with a male companion. Kris assured her it would only be the two of them. She had expressed not wanting to meet his parents or the children this early in their relationship. Kris didn't push the matter and was happy she agreed to look into the properties with him. They had made early appointments each day leaving the afternoons and evenings free. Sage had packed all the information they needed on the properties she researched. Kris looked into land to construct a home as well.

Sage closed her satchel and looked across her desk making sure she had enclosed all the necessary papers. She walked into her living room trying to remember what else she hadn't packed. They decided t stop for dinner before they left. They booked a suite in the Marriott Suites in Virginia. Kris was picking up the groceries for the suite before picking her up. Sage was looking into her DVD collection when Dionne called her from the front door.

"Ma, where are you?"

"Hey baby, I'm in the living room."

"Hey, did Trevon call you."

Sage stood with a look of worry across her face. She didn't know what to expect.

"Oh, Ma there's nothing wrong. He's thinking about staying a little longer after the wedding. I told him Jarad and I probably wouldn't be going on a honeymoon. Jarad's dad is not doing well so we'll still be around. I think he wanted to know if he could stay here. I told him to call you."

"He knows he can stay here. That's why I have this place. I don't need all this room for myself. It's for us to share as a family."

"Well, he's gonna call you. I didn't know you were going away though."

"He'll call on my cell. He doesn't call on this phone often. Why haven't you called? Karen said you were looking for me a couple of times. I always answer my cell."

"You seem so busy. I guess business is jumping."

"A few new deals but I've had a lot of closings. My day is longer than usual but hey it goes with the territory."

"How's everything else going?"

"Everything else?"

"Yeah are you still dating?"

"Yes, that's going well too. As a matter of a fact I'm looking into property for his parents and their grandchildren."

"He has children?"

"No, they're his sister's children; she and her husband died in an accident."

"Oh, that's got to be difficult."

"What?"

"Knowing that he could have an instant family when his parents die."

"Dionne, they're his family already. Anyway we're looking in Virginia. They chose a few spots, and we're going to check them out."

"So I guess you two are an item now?"

Sage smiled, she was pleased to answer the question with confidence.

"Yes. It feels good to be able to say that too. Anyway how are things going with Jarad, his parents and the wedding?"

"Jarad is scared about his dad's condition. That's all he talks about. When is it gonna be over? You know, something no one can answer. I'm trying to be there for him, but it's difficult. The wedding is set everything is done. Eight weeks and it will be over. I'll be married and the stress will be a lot less. Jarad hasn't been a part of this whole thing. I understand about his dad, but he doesn't even ask what has been done. Are you still bringing your friend to the wedding?"

"Yes, I gave you the count didn't I?"

"Anyone else, I mean from your job or clients?"

"No, you don't need a count for the ceremony. Any other clients would only be invited to the ceremony, you sent the invitations out didn't you?"

"They went out two weeks ago."

"Good, everything's set. Did you speak with your father?"

"A few times. He's fine. He asked about you."

"Dionne, it's okay if he didn't ask about me. I'm okay with that. Is he still bringing a guest?"

Sage hoped she would answer yes. She wanted to see Brian's face as she introduced Kris as her friend. Sage believed that would close a chapter of her life that should have been closed when she got her divorce.

"He wasn't sure. I told him it was okay, but he said he didn't want it to be a problem for you. Mom, it's been a long time you guys should be able to accept things and move on."

"I have moved on. I'm not stopping your father from bringing a guest."

The door bell rang and Sage told Dionne to get the door while she grabbed her other bags from upstairs. Dionne opened the door and was greeted with a smile from Kris.

"Hello, you must be Dionne. I'm Kris Randall a friend of your mother's."

"Yes, come in. She went upstairs."

"I'm glad to meet you your mother talks about you often. Your big day is coming soon."

"My mother and I were just talking about the finishing touches, the guest, and the ceremony; that kind of stuff. But let me ask you something before my mother comes down the stairs."

They walked into the living room. Kris took a seat on the couch and Dionne sat next to him looking back at the steps hoping her mother would be upstairs a while longer.

"I know you from somewhere Mr. Randall. It has bothered me since my mother first mentioned your name. I don't know where I know you from, but I do. Then I thought about it. You know my father. Mr. Randall that's not good for my mother. You're not one of his business associates, and if I recall correctly you were with him casually. My father has lived his life on the DL for years. What about you?"

"I am not on the DL. I don't have any interest in men or your father."

"Are you denying you know my father?"

"No, I know him. I have been to different events with him. It's obvious you know about his lifestyle too. I was working for an escort service and your father hired me as an escort."

"You escorted men, and you're not on the DL?"

"Escort only nothing else. Your mother knows about all about it."

Kris didn't mention Brian's threats, and he didn't want to know why Dionne hadn't told her mother, she knew about Brian's way of living.

"So what happens Mr. Randall when my father sees you with my mother at the wedding?"

"Your mother and I talked about it, and I guess that's when they both realize that they have moved on."

"Are you trying to insult my father in some way?"

"No, Dionne. I wouldn't do that."

"My mother doesn't know we know Mr. Randall. My brother doesn't speak to my dad because he knows. My father was caught once by my brother and then my mother. My father has problems and now you're a part of them."

"How's that?"

"You escorted my father in his desperate moments. Now you're with my mother? I don't see how you don't think you will insult him. It's my day Mr. Randall, and I want my father's memories of that day to be pleasant. Find another way to hit him below the belt."

"Your mother suggested I be her guest at your wedding. I didn't know who your father was until recently. Meaning I didn't date your mother because of your father. Your father has his own problems, and I am not trying to be a part of them, one way or the other. Dionne I really think you need to discuss this with your mother."

"I can't."

"Why?"

"He told me to promise I wouldn't tell my mother I knew. My brother and I both promised."

"So your mother's life is subject to being criticized but your father's choices are protected?"

"Mr. Randall my father hurt our family. My brother more so than me and I guess my mother more so than my brother. I love my father and my mother, but I need to stop them from hurting each other. I couldn't stop my father and his bedroom ventures, but I can stop my mother from serving him a plate of public humiliation."

"Bedroom ventures?"

"Mr. Randall, there are more secrets in his life than him living on the DL. We just want to get on with our life."

"And your mother?"

"Until you came along it wasn't an issue?"

"So I'm the problem?"

"My father's the problem, but he's my father."

"Dionne, I don't know how to solve this for you. I am a part of your mother's life until she tells me different. Not you or your father has a say in that. If your mother doesn't want to invite me to the wedding, than I won't go. You explain the issue you have, and I'm sure she'll agree, but the issue is yours."

"Mr. Randall she won't like the fact that you knew and didn't mention it to her. She doesn't like secrets. You should know that."

"You're right. I wouldn't tell her I wasn't coming to the wedding without mentioning the secrets you've told me today. It's up to you Ms. Drakeford. Either you tell your mother, or I tell her. If you don't want her to know that you've known about your father for some years now than I'll see you at your wedding. The choice is yours."

"Hmm … we'll talk." Dionne went to the bottom of the stairs and yelled. "Mom, I'm going now. I've met Mr. Randall. I'll see you guys later, have a good time."

Chapter 28

Kris needed fresh air. Sage was talking to him off and on from the bedroom but her voice was muffled as though she had her head in a closet. Kris walked up the stairs to tell her he was going to the store for drinks to put in the cooler. It was the only excuse he could think of to leave the house and call Greg. Dionne gave Kris a few things to consider. Kris hadn't thought about Sage's reaction to Carla and Demarest or the child that Brian wasn't supposed to know about. Dionne knew more than Sage thought, which meant Brian could have told Dionne and Trevon about Carla and the child. Kris didn't want to be the one to tell Sage anything else about Brian's past. It wasn't his job. He was beginning to love her and didn't want the past to be a burden to their relationship. He needed to talk to someone about it. Kris chose Greg.

Sage looked up as Kris walked into the bedroom.

"What did you say Kris?"

"I'm going to the store. Take your time it's early. What are you looking for?"

"I had a map that was marked with properties in the Richmond area it could have helped us. I had marked it for a client about four months ago. He bought a home in a small town outside of Richmond, but we could use the research that I did. I thought about it at the last minute. You know what, I know where I put it. It's downstairs in the bookcase."

Sage began putting back the papers and folders she had placed on the bed. Kris waved his hand indicating he was leaving.

"I'll be back in a minute."

"How did you like meeting Dionne?"

Kris hesitated not knowing how to hide what he felt about the conversation, he and Dionne had.

"She's pretty; seems to be a smart young lady. I asked her was she ready for her big day, she blushed just like you."

Kris hoped his answer wouldn't lead into Sage questioning about the rest of their conversation.

"She's her father's child though. They've always been closer than she and I. Trevon and I are close, but Dionne truly loves her father. I guess it's that father daughter thing. I'm glad the two of you talked, maybe now she'll be more relaxed about you coming to the wedding."

"Maybe, you go ahead and I'll be right back. Do you want anything special from the store?"

"No thanks."

Kris walked outside and decided to walk to the deli a few blocks from the house. He had filled the cooler and since the excuse worked, he would get a bag of chips to keep Sage from being suspicious. He bought a bag of chips and a Pepsi and dialed Greg's number as he took a slow walk back to Sage's house.

"Tempting Escorts, Greg speaking."

"Hey Tempting."

"Hey dark and handsome."

They both laughed.

"What's up man? Did you and Sage meet up yet?"

"Yea, but listen. There's more shit piling up."

"More? Impossible, did that dude call you again?"

"No. I met his daughter. I think she's as bad as he is."

"Can't be. What's up with her?"

"She tried to get me out of coming to the wedding with her mom. I mean to the point of threatening to tell her mother, she knew who I was. Greg I don't remember meeting this kid. She called it right though. She said I was with her father on a casual outing. She thought she had me. Sage didn't tell her much about me and she figured Sage didn't know about the escort service."

"She knew about her father being involved with the escort service?"

"Yea, and check this, both her and Sage's son knew about their father being on the DL before Sage did. They didn't tell her though."

"What? Usually the kids are down with mom."

"Well, they haven't told her they know. So Sage is in the dark again. What if I bring up this guy Demarest and Carla with their shit and everyone knows but Sage again? It looks like if it wasn't for me Sage wouldn't be subjected to her ex's problems."

"It would have surfaced, believe me. Listen let me make a call don't say anything yet. You're in the middle now man. If you don't say anything she will always think you hid something from her too. If you say something, you're..."

"The ass that broke up her dysfunctional family."

"Remember you said it. Listen do you love the woman or what. I mean where you going with this. I know you Kris. You must care a lot about her to deal with her issues and her family issues. Is it getting serious?"

"I hope so. I don't want to rush things, but I need a stable woman in my life. There's some things that I need to settle before my people get this property."

"Kris, you're not thinking about rushing into anything are you."

"Man, I need someone to understand what my future may be. I may have to raise those kids man. I don't want to be dating this one and that one while raising four kids."

"Do you think Sage wants to raise someone else's kids?"

"It may give her a second chance."

"What do you mean by that?"

"Greg, Brian Drakeford has his kids still keeping his secrets from their mother. I don't think Sage ever had a great relationship with her family, her kids or her husband."

"I don't know man, four children and a new man?"

"I plan on making it work Greg, if she'll have me. I do care for her, love her, whatever. I got feelings for the woman. It's fucked up what her husband did to her and her kids knew about it. I don't know whether I want to bring another secret out in the open."

"So what do you say when the daughter tells you knew about Carla and Demarest or the kid."

"No one knows I know about them but you. Shit let Brian's cards fall without me dealing them."

"Think about it man. Let me make this call. Carla will tell me if they know or not. My bet is that nobody knows."

"Let me know. If I don't answer the phone I'll call you back when I can talk."

"Oh, it will be in the next half hour or so."

"Bet. I don't think Sage will be ready anyway."

Chapter 29

Kris's phone rang and when he saw the name on the caller ID, he was glad he was still walking back from the deli. He slowed his pace more answering the call.

"Yeah, what's up Brian?"

"You, what the hell do you think you're doing?"

"This moment or when? What are we talking about?"

"Listen you sarcastic fuck. I told you I would ruin you. If you're trying to turn the tables you better think twice about it. I think we need to talk and this time you need to hear the entire conversation so that you know what you're dealing with. I can make you or break you."

"I don't want to get vulgar. Let me see if I can explain this with a civil tone first. I don't fuck men!"

"I'll do the fucking. Be at the diner by seven tonight. Then we'll talk about positions."

"You amaze me, you little shit. I don't want you and you don't really want me. You don't know me obviously, or you wouldn't keep calling and annoying me. You do you. If you think you can ruin me go on. I've had enough business in this area to carry me through your worst rumors. And I've heard you've had a few bad ones yourself. Harassment and abuse, I'd kill you first. Anyway do you sweetie. Lose my number or you'll wish you had. Threat for threat Mr. Drakeford you don't scare me."

"Kris, listen, maybe we got off on the wrong foot. I know you have had your rounds with men like me. I mean your boy Greg, for instance. When you first met he wanted you. There are others and I know it. Some of them still want you. Are you sure you want to battle with what may become a living nightmare?"

"Dealing with you and your shit is a living nightmare? Once I get through it though, I believe I will have peaceful dreams. Something you won't understand Brian. But I promise you if you keep pushing my nerves, I may have to invite you into my world."

"That's exactly where I want to be."

"Keep your eyes open"

Kris hung up angry that he didn't say he was with Sage and how much he enjoyed the love making sessions they had. He wanted to tell Brian that Sage could call him during the day and cause him to feel her warmth. Kris could go on and on explaining how his ex-wife fulfilled the man in him like no other woman had.

"Shit!"

Kris promised himself that he wasn't going to let Brian separate his relationship with Sage. He was being pushed. It would be easier to tell Sage it was too much. She couldn't expect anyone to deal with her and the baggage that kept turning up. Then the thought of what Dionne said came to mind. Maybe no one would notice if he wasn't in the picture. He would walk away and the only one that would know what was really going on would be Dionne. Sage would be hurt again. Kris couldn't do that to her. He couldn't do that to himself. He realized he was in love with Sage. He returned to the house and saw Sage at the car packing her garment bag into the back seat. He shook his head hoping she hadn't checked the cooler.

Chapter 30

Carla answered her phone on the fourth ring. She yelled for Demarest or Carl to grab it but the phone rang again letting her know they hadn't heard her. She picked up the cordless line in the kitchen, which allowed her to continue preparing dinner.

"Hello."

"Hello Carla?"

"Hey Greg, how are you?"

"Fine baby and you?"

"Okay, what's up with that crazy ass Brian? Has he given up on Kris?"

"I'm afraid not he called today. I thought the two week gap meant it was a game of chase for him, obviously not. Listen, does he know about Carl?"

"He knows I have a son. He doesn't know Carl is his."

"How's that I mean he can count can't he?"

"I told him Demarest was Carl's father."

"You're joking right?"

"I said it as a joke and that ass didn't ask any more questions. Every time he would bring up Carl, I would bring up Demarest. I never told him anything else."

"Carla, really Brian can't possibly think that Demarest is Carl's father."

"Greg, I don't know. He never said anything to me or Demarest if he did know."

"So Brian thinks you and Demarest got together, and are still together? Carla, everyone knows Demarest is gay. I bet even Carl knows Demarest is gay."

"He knows Demarest is different that's for sure."

"How old is he now?"

"He'll be eleven this year."

"You were with Brian when he was married?"

"Yea, that was the reason I never said anything. After Sage caught him with that damn Zach I was done and I knew Sage was done too."

"Wait, you didn't know he was into men?"

"Hell no! We had been together off and on for more than a year. It started out as the escort thing then he would take me with him on business trips, and I would wait for him in the hotels while he was at meetings. Zach introduced himself at one of the conferences and hooked him up with a couple of good business prospects. My traveling with him stopped. That night that Demarest and I wound up together with him, I had no idea that Demarest was his entertainment. I barely knew Demarest but it didn't take long for me to realize that Demarest was more than a one-night thing for Brian. I went along with the night thinking Demarest was there for me. Brian and I got our thing off; afterward it was supposed to be me and Demarest, but he couldn't even get a hard on. Brian insisted and he tried forcing Demarest on me. When Demarest still couldn't perform Brian raped him right in front of me. Beat his ass and raped him. Demarest held back his tears and anger. He was moaning in pain and telling Brian how sorry he was. I left the two of them there. That was the last night I was with Brian. I thought about Demarest for weeks. When I finally called him, he told me about Brian harassing him on his job. Greg, Demarest and Brian had been an item for about five months on the DL before I started dealing with him, and that bastard had the nerve to be harassing Demarest after that night of humiliation. Demarest said he didn't want to be bothered with him, but he was scared he didn't have a choice. Greg he really loved Brian. I thought I was falling too until that night. The next week when Sage caught him and Zach in her bedroom Zach told everyone on his job about it. Brian got transferred before the big boys found out, and I told Demarest to tell him he would file a harassment charge against his ass if he didn't leave him alone. We've been friends ever since."

"So Brian can't believe that Carl is Demarest's."

"I think he knows better, but he doesn't know who the father is. That's why we moved to keep people from prying. He doesn't know when Carl was born."

"Did he contact you after you moved?"

"He called once or twice. He was calling Demarest more, claiming he wanted to know where his money was going. We've always had separate phone lines, so he has no idea that we live in the same home. Demarest is dating a guy he met here, and he's barely home but this is his home."

"What about you? Are you dating, I mean what does Brian think you're doing?"

"I don't give a damn what he thinks. But Mr. Tempts you are another subject," she teased. "I'm not dating seriously and I could change my mind for you. Carl takes up a lot of my time. We're really close. I spend a lot of time working and enjoying my son. Not that I couldn't fit you in every now and then."

Greg laughed ignoring Carla's comments. He dated her when he first hired her to work at Tempting Escorts. She was an escort he would book for himself and surprise her. When he thought he was falling in love he called it off. He explained his life was complicated and there wasn't much room for a serious relationship. Greg regretted it ever since.

"Carla, I don't know how to stop Brian, but he's got to stop this shit. He harasses people and causes unnecessary drama and moves on leaving their lives fucked up. Kris is about to explode."

"A good ass whooping would do Brian some good. I can picture that."

"A dose of his own medicine would be better. Does Dionne know you?"

"Dionne? Who's Dionne?"

"Brian's daughter."

"No, I knew he had two kids, but I don't know them."

"Good."

"What's up with his daughter?"

"She's not happy about Kris dealing with her mother. Same shit. She wants Kris to leave her mother alone, or she'll ruin his rep with Sage. She told him she would tell her he knew about her father and his lifestyle. Kris has her at bay, for the moment, but we need to knock her and her punk ass father on their asses."

"They've been divorced for what, seven years? Why would his daughter care who her mother dates?"

"We don't know that yet, but we wanted to make sure she didn't know about you. Apparently, both her and her brother knows about his lifestyle."

"Really?"

"Yea, but you, Demarest and Carl would make the drama cease. The secrets need to stop. If Sage knew about you already maybe they would stop spoon feeding them to her, and she could get on with her life."

"Greg, what's in all this for you?"

"Kris, I really like him. He doesn't deserve this shit. Just like you and Demarest didn't. Neither does Sage. You're right, Brian needs his ass whooped but if Sage knew about you and Carl, and she could reveal his own secret that would kill him."

Greg and Carla talked a while longer discussing how they could arrange a meeting that wouldn't cause Sage discomfort. They all wanted Brian to be devastated; they weren't trying to embarrass Sage. Carla promised to discuss their conversation with Demarest, and maybe they could all meet while Sage and Kris were looking at properties.

"I'll call Kris and see how he feels about it."

"It will be good to see you. Greg, tell Kris we all feel the same way."

Chapter 31

Dionne arrived at her apartment before Jarad got there. The two of them had planned to go to the movies and dinner. They hadn't been out in months but Dionne had other business she preferred to take care of. It was close to five thirty and dinner was planned for seven. Dionne had two calls to make before leaving. She dialed her brother's number hoping he would answer and be able to talk. While she listened to the ringing on the line, she kicked off her shoes and settled on her couch.

"Hey Sis."

"Hey Tre. How's things going?"

"Fine, I talked to Ma about staying with her after the wedding, she said it was okay. She didn't seem to mind at all. I was waiting for the excuses you said I would hear. Anyway it's set. I'll be in town for a little over a month."

"Is Lynn gonna stay that long too?"

"No, I don't think so. She's coming to the wedding and then going to visit her family. Then we'll go back home together."

"So you're cool with that?"

"Yea, it's cool. What's up with you? How's the plans going?"

"Just waiting for the day now. Tre, Mom is thinking about bringing a guest."

"That's good. Have you met him?"

"He knows dad. As a matter of a fact he has escorted him through that escorting service."

"Really, the guy is gay or something?"

"No, he says he's not but who knows, Dad said the same thing."

"Dionne, listen, I don't won't to talk about dad and his issues. Who is this guy and how did he meet Mom?"

"Kris Randall, I've checked him out. He's got his own company. He deals with investors that are seeking property. That's how he met Mom. She sold his client his last big deal. I don't know how long they dealt with each other on a business level, but they've been in a relationship for about three or four months."

"Okay, so what's the problem?"

"Trevon, he knows about Dad and Zach; the whole thing. Mom wants to bring him to the wedding. The problem is Dad doesn't know they're dealing with each other. I guess Mom thinks she can get back at him."

"Does she know this guy knows Dad?"

"Yea, that's why I said she's just dating him to get back at Dad."

"Well if it will help her get over his ass than I say let her do what she wants to do."

"Tre! It's my wedding day. Dad will be humiliated!"

"He knows how to keep his emotions on the DL. He can ignore Mom and her date for the day. Dionne I don't see

the problem. I'm not about to help you protect Dad. I told you I've disowned him. He made a promise to us...."

"Trevon you and I both know he couldn't keep that promise."

"Dionne, I was fifteen. My father promised me and I believed in his promise. Two years later he's caught in bed with a man! Fuck him Dionne, he hurt me and my mother. He can't be trusted. You protect him on your wedding day, and he'll do your dirty before you and Jarad have your first child. The only reason he seems innocent to you is because you haven't seen it first hand. It has a different effect than hearing it."

"What's the difference Tre? I understand the hurt you feel; I feel it, too. Do you think I sleep well knowing my father and mother broke up a marriage because he cheated with another man?"

"Well try topping that with him sneaking into your bed at night."

"What?"

"You heard me."

"Tre, you said…"

"I know the lie I told for years. It kept things together between you and him, and for that matter, I thought it would help cover my feelings for him. Dionne, that's why I can't be around him. Yea, he did it a few times and stood watching me at the door. I would always stop him by questioning what he wanted. I waited the night it happened, and he pulled back the sheets got in the bed and began kissing me gently, like a girl would. We fought. I fought. He tried talking to me promising it wasn't what I thought."

"You didn't tell Mom?"

"No, and I told you I saw him kissing a man in his car. I did, that was Zach. I approached his ass about that, and he told me if I told Mama I wouldn't have a place to stay. He said that was their farewell, the last time they would be together. I cried. I was coming of age enjoying my new sexual awareness and the only man I knew to talk to about it was gay. He promised his life wouldn't interfere with ours, our home, our mother. Two years later she caught him with Zach. Dionne, if I had been home and knew it was Zach, I would have killed him. Now you want me to protect his ass? Hell no. Mom needs to be able to get this off."

Dionne was silently crying and wiping her face. She didn't know what to say. Over the years, she thought her father was misunderstood. Confused, she had no idea he had attempted to molest Trevon. Their father was sicker than she imagined.

"Tre, I didn't know he was capable of something like that or even abuse. He told me about the guy on his job trying to get him fired by filing a harassment complaint. I didn't believe that either. I didn't think Dad could do something like that."

"Now you know. I wouldn't put it past him. The more I hear about his lifestyle, the things he does to others and the secrets he hides, the more he disgusts me."

"Damn Tre. Did you tell Ma anything?"

"No, I kept it to myself. Like I said I told you what I wanted you to know and the rest you found out on your own."

"Yeah, I started looking into things when that damn guy on the job wanted to file that complaint. I think the guy wanted money or something."

"Is that what Dad said, or what you found out."

"I never found out anything. Dad didn't know I was looking into it. Anyway, I never found out what the complaint was. I think it was just a threat."

"Dad did something, trust me. So your plans are to tell Mom she can't bring a guest?"

"No, I don't know what to do. I don't want my wedding to be Dad's coming out party."

"How? Dad won't say anything and I doubt if Kris will either. The shit will hit the fan the next day if not later that night."

"I guess you're right. I'm gonna ask Dad about Kris."

"Ask him what? You can't ask him is he dealing with him."

"Why not? He told me about Zach when I questioned what you said."

"Dionne, admit it. You want to warn him. You want to give him the upper hand on Mom again. If Jarad was on the DL would you want to know?"

"Yea, and you better tell me."

"Why didn't you tell your mother?"

"She saw it for herself. We didn't have to tell her."

"We should have. It would have saved her from seeing it in her bedroom."

"So what do I do Tre?"

"Mind your business, enjoy your day. Let Dad get what's coming to him."

Dionne didn't tell her brother, she threatened Kris. She told him that Kris and Sage were going to be in Virginia for the next couple of days. They laughed and talked a few minutes longer without mentioning their father again.

Chapter 32

Dionne looked at the clock and decided she had time to call her father. The conversation would not be the same as she intended. Trevon had given her other things to question her father about. She loved her father, and her brother was right, she did want to warn him. Trevon wouldn't forgive her though so she would leave it up to fate. If her father found out her mother was dating maybe he would look into who her love interest was without Dionne telling him.

"Dad, it's me, Dionne call me."

Dionne left the message on Brian's cell phone. She dialed his home line thinking she would get his answering machine as well.

"Yes."

"Hey Dad, did I disturb you?"

"No, I was getting ready to make a call, but it can wait. What's up baby?"

"You, I figured I would call you before I went to the movies with Jarad. What's your night looking like?"

"Nothing, I'm staying in tonight. I have a dinner to attend tomorrow, business dinner."

"You didn't have to say that. You are entitled to go out you know. Mom does now."

"What?"

"Yea, she's finally dating on the regular now."

"Hmmm, good for her, she deserves it."

"Dad you don't really mean that. I mean, don't you feel a twinge of jealousy?"

"No, Dionne you and I have had this conversation. Unfortunately, your mother and I are no longer an item."

"Listen to you, why are you saying unfortunately? I bet you could step right in and win her over."

"I don't think so, anyway I don't want to."

"Wow, so it's final for both of you."

Dionne hashed this argument once a month with Brian. She said it was a way that he could confess, but he never did. Dionne had told him that she and Tre knew about Zach. She wanted to tell him she knew about Tre too. Dionne decided it would be the last time she talked about him and her mother as a couple.

"It's been final honey for a long time. I'm glad we can still talk to each other. Your mother's a great woman, I hope she finds happiness."

"Like you did with Zach?"

"I'm not with Zach anymore?"

"Dad, I can't do this. What went on between you and Tre? Why doesn't he trust or believe in you?"

"Dionne what's up, I mean, why all the questions? You keep rehashing the past as though it's still repairable, or that it matters. I can't fix the mess I made and talking about it only keeps the hurt new."

"Dad, you hurt all of us, but I didn't know how Tre felt about you or why. I asked him and he told me."

"Did he now? And you say that to say what?"

"I don't know what to say. I thought I was surprised when Tre said he caught you kissing Zach, or when you told us it wasn't easy pretending to be satisfied in your marriage, or when you told us you wouldn't hide anything else from us. But Dad you didn't mention you tried to molest your own son. What else haven't you told us?"

"I thought Tre told you about that too. And it didn't happen like that."

"Like what Dad? How can you be trusted? No wonder Tre wants me to be with his children at all times when they visit you. You need help Dad, professional help."

"I did get help. I went through counseling and I deal with group sessions now. Dionne I don't need you running a 'Save Brian Drakeford's Life' campaign. It's done. I've apologized and that's all I can do. I'm sorry."

Dionne didn't know what else to say. She listened, determined that after the wedding she would be like Tre and keep her distance from her father. She never mentioned Kris Randall.

Chapter 33

Brian hung up the phone disgusted that he allowed Dionne to get him upset. He had gone through the pain of losing his family. Brian knew he lost his relationship with Tre years prior. He hadn't thought of that night for almost five years. It was the first break in his counseling session. Once he admitted how he destroyed his relationship with his son, he could admit to his betrayal of his wife's trust. Brian started therapy shortly after Sage walked in on his rendezvous with Zach. His sessions lasted for more than six years and after the divorce was final he stopped going to the sessions entirely.

After he lost his family and the possibility of losing his job taunted him daily, the things he lived for, he gave in to who he considered he was supposed to be. Brian sought Zach's affection only to be told he loved him but couldn't trust him. Brian began dating and socializing more with people he didn't know and found out a lot of his business clients were on the DL as well. They introduced him to the clubs, invited him to social events and told him about Tempting Escorts.

Brian's anger and feelings of desperation hadn't diminished. He worked through them during the day and at night he took it out on his various dates. Demarest, an intern at Kilmore became a regular. Brian could have had a relationship with Demarest, but he wanted Zach. It was easier to use Demarest sexually and abuse him mentally. This became Brian's game. He introduced Demarest to his clients that dealt with Tempting Escorts and even encouraged Demarest to escort them part time. As a young lover Demarest fulfilled Brian's needs, but every now and then he would slip and moan Zach's name. It became the norm and Demarest screamed the same words that Brian heard Dionne say over the phone, "… you need help". He lost his control of Demarest the night, he introduced him to Carla. He searched his soul many nights after that trying to find the roots of his issues.

Brian thought about his past as far back as he could remember. The time before he met Sage, before he went to college, he thought about his father abusing his mother and him. Brian began to cry. The phone rang and he wiped his eyes as though the caller would be able to see his tears.

"Hey, Brian, it's Zach."

"Yeah, what's up?"

"Listen, I was thinking. Do you think it would be too much if I invited another couple to join us at the table? You know Doug, he dates that nerd Lamont from Tempting Escorts anyway he has tickets for the dinner too."

"How do you know Doug?"

"C'mon sweetie, do we need to go there?"

"Yeah, we do. What's the plans for later? I hope they don't include Doug and Lamont."

"No, they don't. There's some things I just won't do, especially with Lamont."

"What about with Doug?"

"Brian, are you jealous? We're not an item, you and I. Why? Because you can't be trusted remember?"

"I remember and I've tried to make up for that."

"Yes, you have. And I've thanked you over and over again."

"Zach, you know how I feel. Why do you continue to string me along?"

"Cause you love those who don't love you."

Zach hung up the phone without Brian agreeing to share the table with Doug and his date. He hoped it he wouldn't bring Lamont. He was sure Greg told Lamont about his requests for Kris. He didn't need that to be the topic at dinner. Brian thought about Kris. He wanted him if only for a night. Dionne might have been right. He still needed help.

Chapter 34

Sage pulled out her CD case searching for CD's to load into the radio. Kris drove in silence for more than thirty minutes, and it was beginning to bother her. They stopped for dinner on Interstate 95 and Sage was looking forward to his explanation.

"Did you want to stop at the diner or do you feel like fast food?"

"We need to stop at the diner."

Kris gave Sage a confused look wondering what she meant by her statement. He pulled into the parking lot of the first diner after exiting the highway. They got out of the car, entered and waited for the hostess to seat them.

"Are you hungry?"

Kris asked, as Sage looked pass him pointing to the table where the waitress stood beckoning them to come and be seated.

"Thank you. We'll take a look at the menu's for a minute please."

"Sure, can I bring you anything to drink right away?"

"Water will be fine."

Kris watched allowing Sage to speak for both of them. She smiled at the waitress and handed Kris his menu.

"Is there something wrong lady?"

"You tell me. You haven't said a word since you got into the car."

"You're right. There's a lot on my mind."

"So you block me out. I mean, Kris, I can't do this again. We need an open relationship."

"You're right Lady, you're right. I didn't want to burden you with more about your ex or the past."

"More what?"

"He called today, again; more of the same threats."

"I understand why now."

Sage smiled and Kris knew she was referring to his bedroom performance.

"Sage, your ex knows nothing about my bedroom actions, that I can assure you."

"Okay, maybe he heard about you."

"No, that's not true either. I never dealt with anyone in this town. Brian is just … well he's Brian. The more I learn about him the more I feel sorry for him."

"Sorry? Wait she's here for our order."

The waitress took their order and the conversation went on after she placed their water on the table.

"Now, tell me why you feel sorry for Brian."

"He lost the best woman ever for one, a beautiful family, and if he keeps messing with me, he may not like the repercussions."

"Repercussions?"

"Sage, you already know Brian was not truthful about a lot of things. One of them being his sexuality. There are other things, but baby I swear I don't know how to tell you."

"What other things Kris?"

"Did you know about a guy named Demarest? He worked with him on his job?"

"I've heard that name. Yes, that's the man who Brian said was upset about getting a position and threatened to file charges against him."

"Did he tell you the type of charges?"

"No, I think discrimination because he was gay?"

"Was it before or after Zach, Sage."

"The first time I heard about it, I think was after....no before the Zach thing. Zach topped it all. Brian tried to tell me that the complaint that Demarest was filing and his transfer was how he was being punished for hurting me. He tried to get spiritual about it. Why, what secret lies there? I already figured that Demarest wasn't lying although I couldn't see why Brian was against anyone being gay."

"No, I guess he wouldn't be. Brian helped move him to Virginia and was paying for his expenses for years."

"Really? Okay and why would I find that secret a problem? I'm sure he paid a few more not to tell."

"I guess you're right."

"So, is that all that worried you?"

"No babe, it's not that simple."

"You're joking!"

The waitress returned with their food causing a pausing in their conversation again. Kris's phone rang and the called ID showed Greg's number. Kris excused himself from the table to take the call. It was dark outside but Kris stood close to the front door of the diner where the light gave way to the darkness.

"Hey man."

"Yea, what's up Greg?"

"Carla's willing to meet up with you guys. Did you decide whether or not to tell Sage?"

"I was talking to her about Demarest before you called. I didn't mention Carla and her son yet."

"Are you?"

"I've got to man. It's bothering me. I guess I'm easy to read because Sage knew something was up. So I began telling her. I'm not going to mention Dionne's take on all this. Sage seems to be taking this thing about Demarest better than I thought she would."

"You told her he was dealing with Demarest while they were married?"

"I didn't give her a time frame."

"Carla's son is eleven. Sage will figure it out and then the shit will hit the fan."

"Listen, I'll be there for her, but she'll have to deal with what her children know and why they didn't tell her."

"Understood. Listen Carla invited me down so let me know when the coast is clear."

"You're stepping into forbidden territory."

"Forbidden for who? Man I've explored that territory already."

"Maybe she can keep you on this side of the world. Does she know you travel to the dark side?"

"Yes. What the fuck do you mean the dark side?"

"I can't fuck with you guys. In order for me to deal with another man it would have to be dark, real dark."

"Be careful, Brian knows how to turn off the lights."

"Fuck you Greg."

Chapter 35

Sage was sipping her coffee when Kris returned to the table. They exchanged smiles and Kris put his phone on vibrate so they wouldn't be disturbed again.

"Greg said to tell you hello."

Kris wanted to soften the conversation before suggesting they meet Carla.

"And what was he talking about?"

"The same thing we're talking about. He was checking on something in Virginia."

"Information about Brian in Virginia?"

"Yea, that's where Demarest lives."

"Kris, just tell me without the riddles."

"Demarest lives with the woman who encouraged him to file harassment on Brian. They met years ago. Brian introduced them. Sage I really want them to explain this situation to you."

"Why, that was years ago? I'm no longer connected to Brian's past; some things are better unknown."

"Some things have a way of resurfacing. I think you were caught off guard enough and maintained your balance well. But baby, this might unnerve you, and I want you to be prepared."

The waitress returned to the table. She gave the check to Kris. He handed her the check and his credit card. Sage wiped her mouth and drank the rest of her coffee.

They returned to the car continuing the conversation.

"Say what it is Kris, please."

"Tell me you'll be willing to talk with the people who can answer all your questions. Listen, the woman who told Demarest to file charges was dealing with Brian during the time that Demarest was. She and Brian have an eleven-year-old son. I don't think Brian knows about it. The money that he was sending Demarest was spent on a home the three of them live in. Demarest is gay but he and the woman have remained friends all these years. They want to meet you."

Kris didn't wait for her response. He started the car and headed for the highway. Sage was silent; her thoughts had taken her over. She was at a lost for words.

"Kris, call the woman, Demarest or Greg. It's time to bury the past. I have a few questions and maybe after all this time I will finally hear the answers. Tell them I'll meet with them, I guess when we're free one of these evenings."

"I'll call Greg. Thanks Sage."

"No, thank you. It's time I move on, and I need to let go."

Chapter 36

Lamont waited in the foyer of his apartment complex for Doug. Dinner started at eight but they both wanted to be there for the cocktail hour. Lamont loved going to these affairs. Doug worked with clients who paid good money for escort services, and it was another chance to promote Tempting Escorts. Lamont made sure he had plenty of business cards. Although Doug and Lamont had been a couple for more than three years, there was never any display of public affection at these events. Most people assumed they were a couple but they both agreed it was better for business if they were considered close friends. Because of their agreement, Lamont was surprised when Doug told him they would be sharing a table with Zachary Blanding and his guest. Lamont and Zach had met on a few occasions, and they tolerated each other for the sake of Doug.

Two queens at a table always brought drama and Doug would laugh and smile at the snide remarks and facial gestures made between Zach and Lamont. Lamont asked who Zach's guest was, hoping it was someone he knew. Doug told him he never asked and whoever it was, he was sure they understood Zach.

Doug arrived closer to seven o'clock than Lamont liked but when he got out to open the passenger door for Lamont his appearance made up for his lateness.

"You clean up well. Damn, I might have to forget our little agreement about business dates."

Doug smiled and closed the door behind Lamont and got in on the driver's side.

"There will be time for you to admire me. You look good yourself. That suit is nice. Is that the tie I gave you?"

"It is. This suit is the one I told you I had tailored. Thank you."

"Fits you well, let's go and make someone upset."

"Are we waiting for Zach before going in?"

"No, we're sitting at the same table. We'll catch up with them there."

"Did you find out who his guest is?"

"Is that bothering you? I mean you keep asking like you're worried about who he may be with. What's up with that?"

"Zach is a problem. I can put up with him, but I would like to know who else I have to deal with."

"No one, just me. Let's not start the night thinking there's gonna be drama."

"Baby, Zach is always bringing the drama. Humph, I hope he didn't invite you thinking he was gonna grandstand me tonight."

"Lamont, he doesn't think that."

"Doug, that bitch don't fool me. He wants you and I know it. It's okay though, I'm secure in my spot. Let him try his best shit."

"Lamont, forget about it. I'm not interested in Zach, and you know it. Anyway, I think his date will keep him busy. It's somebody he's dealing with."

"Oh, okay we'll see. Maybe he's trying to get your attention by bringing someone else."

"You have my attention, remember that."

Doug drove to the sign indicating valet parking. They got out of the car and Doug gave the parking attendant the keys and a tip. Cars were filling the parking lot quickly. The makes and models of the cars gave a visual of the quality of the business owners, entrepreneurs, and clients in attendance. Lamont was pleased knowing there were plenty of prospects for the escorting service.

"Doug, hey man. How's it going?"

Doug turned touching Lamont on his arm, to let him know he stopped. The man who called his name was his boss, Mr. Washington, CEO of WMC Architectural Designs.

"Mr. Washington, how are you this evening."

"Man, I can't wait for this to be over. This event is once a year for a reason. It's a pain in the ass. But it makes the business for us. How's your project coming along? I hear you're working on that Desmond presentation."

"It's coming along, there's some rough edges, but I have time. We'll get the account."

"That's what I like to hear. Listen, I'll see you inside. If not, I'll see you in passing on Monday."

"Good seeing you sir."

Mr. Washington waved his hand as he left Doug and Lamont watching him walk off. The man walked slowly showing his age. The rumor was he was the oldest CEO in town still working.

"Why does he bother coming to these dinners?"

"Lamont, it's probably his only chance to socialize. He doesn't need to be by himself though. I don't know where his assistant is. They hired him to escort him around for events like this."

"Do you think he'd be interested in our service?"

"No that old man?"

"Fool. We could provide a service for him. Something like what that assistant is supposed to be doing. I mean the person doesn't have to know the business, similar to a bodyguard, a personal escort to help him to events and meetings."

"I don't know. I'll find out what's up with the assistant and let you know. That punk will show up tonight, he should have been riding with him."

"Doug, hey, I thought you said we would meet at the table, how sweet of you guys to wait for us."

Doug and Lamont hadn't given Zach a second thought after talking about him in the car. They were standing where Mr. Washington spotted Doug.

"Zach, yeah, well we were on our way in. Hey man, I'm Doug Carver and this is Lamont Fields."

"How rude of me, yes, Brian Drakeford, this is Doug and Lamont."

Lamont tried to restrain from giving Brian an inquisitive look, but he needed the name repeated to be sure.

"Did you say Drakeford?"

"Yes, Brian Drakeford. Is there a problem?"

Zach was prepared for the drama. He knew Lamont worked for the escort service. He hoped Lamont would tell who Brian had been spending some of his time with.

"Lamont, I recognize your voice now. How are you? I'm a client of Tempting Escorts."

"Yes, Mr. Drakeford, a pleasure to finally meet you."

Lamont's tone let Brian know there would be no exposure of his affairs tonight. Brian gave Lamont a nod of acknowledgment as they all entered the reception hall. The room was huge and their table was on the opposite side of the entrance. The four men walked across the dance floor as people yelled hellos to Brian, Zach and Doug. Lamont could tell the ones who spoke knew that Brian and Zach were or had been a couple. As they approached their table Lamont could see there were two couples seated there already.

"Good evening people. How is everyone? This is Brian Drakeford, Douglas Carver and Lamont Fields. This is Mr. Anthony Smalls and his wife Cassie and this is Mr. Walter Clousing and his wife Maria. I hope the table suits you both. I tried to get your tickets close to the dais. The Smalls and the Clousings are being honored for community service in small business tonight."

Brian, Lamont and Doug said their hellos and congratulations while they took their seats. The couples politely said thank you adjusting their chairs making room. Lamont gazed around the room looking for a place his business cards would be most visible. There were two bars and he would venture over and talk to the bartenders about leaving his cards where people could pick one up while waiting for their drinks to be prepared. Zach excused himself from the table when he spotted a client he knew. The Smalls and Clousings were called to the dais for presentation directions, while Doug went to get a drink for himself and Lamont. Brian and Lamont were left at the table, giving them a moment to talk.

"How's business?"

"Meaning?"

"Don't' be on the defensive Lamont. I'm just making small talk."

"Small talk is, how's the weather? Business is fine. How's your business?"

"Meaning?"

"Did you straighten things out?"

"What things would you be talking about?"

"Sweetie, your phone calls indicated you were having some trouble. We don't get many clients who have a hold put on their account."

"Well if that's what you're talking about, yes, I did talk with Mr. Tempts."

"Okay, I'm glad you got things straight."

Brian didn't know what to say. Lamont didn't give any indication he knew what the problem with his account was. He didn't want to tell Lamont anything about his requests for Kris if Lamont didn't already know the situation.

"Are you losing a lot of your escorts?"

"No, not at all, as a matter of a fact we just hired a few last week. It takes a while to get the right people, but we always have people seeking employment."

"Really, I would think it would be hard to fill the vacant positions."

"Not really we pay well. There are people who misunderstand the type of agency Tempting Escorts is. We are not a dating service, we don't provide match making. If that's what they think they're looking for work in the wrong place."

"For a moment I thought you were talking about the clients and not the escorts."

"The clients are confused too. I mean what goes on afterward is not our business, but people shouldn't be calling us thinking we're going to help them build a relationship with our escorts."

"That happens often?"

"Brian, you know it does. You know it first hand."

"Why do you say that?"

"I play many games, none that I would play with you. Like I said, Tempting Escorts is not a dating service. If someone can't get the escorts to deal with them outside of the paid hours of service, they need to leave the service out of it. It's outside the realm of our business. That's why clients who get involved like that are denied the service."

"And it was determined that I fit into that category?"

"I wouldn't know. That's handled by upper management. That's why you were told to speak with Greg Tempts. He makes those decisions. I don't know the depth of the problem. I do know your file was pulled because of a problem though."

"Lamont, Tempting Escorts is a small business. I know the talk has gone through the office. I appreciate you trying to keep the information confidential. It's just you and me at the table now. Do you know about me and Kris Randall or not?"

"Brian, I don't know anything about you and Kris Randall. What I do know is business, business that I will not talk about in a casual setting with you or anyone else. Company policy won't allow it. It's your business. If you want to discuss it, you tell me about it, and we'll talk. Other than that sweetie, drop the subject."

Brian was furious. He didn't know what Lamont would or wouldn't tell. If he openly admitted to wanting to deal with Kris or the threats he made Lamont would have a platform to talk about it all night. He was sure that the feeling between Zach and Lamont was mutual and Lamont would use the conversation against Zach.

"We'll drop the subject for now, but Lamont, I know you know more than you're saying."

"Excuse me Brian. Doug is calling me at the bar."

Lamont got up leaving Brian watching him cross the dance floor. Zach returned to the table bringing him a needed drink. The house lights brightened indicating the presentations were about to begin. Everyone returned to their seats Lamont made sure he and Doug sat across from Zach and Brian putting the married couples between them on both sides.

The program was beautiful; the dinner was better than the usual banquet dinners. Networking and the music for dancing began. The Smalls and the Clousings said their goodbyes shortly after the music began leaving Doug, Lamont, Zach and Brian at the table. Brian excused himself to mix and mingle with clients.

"So Doug, did you see the gentlemen from Baltimore Heights? They were looking for a representative from your company."

"I spoke to them briefly. Thanks for the hook. I believe we'll be able to work the project for them."

"It's hard to get in the door with some of these folks. If I get in, I'll let you know."

"Aren't you playing two sides Zach?"

"What are you talking about Lamont?"

"Brian and Doug are competitors. Did you give Brian the same opportunity? Or are you just throwing Doug a hook to see if you can bait him?"

"Stop it. This bullshit here, is my job honey, it's what I do. I search the businesses and give them to the companies that can provide the service. Similar to your business, you get a profile and match them to who can provide the service. You understand that don't you sweetie."

Lamont's blood pressure was rising. He could feel the heat around his neck.

"You're right, especially when the service that the client has been dealing with just isn't enough or doesn't stand up to par."

Doug knew Lamont had touched a nerve. He didn't know why. Lamont hadn't told him the full story regarding Brian and Kris. Brian was returning to the table as Zach responded.

"What the fuck are you saying bitch? You've been providing some service, to who?"

"I never said that. I merely was agreeing with you that we do the same job, my company and yours. I just don't understand why you would throw this client at Doug when your man is in architectural designing himself. I'm sure Doug appreciates the lead, but I don't think you should bait him for your personal reasons."

"Wait a minute Lamont. Who said he was baiting me?"

"Doug, no let's ask Brian. Brian, did you get a chance to talk to the men from Baltimore Heights? We were discussing the fact that Zach put in a good word for Doug to talk to them. Has your company had the opportunity to talk with them? I would think he would hook you up too or first, you know what I mean?"

Brian looked at Zach giving him a look of frustration and embarrassment. Zach had given Doug a door opener; if the deal was closed it would be huge for his career. Most designers would kill for the opportunity to sit with the planners and developers for Baltimore Heights.

"No he didn't mention it."

"I told Doug that. Anyway Doug thanked Zach and I thank him too. It proved a point I wanted to make to Doug all along. Back off Zach. You can't buy him."

Lamont got to his feet.

"The two of you belong together. When you can't get what you want you turn tricks."

Lamont left the table. Doug knew that meant he would be sitting at the bar or the lounge the rest of the night.

"Zach, man I'm sorry. We'll talk. Again, thanks for the hook."

Zach couldn't look at Brian. He knew what the rest of the night would be like. Brian left him sitting at the table and went to the bar. Zach would have to make up for his mistake.

Chapter 37

Doug didn't have much to say on the ride back to Lamont's apartment, there was little he could say after Lamont exposed Zach's intentions. Doug denied knowing what Zach was doing or any other advances he had made. Lamont didn't want to argue.

"Are you up to company for the night or am I going home wondering why I'm being punished?"

"Doug, wake up. Zach has been coming on to you for months. You can't possibly be that naïve, or think that I am. It's okay, though, I knew it was coming to this. He's knows I know now. The next move is on you."

"Me?"

Doug parked the car in the front of the apartment where he picked Lamont up six hours earlier. Lamont didn't tell him to drive to the parking lot, which answered Doug's question about him spending the night.

"Yes you. Doug for the sake of business you don't tell Zach to back up. You accept his passes, compliments and advances knowing damn well if you took it further he would pounce at the opportunity."

"The key word in that is "if". I don't take it further. I don't do anything more with him, then you do with the clients you deal with."

"Doug, be real. I don't deal with them on that level. What, I talk to them on the phone and that's it."

"You flirt on the phone and if they took it further?"

"What are you talking about? Don't turn this on me!"

"It's the same man. You flirt and if they pursued it, 'because of business', you would continue to get their business."

"I really don't think it's the same. Some of the clients we have I don't even meet."

"Yeah, that's another thing. What's up with you and Brian? Why did you include him in your stab at Zach?"

"What?"

"The two of you belong together thing? What was that about?"

"Listen that damn Brian is as bad as Zach. Neither of them can take no for an answer. Don't change the subject either. I don't want to be used Doug. It's bad enough that we go to these events as just friends. I thought we had got beyond that."

"We did. I thought you said you were secure in your spot. Didn't I leave with you? Aren't I here with you now? Lamont I told you there's people who I deal with that still think our love is forbidden. Unfortunately, some of them are the clients that pay the most. Don't get caught up in the bull."

"I won't. You remember the same thing."

Lamont opened his door and got out of the car. Doug opened the window to make one last plea to stay over night.

"Lamont, call me if you can't sleep."

"I'll be sleep before you get home."

Chapter 38

Brian hadn't forgotten about his anger when Zach promised there was nothing between him and Douglas. Brian wanted to keep their relationship. His head was beginning to hurt from the champagne he drank and his frustration was building.

"Zach, do you have anything for a headache."

Zach smiled as he turned the key in his apartment door. He hit the light switch and proceeded to the bathroom without saying a word.

"I guess you're getting them for me?"

"Yeah, I have them here sweetie, let me get you a glass of water."

"Zach we really need to talk before starting our relationship again. I don't want this to be a surface thing anymore, but there's some things I need to tell you."

"Honey look, I couldn't talk serious tonight if I wanted to. Your head hurts and I know mine will in the morning. Can we talk then, will that be a problem?"

"I guess not. If you promise we'll talk then."

"We will, promise. Do you need something else?"

"No thanks. I do want you to know that I didn't appreciate you offering a deal to Doug before offering it to me. Why wasn't I told what was going on?"

"Brian, we'll talk in the morning. You already said your head was hurting. Don't blow this thing out of proportion. Remember we haven't been dealing with each other for the last five months. I really didn't think you would go to the dinner with me. I did what I get paid to do. I found a company to complete the project for my client. I didn't want to go through the drama with you and have you hold the account over my head. It's done now Brian. I told you I have no desire to be with Doug. Let it rest."

"I don't think I'll be staying tonight. Call me in the morning so we can meet for breakfast and talk."

Zach walked toward his apartment door and opened it wide so Brian could leave, exaggerating a careless attitude. Brain left without saying goodbye. Zach watched as Brian walked down the hall toward the elevator.

"I wish I would call your ass, please!" Zach slammed the door closed.

Chapter 39

Lamont got out of the bed on Monday morning with the intention of calling the office. He had a headache since Saturday night, after the dinner. Doug tried to talk him into going to breakfast on Sunday and a movie Sunday afternoon, but Lamont declined both offers. The last thing he wanted to deal with was Doug's pleas for him to understand the situation between him and Zach.

Sharonda answered the phone ready to fuss. She knew he was calling to say he wouldn't be in.

"What the hell is your problem today?"

"An intense headache girl, I've had it since Saturday night. I'm taking a shower and going back to bed."

"Did you take anything for it? I know you did."

"I took enough to stiffen a horse. I'm doped up but my head still hurts. I just need to recoup, I guess my body is tired."

"It doesn't sound normal Lamont. Did you call the doctor? Your blood pressure might be up or something."

"Well if I'm not better by tomorrow I'll consider going to the doctor."

"You won't go to the doctor. You are horrible. What's wrong with you and doctors?"

"Listen, is Greg there? We won't be going there right now. I told you my head is hurting, that's all. Let me speak to Greg."

"He's in Virginia. He left yesterday."

"Virginia? Carla's house?"

"I guess. He did say that Sage and Kris would be meeting with Carla some time today."

"Girl is he getting involved with her again?"

"Lamont, go take your shower."

"Gossip cures girl. You don't know?"

"Later, call if you need anything."

"Alright, I'll see you tomorrow."

Lamont hung up the phone and thought about Greg being in Virginia a day early. Curiosity got the best of him and he dialed Greg's number.

"Hey Lamont, how was the dinner?"

"I met Mr. Wonderful."

"Who?"

"Brian Drakeford. That ass was Zach's date. We sat at the same table."

"Did you tell him where you worked?"

"After going around the bush; he wanted me to admit to knowing about Kris. I told him I wouldn't discuss business with him. If he wanted to tell it, I would discuss it. He chose not to say anything. I was hoping he would."

"So the rest of the night went on without any other conversation about him and Kris?"

"He was with Zach, I think he was scared I would mention it around Zach and blow his thing. Zach blew his thing though. Greg, I finally got that bitch. He hooked that damn Doug up with some business deal. He hadn't mentioned it to Brian. You know I told it. I put that bitch on front street. Yes, I did. I asked his ass was the business deal offered to bait Doug? You know he denied it. So I asked him had he offered the same deal to Brian. Silence, you know that's what we heard, silence. I went on from there. I told him I found it hard to believe that he didn't offer his own damn man the deal first. But I let both of their asses know they deserved each other. It got heated. I left the table and told Doug's ass off afterward. He's so fucking naïve. He claims it was all business. Doug doesn't even see what Zach's plan was."

"Maybe I'm as naïve as Doug, what was Zach's plan?"

"Greg, sweetie, it was simple. Doug accepts the lead Zach gave him, whether or not he lands the deal Zach opened the door for him. If the deal goes sour, Zach is in the wings waiting for Doug to complain and then he would probably offer to make it up to him. If the deal goes through, the offer would be to celebrate. Either of which he would spend time in a one on one with my man. Shit, that bitch ain't fooling me."

"Oh. I guess you could have a point. So you and Doug left together on good terms right? I mean, it wasn't Doug's fault."

"Greg, I told you, Doug lives his life with blinders on. Anyone could have seen that shit coming. Not Doug. Just like that swapping shit he always wants to do. Set up for problems. I needed a break so I told him good night. I'll deal with him later this week."

"Your game player. So I see you're calling me from your home phone. What's up with that?"

"I have this headache I can't get rid of."

"So you could have called me later. Go take care of yourself."

"I wanna know what is your ass doing in Virginia?"

Greg laughed. Lamont loved gossip and Greg loved hearing him relay it. The thought of Lamont telling the story without the details would be better than the truth.

"What do you think?"

"I know you ain't thinking about Ms. Carla again. I thought that was the Carla you were dealing with at one time; I didn't want to say anything just in case I was wrong. Didn't she have that child then?"

"No, not when we started dealing with each other. I hadn't heard from her after she moved. We talked off and on and I knew she had a child but I thought she was in a relationship headed for marriage so I backed off."

"So, answer the question, why are you in Virginia?"

"She invited me."

"My ass, you invited yourself. What makes you think that Sage wants you in on their meeting?"

"I'll be there before and after not during."

"What kind of shit? What are you talking about?"

"I'm not here because of the meeting."

"Greg, why then?"

"I don't know. I guess to see what's up with us. You know I really liked her but I had my reservations. Now I'm not sure I didn't make a mistake."

"Greg, that woman don't want a man who can't make up his mind about his pleasures. Ask Sage."

"Lamont, listen, I want to explore the possibilities."

"Say what you want, that's dangerous. You be careful."

"What's dangerous? She knows about my desires."

"Let her play you, hear? Listen my head is killing me. You come on home. When are you leaving there?"

"Probably tomorrow, we're going to dinner tonight with Sage and Kris."

"Where's Demarest?"

"I guess he's around. I didn't ask. He'll meet Sage though, if that's what you mean. He wasn't included in our dinner plans."

"Well, you come on home. Let that past die. I don't think it needs revisiting."

"It may change my feelings about who I really am."

"Greg, you are who you are. That's that damn man's problem, that damn Brian. He thought being married would change him. Don't drag that woman into your world of confusion. Get yourself together first. If she's truly who you want to be with, realize your past fantasies can't continue into the relationship you'll have with her. If you can't let go of those fantasies, then the straight life ain't for you."

"Thanks, I'll talk with you later. Go and take care of your headache."

"Call me and let me know how things go."

"I will."

Chapter 40

Sage and Kris spent most of the morning looking over the information about the properties they had seen over the weekend. Sage had taken notes and collected presentation material on the properties they thought would best suit Kris's parents and his sister's children. They checked the neighborhood, schools, and store locations to be sure things were convenient for his parents and the children to get to. Sage loved the countryside, while Kris thought it would be better to look at the property that wasn't too far from the city. Papers were spread over the king size bed in their suite while they sat at the kitchenette table looking at the figures.

The weekend had been about business as planned during the day and they looked for activities to entertain themselves in the evenings. Saturday night they went to the movies and Sunday they combined house hunting with touring the historic sites of Virginia. They spent the Sunday evening having a beautiful dinner. Kris made reservations and asked Sage to get dressed without telling her where they were headed. The restaurant was beautiful, the food was delicious and the jazz band set off the mood for romance. Sage was pleased she chose to accompany Kris on the trip. The appointment for Monday was at two o'clock and afterward they would be meeting Carla and Demarest at their home. They agreed to go to dinner with Greg and Carla later in the evening.

Sage called Karen three times over the past three days keeping her abreast of the happenings and her fears. Karen agreed with Sage, the meeting with Carla may answer questions that were needed to be answered years prior. Sage wanted to meet Carla and Demarest, but she still had fears about uncovering more of Brian's problems.

Kris leaned back in the chair stretching and winked at Sage when he noticed her glance. She returned his gesture with a smile.

"Kris, do you think your parents will like what you've picked?"

"I hope so. My mother's choices would probably have been the same as yours. The country, the open air and away from the hustle and bustle of the city, but if the children get involved in extra activities she'll appreciate being close to where they may have to go."

"She'll understand. The houses are really nice and the prices are in the range they're looking to spend. Once the kids get older they can sell and move further out."

Kris's expressions changed and he picked up the papers of the last house they had to review.

"What's the face for? You act as though they won't be happy to move or sell again."

"No, I don't know how long they'll be able to keep the kids."

"What?"

"Yeah, that was the other problem. My parents are up in age. They've done a lot for the children and my sister's husband's side of the family sends what they can. But the reality is I may be raising those kids in the next couple of years."

"They'll have to adjust again in a few years? That's rough, you know going from place to place."

"They've been in the same school since they started. This will be their first major move. Moving in with my mom and Dad reminded them of a weekend or school break. My sister's home was near my parents."

"So you plan on taking in four children?"

"No, I'm prepared if I have to. If either of my parents got sick, I will take over the rearing of the children. I don't want them to be burdened with choosing between their health and raising the children."

Sage thought a moment about what Kris was saying. She didn't want to dwell on the topic, but it was true Kris would be the guardian for four children at some point in their lives. "Are your parents ill now?"

"No, and hopefully they will remain healthy throughout their lives and die of natural causes. I don't think there are any major health issues, but I keep myself mentally prepared for the kids."

Sage was relieved. She thought the buying of the new home was tied into some health issues that would become a problem from now on for Kris. If it had been a problem she knew it would trickle into their relationship. Sage wasn't quite ready for the connection to a new family of four.

"I'm glad they're fine. Didn't you say the youngest was seven?"

"Yeah, Nicki is seven, Derrick and Erik are ten and Maurice is thirteen. I think I got it right."

"Twins?"

"Yeah, runs in the family somewhere or maybe it was their father's family. Anyway, they're good kids; they make good grades, participate in school activities and obey their grandparents well. Better than well. I'm really amazed at their attitudes, I mean, I expected them to act out considering how strict my parents are."

"Well, they might figure they have no other home to go to."

"When we found out they would be with us instead of their dad's family we gave them a choice. They chose my parents. I was surprised they didn't want to live with me all the time. They love to visit but they love to go home."

"It could be worst. They could be uncomfortable living with older people, maybe they'll choose to live with you when they become teens and want to do other things."

"Well, whatever they choose I want to be able to handle it as much as I can. I've never been in that position so I know I'll need help."

Kris gave Sage a look that said he wanted her help. Sage responded with a smile.

"You'll be fine, there's no rule book. Lord knows you can't be prepared for everything."

"I think if I know you're in my world it will remain balanced."

Sage got up from her seat and kissed Kris on the forehead and went into the kitchenette.

"Do you want anything from the refrigerator?"

"No, what time do you want to leave?"

"Kris, do you think this last house would be as good as the others. I was thinking about riding by and seeing it first. If we don't like the area or the look we can call them and cancel."

"I don't know. Are you anxious about meeting with Carla and what's the guy's name?"

"Demarest, I think, weird name for a man."

"Well, you know how that goes. He probably changed his name. So how do you feel about this meeting?"

"To be honest with you, I'm looking forward to getting this chapter of my life closed. Usually after a divorce the husband and wife either come to terms and leave the past alone or don't deal with each other at all. I keep finding pieces of what happened while we were married. I think that's keeping me emotionally attached to Brian. I need that part of my life to be closed. I want to move on it's been seven years and then some."

"Well, let's hope that this meeting with them gives you that needed closer."

Chapter 41

Carla prepared snack trays and set up other refreshments on her dinning room table. She wanted the talk with Sage to be informal and welcoming. Demarest had cleaned the house for her and the aroma from the candles added to the clean smell. Carl wouldn't be home from school until after they had talked for at least an hour and a half. Carla was a little nervous. She thought of the days, years ago, that she wanted to meet Brian's wife. Now it seemed unnecessary but as she and Demarest talked more about it, she realized that Brian would go on abusing people. Their conclusion was he didn't understand the hurt he left them with. If this introduction would make him understand and stop him from hurting others in the future than it was worth it.

Greg called earlier checking to see if her nerves had settled. Seeing him again after eleven years was refreshing. Carla cooked dinner for the two of them on Sunday afternoon. Carl spent his day with friends leaving his mom to the first home date she had in years. They enjoyed dinner and wine, watched a movie and caught up on the gossip and goings on of Tempting Escorts. Carla was surprised that Greg wasn't forward about spending the night or starting a relationship. He had expressed wanting to be with her again during their phone conversations. She told him she doubted his interest extended beyond the bedroom. Greg told her he had changed. Carla had heard it before. She wished she could trust his word.

Sage and Kris arrived a little after four. They decided to go and see the house at two o'clock and found the house to be the best they had seen. They talked to the owners who had lived in the home for the past seven years. After leaving, they toured the neighborhood. Sage suggested they should visit the local grammar school and high school to get an inside look at the programs offered. Carla was pleased when Demarest finally went to answer the door.

"Welcome, come in. It is good to meet you both, I'm Demarest and that's Carla. Come in, have a seat."

"Hello, I'm Carla. Sage and Kris come in."

"Thank you. Thanks for having us."

"Well, I think this meeting has been a long time coming. In a way I'm glad that it has come to this."

Sage took the opportunity to look around the home, a habit she had as a real estate agent. The home was beautiful and comfortable. There was a definite sign that Demarest was a part of the family. Pictures and items in the curios contained his effects. It was apparent that he was openly gay, and it wasn't a hidden topic in their house. Carla was a beautiful woman. She wasn't what Sage thought would visually interest Brian. He always said he loved the darker woman but Carla looked as though she may have been Hispanic. Demarest was light in complexion as well. They were both nice looking people but Sage realized again she didn't know Brian's hidden desires.

"Sage, I understand your daughter is getting married in June. Do you think this news would be taken better before or after the wedding?"

"Carla, I don't know. It's hard for me to get a grasp of what has happened."

"It took us a while too. It all happened so fast."

Kris watched Demarest as he spoke. Until he spoke, there were no signs of him being gay. His voice was softer than the average man, and he didn't try to project it any other way. After they all got comfortable sitting in the living room, Carla offered soda and refreshments. Kris and Sage declined anxious to hear the story that was told by Greg. Demarest told the story just as Greg repeated it.

Demarest began working at Kilmore with Brian and in a matter of months was approached by him for a date. They dated for more than eight months before he started abusing him in the bedroom. Demarest thought it was a dominance thing and tried to be comfortable with it. Brian didn't always act that way, but it was enough to give Demarest a reason to complain. Brian didn't listen or make an effort to change things and two weeks later Brian told Demarest there would be a woman joining them at this party they were going to. Demarest continued to describe the evening including his feelings and his embarrassment. He had to take a moment to collect his emotions when he described the rape and the shame he felt afterward.

Carla became his friend. She called to check on him.

When she called, he had been to the doctors for the anal ruptures he sustained and counseling, which allowed him to continue working at Kilmore. He tried to avoid Brian, who saw no fault in his actions. Carla told Demarest about the pregnancy and they used it. He would file harassment if Brian didn't leave him alone and if he tried to retaliate they had a back up. Carla would reveal her pregnancy and expose the rape to his superiors. It never got that far Brian stopped after being threatened with harassment. He never found out about the pregnancy and when he did Carla lied.

Carla excused herself and went into the dinning room to get the tray of refreshments. Sage got up to help her bring in the sodas and cups. When Sage got to the dining room, she found Carla softly crying seated at the table.

"I'm sorry. It bothers me every time I hear him have to go through that story. He's getting better with it and the counselors have told him it will get better each time. But Sage, it's so ugly for someone to do that to anyone. I can remember him screaming, begging Brian to stop. That's the only thing about this whole thing. I don't know if I want to look at Brian. He was a monster that night."

"Carla, I understand. I've seen that monster in a mild form. I just don't want him doing that or anything else to others. Now that I've heard it, I agree he needs to feel how it feels to get blind-sided by someone you love. It's his dirt and it needs to be thrown in his face."

They returned to the living room where Kris and Demarest, were talking.

"I've only dealt with him on the surface. He's kinda been threatening me."

"Are you gay?"

Demarest asked the question, as though he hoped Kris was.

"No, not even bi. He claims I'm confused because I did the escorting thing."

"There were plenty of straight men working at Tempting; even those that escorted the men."

"I know but he's chosen me to make his next love interest."

"Well you don't want that shit. That's for sure."

"Carla, you were seeing Brian at the same time as Demarest?"

Kris was glad Sage broke in changing the questions. He was a little nervous about Demarest's interest in his sexual preferences.

"I guess so Sage. Brian and I went on a few dinner dates where I was the escort. I would always meet him at a designated location, and we would leave from there. One night I was running late, and I gave him my number and address, so he would pick me up to make up the time. We returned to my place and the relationship began that night. It lasted until that night with Demarest. I wouldn't see him after that. It must have been close to five or six months. I found out about three, maybe four weeks later I was pregnant. They said I was eight weeks along. I never told him. I didn't want him in Carl's life at all, and I still don't. That's what has kept me from coming forward. That and I didn't want your home to be wrecked anymore than it was."

"Carla, how old is Carl?"

"He's eleven, he'll be twelve."

Just hearing the age told Sage he had been dealing with Demarest, Carla and Zach at the same time. He was coming home to her in their bed begging to make love to her knowing he had three sexual affairs going on. Her walking in on Zach was the tip of the iceberg. Brian had major issues; he was abusive, gay, and the father of a child outside of their marriage. Kris put his arm around Sage giving her comforting support.

"He looks more like me, I think, but he does have a few of Brian's looks when his moods change."

Sage got up to look at a few of the pictures that were in the room. She could see the resemblance in Carl of his mother, but she didn't see Brian's features at all. Carla walked up behind her with a picture of Carl in his baseball uniform and tears dropped from Sage's eyes.

"He had a little attitude about going to practice just for pictures. When his moods change, he looks more like Brian. It's funny but it's true. His moods change his looks. If you need more proof, we'll submit to DNA testing."

"No, girl, Brian might need proof but I don't. I've been divorced for over seven years. It's time to close the book on Mr. Drakeford. So can you, Demarest and Carl make the wedding?"

Chapter 42

"Karen, the question is not whether or not to invite them to the wedding. I just want to know if you think the wedding is the place for Brian's embarrassment. Kris said no one will really know. Brian will be too engrossed in the moment during the ceremony and a little uncomfortable at the wedding. It will probably be something he will address with me and Kris days later. That's not what I want. That bastard needs to be put in a situation that he has to squirm out of. That's how each of us felt. I don't think it will affect him like that at the wedding, not to mention I really didn't want to ruin Dionne's memories of her wedding day."

"Yeah, what will Trevon and Dionne think? You'll be the one who ruined the day. Do you think if they knew before hand it would make it easier?"

"I don't know that Dionne would go with it. You know how she feels about her father. Trevon will probably say he could care less. He doesn't care how his father feels, or what he thinks. I wanted to persuade him to think differently about Brian, but I couldn't bring myself up to it. Karen, they have to know, but you're right, they shouldn't have to find out that way."

"Listen girl, talk to your son first. Maybe he can help you bring this matter up to Dionne, and together you can come up with where Brian will have to face you guys with his nasty issues he tried to cover."

"I hear you Karen, but I don't want to give Brian a chance to prepare an answer. I don't want to hear his excuses. I want him to have to answer right then and there in front of us all. How will he explain the three of them and the havoc he has caused in all of our lives?"

"You know the answer to that Sage. He can't explain it. There is no explanation when you cause pain to people you claim to love. He'll look at all of you and wonder why, no how, you could do this to him? How did you all get together? Why you were out hurt him?"

"Karen, after hearing Demarest and knowing what I know about Brian's past, I don't want him hurting anyone else. He should be in jail. He raped that man. How do we know who else he's victimized? Shit, if Kris was as weak as Demarest it could have been him. It could be Zach. I could have been on that list."

"Sage, talk to Trevon. Will he be here before the wedding? I mean enough time to talk with them and maybe Brian if you need to?"

"I won't deal with Brian. They can, but I'm like Carla, I don't want to be around him if I don't have to."

"Well, girlfriend that's my only advice. I wouldn't put it in Dionne and Trevon's face like that. It may ruin your relationship with them."

"I'll call Trevon."

"How did you and Kris make out with the properties?"

"Girl the homes were nice. The last one we went to was our choice. He's going to see them this weekend and show them our findings."

"I'm glad you're back. Things around here have been too quiet."

"Quiet? I've got a desk full of messages."

"I know we didn't want to dip into your appointments, so we waited."

"Girl, y'all are too much. Look at this. Ms. Wright, please call, needs appointment. I've got five of those type messages alone. You could have set up an appointment for her."

Sage handed Karen the messages.

"See, not five, eight, that's half the pile."

"Girl, Carmen made it seem like they needed your attention."

"Well, not that I can see. What's up with Carmen?"

"That damn boyfriend of hers I bet. Everyone else had appointments scheduled. I told her to cover for you."

"Well, let girlfriend know, she'll still be handling these. What the hell is she thinking?"

"That you were out of town."

"She better ask somebody."

"Give them to me. I'll take them to her with a note from me."

Sage handed the messages to Karen and picked up the phone on her desk to call Trevon. She looked at the clock on her wall. She still had two hours of office time left. Kris was meeting her at the house.

Chapter 43

Sage put her robe on before going downstairs. She thought she heard Dionne's voice, and she hurried to meet her at the bottom of the steps.

"Mom, I was on my way up the stairs. I figured I would catch you sleeping. I just wanted to go over the seating arrangement. I have to take a final head count and seating to the coordinator today. You didn't answer your phone last night."

"Aren't you working today?"

"No, I took off today to wrap up some last minute things. Jarad finally realized he was getting married in less than four weeks. I don't know what kicked him in his head but he's been getting things together that he let go for months."

Sage made her way to the kitchen hoping Dionne wouldn't linger at the stairs or go into the living room where Kris left his jacket. She noticed as she walked by it was left in the recliner where he sat after they returned from the movies. Kris was upstairs sleeping. Sage made sure she closed the door.

"How are Jarad's parents? Is his father doing better?"

"As a matter of a fact, I believe he'll live longer than all of us. He's up and around now. Not fully himself though. He spends the day sitting up, but he still needs close attention. I don't know if he'll live through another episode like the last one."

"I'm glad he's doing better. Give his mother my regards."

"Sure, sure. How's Kris?"

"Good, thanks. Can I get you coffee or something? Where's your papers or the seating you wanted to go over?"

"It's in the computer. I can pull it up on yours."

Sage wanted to stop Dionne, but she was headed for the sitting room. Dionne returned shortly after she left smiling and holding Kris's leather jacket.

"Why didn't you say I was interrupting?"

"Cause you're not. He's here but believe me, you didn't interrupt anything."

"Hmmm, I guess I might as well get use to this huh?"

"Well, yes, Dionne I don't know what to tell you. I understand how you feel about your father and I but believe me that's over."

"I know it is Ma, and I'm learning to deal with it. I had my hopes and wishes, but I've accepted it better in the last two weeks than before."

Dionne thought about Trevon and the conversation they had. She didn't know when she could bring herself to talk to her mother about her father and what she and her brother knew.

"When is Trevon coming in?"

"He said the week before the wedding. Why?"

"I think we all need to sit and talk."

"We all? Mom who is all? Me, you, Trevon and who?"

"No that's it just the three of us. I think before the wedding would be good. Then we can understand each other. A lot has changed over the years."

"Ma, remember when we used to have the late night talks on your bed?"

"Yes, you and Tre used to ask the weirdest questions."

"Just to stay up longer. We hated when the questions were over, and we had to leave your bed."

"Well this conversation won't be in my bed either."

They both laughed. Sage made a pot of coffee to go along with their conversation. Dionne printed her seating arrangements on the computer, and they sat at the table laughing and discussing who would be disappointed in their seat. Two hours passed before Sage realized Kris was still upstairs.

"Dionne I forgot about Kris. I'll be back down in a minute."

"No, Ma really, I have to go. Talk to Tre and confirm the night we'll talk. Don't forget the rehearsal and the rehearsal dinner, and the stupid bachelor party is that week."

"You won't be going to the bachelor party."

"No, but I think Tre will. He's in the wedding. Remember?"

"Wow that cuts the week in half. Let me see when Tre is coming. I'll call you."

Dionne went to the front door looking back watching her mother climb the stairs. Sage entered her bedroom and heard the shower.

"Kris, I'm sorry honey. Dionne and I got caught up with the guest list."

"Listen, I have to go."

Kris came out of the shower with the towel wrapped around his waist. His answer gave a tone of slight disgust. Sage didn't want to think he was mad because Dionne showed up.

"What's wrong with you?"

"Your damn husband, I may have to really hurt that nigger."

"What's wrong Kris?"

Kris hadn't paused to talk. He continued to put on his clothes.

"He called you again?"

"No, how about he called my office and told the staff I wouldn't be in, but they could call his home if they were looking for me." "Why would he do that?"

"Cause his faggot ass loves bullshit. He knew it would make me call him to tell his ass off."

"And that's what you're going to do."

"You're damn right!"

"Just what he wants."

"Fuck the dumb shit Sage. He needs to be told enough of this bullshit already. Last week I had a client ask why didn't I favor doing business within the gay community?"

"What, Kris wait? He just wants to see you and you're running, not thinking."

For the first time since the phone call Kris stopped moving and collected his thoughts. He went over the phone call in his mind. The call wasn't from Brian it was from Kris's Washington office. The secretary was verifying where she should call with his messages. Kris told her to call him on his cell or leave a message at his place as usual. He told her to inform all the staff. There were to be no changes of anything unless they heard it from him.

"You're right. He knew it would upset me enough to confront him. Sage, I don't want to bring you into this but did you decide whether or not you would be talking to Trevon and Dionne. If not baby, I've got to stop this dude from thinking he can interfere with my life whenever he wants."

"I'll be calling Tre today. We're going to get together before the wedding. Then I'll introduce you to Trevon."

Sage fell back on the bed letting her robe fall open bearing her breast and thighs. Kris smiled and dropped the pants he had put on hurriedly. Sage and Kris knew without a word that all phone calls would be delayed.

Chapter 44

Trevon thought about his mother asking him to come home earlier and called his job changing his days to fit in another week. He had plenty of leave time and needed to relax. Lately, it had been hard for him to sleep. His therapist said it was the anticipation of spending time with his father. Trevon got sick each time he visited his mother or sister. He wouldn't feel better until he returned to his home in Oklahoma. After one of his visits when he got sick enough to be put on bed rest. He told his doctor about the feeling he got and why. His doctor referred him to a therapist.

That had been four years ago and Trevon still had problems dealing with the idea of returning home. Sage wanted Trevon and his family to stay with her, whenever they came back home, but he usually refused the invitation. It was easier for him to stay at a hotel. Trevon and the therapist agreed it was time he told his sister and his mother about the attempt his father made to get in his bed. He took the first step and told Dionne, but she hadn't called him again since that call. Trevon wasn't sure telling them would be the solution. He tried calling her and left messages but she still hadn't called him. The doctor told him it was her way of dealing with the trust that was broken by their father. He was determined to overcome his past and begin to heal. The next step was to tell his mother. Trevon was glad Sage wanted him home a week earlier to talk with him and Dionne before the wedding.

Lynn, Trevon's wife, wouldn't mind leaving a week earlier. Their visits home to his parents and hers were only twice a year at the most, and she was glad to spend more time with her parents.

"Hey honey, when do you think would be the earliest we could leave for your parents?"

"I don't know if I can get more days off. My supervisor said she would check the schedules and let me know. I don't want her to tell me she'll give me the week earlier and take the week after the wedding. I wanted us to see my parents that week."

"Listen, if that's what you want, don't worry about leaving early. I'll go up the week ahead, and you keep your plans the way you have them. My mom wants us to have a family discussion before the wedding."

Lynn turned from the stove where she was cleaning the remains of the family's breakfast. She dreaded the answer to her question, but she had to ask it.

"Tre, are you going to mention the problem you have with your father?"

"I think so, Lynn. It's time. It's killing me and it has been for years. I told you I told Dionne right? She hasn't called me since I told her. I've even called her back. I don't know what she feels. I'm gonna tell my mother when I get home. Since Dionne is aware of the meeting I'll find out about her feelings then."

"Well, then you need to be with your family. I'll keep my schedule as planned. Tre I'm glad you're getting this off your chest."

"Me too baby, me too. I'm tired of being mad."

Chapter 45

Brian looked at his watch. It was close to two o'clock and Kris hadn't called him. He called his office twice and the secretary offered to take a message, she didn't indicate whether Kris would be in or not. Calling the cell number didn't help, Kris had blocked his number. The phone rang and Brian was sure it was the call he was waiting for. Zach's name appeared and Brian had to change his thoughts.

"So, I see you've decided to give in."

"Give in to what? I thought you wanted to talk. I know it's been a couple of days but what the fuck. I'm parking the car, open the door."

The phone went silent. Brian had forgotten about his talk with Zach. Zach was right it had been a few days —enough time for Brian to redirect his attention to Kris. He hadn't thought about Zach since leaving his place the night of the dinner. He hadn't thought much about anything. His psychiatrist would consider his mood a meltdown.

He had magazines all over the floor and an empty bottle of wine he had knocked over in the middle of the night. The place was not clean and hadn't been for more than two weeks. The clothes he wore to the dinner, he and Zach went to the weekend before were still on one end of the couch. Dishes were piled in the sink and Zach wouldn't be pleased to see that the bedroom showed signs of Brian's last fling.

Condom packets were open and thrown on the floor along with the underwear Brian stepped out of before getting into bed. The bathroom still had the towels that were used laying on the floor and sink. The woman left her bra as a souvenir.

Zach rang the bell, interrupting Brian's attempt to straighten up the mess.

"Damn, how long did you think it would take me to park?"

Zach climbed the four stairs that led to the large living room walking pass Brian and stopped gasping in horror at the mess that Brian called his home.

"What have you been up to and how long? Sugar, this is border line disgusting!"

"Look, I've been busy with a few things. Plus, I've had some things on my mind. I've been stressed."

Brian talked as he picked up clothes, shoes, magazines and other items that were clearly out of place.

"Brian, this is not good sweetie. This looks like you went through some sort of a depression phase or something. Is that why you wanted to talk?"

"Well, yea."

"Look, I'll clean up later. What I have to say is more important."

"You talk sweetie and relax. I'll start in this room, and we'll just tackle one room at a time."

"Okay, that's fair. I mean, more than fair. Zach, I've been wanting to talk to you about us. I mean you being in my life again. The way it was before but without the drama of my married life."

"Sweetie that's the past; we've moved on since then. I believe both of us learned a lesson. I don't know that either of us really wants that."

"I do, I love you and need you in my life."

"Brian, you're confused honey. You want someone you can rule. You do know you can't rule me. What ever happened to that poor boy you ran from your job? His name was Demarest, right? I heard he filed charges on your ass while we were dealing with each other, while you were married."

"Like you said that was the past. I've learned from my mistakes." Brian squirmed, feeling his anger mounting.

"You had more affairs going on when you and I were together. How can I trust you after that?"

"I'm different now Zach."

Zach waved a business card he picked up from the table in Brian's face. It had Kris Randall's name on it. He threw it at him and continued to straighten up the papers on the table where he found the card.

"So what does that prove? You know I deal with the escort service."

"Clients talk Brian. You must have forgotten you spoke to them about the service and who you wanted to be your next venture."

"It was talk, Zach that's all."

"I thought about that too until that damn Lamont mentioned we did the same type work. Did you listen to him? He was saying something without telling it all. Then it dawned on me, you were getting service from Tempting Escorts. Is this Kris Randall the man you told I wasn't handling our relationship well?"

"No, we haven't even been in an intimate situation. Zach, don't go through this. What about you and Doug?"

"What about him?"

"You have the hots for him, I know you do."

"And you have it for this Randall guy. Did you know he wasn't gay or bi? What are you gonna do? Rape him too?"

Brian jumped to his feet and grabbed Zach's throat. Zach could feel his hot breath as he spoke through his clinched teeth.

"Shut the fuck up. Say another word and you will be the one who gets raped. That shit never happened and you're gonna forget that anyone told you that. Understood?"

Zach answered gurgling.

"Let me go Brian, yea it's understood."

Brian let him go and went into the bedroom. Zach followed pushing for more answers.

"I won't repeat it but Brian it is the rumor that is going around. That's why your company had you transferred. I didn't want to say anything the other night. That's why I couldn't offer you that deal. This shit is affecting your reputation in the business world and with us. The past does matter sweetie if you're going around using people like us and then raping us."

"Who the fuck is us? I've never raped you. You want to be raped bitch?"

"I want to know the truth and right now it looks like I stumbled upon it."

Zach turned to leave the room. Brian walked ahead of him slamming the bedroom door.

"Strip Mother Fucker. You want to know what he felt? You want to make me feel better about losing my wife, my kids, my job, my world. Strip bitch!"

"Open the damn door Brian. I don't want to fight. This is insane. Open the damn door!"

Brian stepped closed and grabbed Zach's shirt. Zach being the smaller of the two was at a definite disadvantage. He swung a punch wildly at Brian's face as Brian threw him on the bed. Zach reached for the phone and hit Brian in the forehead with the base and the cordless receiver. The fight began; Brian punched Zach in the face and began tearing his shirt off.

"I'm going whoop your ass and then after I fuck you good, you're going to suck my dick and beg me for more."

"Brian, let me up. Get the fuck off me."

Zach kicked and punched until Brian hit him in his nose drawing blood.

"Brian I think you broke my fucking nose."

"Strip bitch, I told you what I want. Now you don't want me to really fuck up your pretty face, so get busy!"

Zach wiped the blood on the pillowcase and began crying. He pretended to give in. He stripped to his underwear and rolled over on his stomach. When Brian stood to unzip his pants, Zach quickly turned over and kicked Brian in his testicles. Brian bent over in pain and Zach made it out of the bedroom; with his clothes in his hands, he ran out the front door. Brian stood and walked to the door. He saw Zach as he got into his truck. Brian returned to his bedroom.

He quickly stripped the bedding and cleaned the apartment. He took the bedding and his garbage to the dumpster watching for anyone who might have seen him. He expected the police to call or come any minute. He dialed Zach's cell number and home phone three times and didn't get an answer. He left a message on his last attempt to call.

"Hey man, I thought we were supposed to meet to talk. I've been home all day waiting. Call me."

Brian left the message on both phones. If the police checked, he would tell them he didn't see Zach at all. His phone rang and he snatched the receiver off the base.

"Yeah, who's this?"

"Daddy?"

"Dionne, yeah baby. How are you?"

"I'm fine, what about you?"

"I'm doing fine baby. What's up? How are the plans for the wedding?"

"Everything's in place, that's what I was calling you for, will you be at the rehearsal Friday night?"

"Is it Friday night?"

"Yea, the Friday before the wedding, three Fridays from this Friday."

"I'll be there baby. How's your mother holding up?"

"What do you mean?"

"Losing you can upset a parent."

"Neither of you are losing me. She's fine. She's ready for the wedding too."

Dionne thought about mentioning Kris, but she held the thought remembering what Trevon said about letting things fall where they may. She had to call Trevon and apologize for not returning his calls.

"How's your brother? I tried calling him but Lynn said he wasn't home."

"He's fine. He's coming here early. Mama wants to talk before the wedding. He said he would come a week early. I was really surprised."

"Why, your brother usually accommodates your mother?"

"It just seems like he doesn't like being home with us, so I was glad when he agreed to come early."

"Well maybe the talk will give him comfort."

"I wish you could be included, but I understand. Maybe we could have the same kind of talk with you."

"Oh, I don't know Dionne. We might want to leave well enough alone. You and I talk often and believe me Trevon, and I are better than before."

"Dad it's just hard for me to believe our lives are so separate. I know we can't be a family, but we should be able to spend time together and get along. I know you and Trevon have had some real problems, but if you don't apologize, how can we get on with being a family?"

"Apologize?"

"Yea, you know. Did you ever say you were sorry?"

"Sorry? Did he tell you to ask me for an apology?"

"No, he didn't. Trevon doesn't even talk about you or what happened. I just thought it would help to open your communication with an apology. I mean for whatever reason you had, let him know you're sorry about the past."

"Dionne, Trevon and I got over it. You should get over it. It doesn't include you or your mother, worry about your big day. That should be enough to keep you occupied these days. You can't fix my relationships. Stop trying."

"I guess you're right." Dionne realized her father didn't know how Trevon felt. "I just thought I would throw in a suggestion to make matters better. I'll see you next week."

Dionne said goodbye and hung up the phone. Brian wiped the tears as they rolled from his face.

Chapter 46

Kris heard his phone ring but didn't answer it before the call went to his voice mail. He didn't recognize the number and his thoughts instantly went to Brian calling from a different number. He waited until the phone signaled the message was there for him to receive. Kris pressed his message button and listened.

"Mr. Randall, this is Zachary Blanding. If you could meet me at University Hospital in the emergency room I have some important information for you. Please come and speak with me, or if you can't come call me. Please."

Kris listened to the message twice. The voice was quivering but clear. He tried to remember if he knew a Zachary Blanding, the name wasn't familiar. He wasn't sure who Zach was, and he definitely didn't want to witness something and be asked about it later. He decided to ask Greg to go with him.

Kris decided not to call Sage, and he tried not to pace while he waited for Greg to arrive. He told Greg the message and Greg confirmed his suspicions by telling him Zach was Brian's friend. Kris imagined the worst. He saw visions of Brian attempting suicide and Zach finding him and calling the ambulance. He didn't know how Zach connected him with Brian but Kris would make it clear that he and Brian did not have a relationship. Greg blew his horn as he promised ten minutes later. Kris walked to his car and Greg could see the concern on his face.

"Man, listen, don't think the worst. We don't know what's at this hospital, and you worrying about it won't help. Pull yourself together man."

"Suppose that dumb ass tried to commit suicide?"

"Whew, you're really reaching. I don't think it would have been his friend calling; the cops maybe, but not his friend."

"You know you could be right. I didn't think of that."

"Let it go man. Did you tell Sage?"

"No, I wanted to know what was going on first."

Greg drove to the hospital as they continued their thoughts in silence. They arrived at the hospital fifteen minutes later.

"Well let's see, you said the ER. I think that's over there. Yeah, there's the sign."

The parking lot was crowded. Kris pointed to a space and Greg parked the car. They walked into the emergency room not knowing who Zach was. Neither of them had met Zach before. Greg walked over to the triage area and spoke to the registration attendant.

"I'm trying to find a friend who called from here. A Mr. Zachary Blanding."

The attendant looked at her list and smiled.

"Yes, I believe he may be admitted already. He was shook up pretty badly. If you just wait a moment I'll check."

"Thank you."

Greg waved Kris over.

"He may be admitted already."

"Who, Brian?"

"No Zach."

"Zach? Why would he call me then?"

"Sir, he's still in the back. You'll need passes. You can get them from the security desk. They'll direct you to the area where you have to go."

"Thank you."

The security guard escorted them through the emergency room past the hustle and bustle of medical staff dealing with different levels of crisis. He hit large buttons on the wall for several doors to open and the sound went from chaos to a quiet calm, which is expected in hospital corridors. The next set of doors opened to what looked like another emergency room. The nurses were still hustling and moving from room to room but there were no visitors interfering with questions or concerns. The security guard pointed to a curtained area, which was identified by a lit number five.

"That's where your friend is."

Greg replied, "Thanks."

Kris and Greg looked around before approaching the closed curtain.

"Zach.", Kris decided to call his name before opening the curtain. "It's Kris."

They could see the curtain moving as though someone was trying to open it. The curtain moved slightly and Greg helped to move it the rest of the way. Zach was lying in the bed with his nose bandaged and packed. Blood covered most of the bandage as it did his shirt. He began to cry.

"Hey man. I'm Kris Randall and this is my friend Greg Tempts. You called me? I'm sorry. I'm a little confused. What happened to you?"

"He's got a broken nose gentleman. Hello, I'm Dr. Norris. Are you friends of Zach's?"

"I guess, sorta, yea."

Greg answered. Kris was in momentary shock.

"Zach came in about two or three hours ago. I think he was in a battle for his life. He was scared to death, and we couldn't get him to calm down. I told him to call someone, and he called you. We've packed his nose but I had to give him something to calm him down. I think he may have been attacked. He won't answer any questions or even nod yes or no. I've called someone to come and talk with him. We can't let him go like this. If you need me, I'm on the floor. Zach is here for observation right now. We haven't decided to keep him yet."

"Thanks."

Greg and Kris looked at Zach, who had closed his eyes, drifting from the medication. Kris didn't know what to say. Greg walked closer to the bed and touched Zach on the shoulder. Zach opened his eyes but didn't try to speak.

"Lamont works for me. He knows you. Would you like me to call him so the two of you can talk?"

"Yes, please, don't tell Brian I'm here."

Zach answered in apparent pain. He spoke softly but both Greg and Kris understood the fear in his answer.

"No, that won't happen. Give me a minute. I'll call Lamont."

Greg pulled out his cell but indicated the connection had failed. Kris tried on his phone and was unable to get a signal.

"There's a phone on the wall in the hall. They let me use that."

Greg went to the phone as Zach had directed him. Kris walked closer to the bed.

"Man, why did you call me?"

"I wanted to see your face. I wanted to know why Brian would do this to me. For who?"

"You don't think he did this for me do you?"

"I don't know. Are you dealing with him?"

"No Zach, man not at all. It's a long story. Brian is trying to blackmail me into a relationship with him. I'm not gay or bi. I don't deal with men intimately. Brian won't take no for an answer."

Zach heard Lamont say the same thing. He realized now what Lamont was talking about. *"Why didn't Lamont tell me?"*

"Were you and Brian lovers at one time?"

"Zach no, never, I don't deal with men."

"You worked for the escort service right?"

"Worked, escorted that's all. Brian wanted more. How did you get my number?"

"I took his phone. You blocked his number, so I called on the hospital phone. I thought you had a relationship with him, and it was on the outs. I wanted to show you where you would wind up if you stayed with him.

He's crazy Kris. He raped that boy from his office and look what he did to me. He tried to rape me." Zach began to cry.

"I would have had to kill him to get out of there, or I would have killed him later. He's crazy. He needs to be put away."

"Lamont's on his way. Listen there's a doctor who wants to talk to you a minute. We'll wait in the room over there a minute. The nurse said they'll call the desk and let them know to let Lamont back here."

Greg and Kris went to the family waiting lounge. Kris sat holding his head. The hurt was spreading. At first he thought it was just him, then he learned about Sage and her family, then Carla and Demarest, and now Zach.

"Greg, Zach's right, Brian needs help. Professionally, you know, in a ward somewhere before someone kills him."

"Lamont said the same thing. Lamont suggested that Zach talk to the police. I don't know if they'll even talk to him about all his issues if Zach files a complaint."

"I don't think it will go that deep, unless Zach mentions he attempted to rape him. Then again, you know how cops feel about gays. They might not even take Zach seriously."

"Gentlemen, I've talked with your friend. I think we'll be watching him for a few days. The x-rays show his nose is broken and chipped in several places. We'll need to watch the bones. If the chips travel, he could have trouble."

"Doctor, has he said what happened?"

"He says he doesn't remember and that concerns us too."

The doctor left Greg and Kris waiting for Lamont. They decided to wait for him before attempting to talk to Zach again. Lamont came through the opening doors asking the nurse for Gregory Tempts.

"We don't have anyone by that name sir. Are you sure you're in the right area?"

"He's here with another friend, they came to see about Zachary Blanding.""Oh yes, they're in the lounge, Mr. Blanding is being checked at the moment you can wait with them."

"Thank you."

Lamont proceeded to the lounge. Greg and Kris stood greeting their friend and telling him what the doctors told them. "Lord, who would think I would be here with Zachary Blanding?"

"You do know him don't you?"

Kris was concerned whether or not Lamont could help. He still was wondering why he was called although Zach explained his reasons.

"Yea, I know him. I just don't understand this mess. This is serious y'all. You know bone chips can kill if they travel to the heart. Lord, he told you about Brian, so he does remember. Why didn't he tell the authorities?"

"That's what you need to make him understand."

The nurse came to the door letting them know they could go and see him. Greg and Kris told Lamont to go. They would give him time to talk to Zach alone. Lamont agreed and went to the pulled curtain and called Zach's name. He opened the curtain slowly and was prepared for the worst. The nurse had cleaned Zach's face. Since he was being kept in the hospital his shirt and other clothes laid in a clear bag under the bed. Lamont could see the blood soaked shirt and the new bandages and packing on his nose that now had new blood stains. He was hooked to an intravenous drip, wire and monitors. Lamont reached for his hand.

"What is this Zach? What happened?"

Lamont pulled up the chair by the bed and listened as Zach repeated his afternoon of horror.

Chapter 47

reg, Lamont and Kris left the hospital shortly after Zach was put in the critical care unit. The doctors spoke to them explaining he needed to be monitored for the next few days to insure, he was stable physically and mentally. Lamont remained quiet when the doctor's asked had Zach revealed what happened. Kris nor Greg knew the full story, so they had no answers. They all agreed to stop by the office to talk.

"Hey man do you think this joker could die?"

"Kris, leave it alone man. We'll see what he told Lamont. It's obvious he doesn't want the cops or anybody with authority to know."

"Man, we can't help him. If someone retaliates on Brian, they could think we're a part of this shit."

"Kris, man, I didn't know you were this shaky."

"Listen man, I'm not down with gay bashing, raping or even assaulting. That's some serious shit. I don't want to be mixed up with it. I'm too old for this kinda shit."

"We all are, even Brian. But if no one stops him then what?"

"It ain't on me. I'm not about finding salvation for his soul. I'm only involved in this because of Sage's connection."

"Bullshit man. If I remember right Brian was on your ass at the same time as you were chasing Sage's ass.

Remember? I didn't know you were dealing with Sage. Things just came together that way."

"Yea, you're right. But I'm saying, I would have been done with that fool after I left Tempting. I'm still connected because of Sage. She wants to get his ass back. If it was dropped Zach wouldn't have called me."

"Zach found you because of Brian's phone not Sage. That's what I'm trying to tell you. Brian wasn't letting you go and Zach knew it. You would be tied to this shit even if you and Sage just did nine to five business."

"Man, this is ridiculous."

"Is there a way to check your blocked calls?"

"No, I don't think so. I guess the company could run the records but there's nothing on my menu to review them. Why?"

"Just wondering if Brian called you."

"Hey look Lamont is still sitting in his car. Is he okay?"

Greg and Kris got out of the car and approached Lamont, who was parked across the lot from them. Greg tapped on the window and Lamont got out of the car.

"The hospital just called. Zach had a seizure they're gonna to operate on him. The bone chips have moved, they want to try to get them before they enter his brain."

The three men went into Greg's office. Lamont told them what Zach told him and why he called Kris.

"He didn't have my number. He said he grabbed Brian's phone thinking he could reach me at the office number. The number wasn't in the phone. So he called you."

"He didn't ask for you. Greg suggested it. He said he called to warn me. Lamont, he thought I was dealing with Brian."

"It doesn't matter Kris. He called for help. Help for him, you and anyone else that deals with that damn Brian Drakeford."

"So what did he say about telling the cops?"

"Greg, he never brought that up. He just kept telling me he needed to be put away. I don't think he means locked up. I think he meant mental help."

"He can't get mental help without a charge."

"Greg, can we get this done if Demarest and Zach talk to each other? Do you think that will work Lamont?"

"Zach does know about Demarest. Why not? Demarest and Carla are still coming up for the wedding right?"

"Yea, the wedding is in another three or four weeks. But did they say Zach is gonna be okay? It sounds as though he might not make it."

"They'll call me. I'll stay in touch with them."

"Lamont where's Zach's family?"

"He's not from here and you know how family can be when you're the gay member of the family. I asked him if he had anyone he wanted me to call, and he said no. He's from Florida. I'll try to talk to him to get some names if necessary, but for now he's not interested in talking to his family either."

Chapter 48

Sage got home after seven thirty. Her open house was successful and she complimented the owners on their preparation. Most homeowners left the small touches of the open house to the realtors. Sage took notes from her client. They served soft drinks and had snacks throughout the rooms in the home. It gave the home a cozy and warming effect. Sage spoke to Kris on the way home and couldn't understand why he told her he was still at Tempting Escorts. Although Sage understood he and Greg were friends she had her own thoughts about males who worked as escorts. Kris told her he would call when he was done.

They hadn't been together since the weekend and Sage was looking forward to his conversation and addictive hugs. Sage walked in her front door and immediately kicked off her heels. Her phone blinked at her, and she pushed the speed dial to retrieve the messages. There were two messages one from Dionne and the other from Trevon. Each was confirming that Trevon would be home a week early for their talk. Sage smiled, she was satisfied that her plan was coming together.

Carla and Demarest called expressing their pleasure in meeting with her and Kris. Sage and Carla talked about getting together so

Carl could meet the other members of the family after the wedding. Sage hoped Dionne and Trevon would take the news well.

Sage picked up her favorite order of Chinese food on her way home and added side dishes that she knew Kris enjoyed. When Kris called, she would ask him to bring a bottle of wine with him. It was eight thirty when the bell rang. Sage opened the door and laughed to herself.

"I was so sure you would call me. That's why I didn't call you. We don't have any wine or beer."

"I'll go to the store in a minute if you want."

Kris's response was so nonchalant that Sage was confused.

"Are you okay? You sound like you're drained."

"I could use something stronger than beer or wine."

"I've got gin, and I even have cranberry juice."

"That will do. I'll still go get the wine and beer. How late does that place on the boulevard stay open?"

"Kris, are you okay?"

"No, babe."

Kris put his arms around Sage and held her. Sage recognized the hug, there were serious problems going on.

After two drinks, dinner and conversation, both Sage and Kris agreed the wine and beer was not missed. They retired to the bedroom to continue the conversation and relax.

"What makes you think Demarest would be able to help?"

"Well before Zach needed the surgery we thought he would be able to help Zach report Brian. Now, who knows if he'll be up to talking to anyone."

"Kris, the hospital will report it, you know that don't you? That's a part of their procedures. I bet there already is a report."

"I hadn't thought about that. We did have to be escorted to the area where Zach was and the nurse had to let security know that Lamont was coming too."

"Didn't you say the doctor thought he fought for his life? They knew something foul happened to him, they just don't know what. The cops may be monitoring his health before they begin questioning people."

"You may be right."

"I just hope Brian doesn't think he got away with this."

"What difference does that make?"

"Kris, if he thinks he got away with it, he'll do it again."

Kris took off his shirt while Sage went into the bathroom and cut on the shower. Kris poured them another drink and sat back on the pillows waiting for Sage to come to bed. He got up before dozing, and decided to join Sage in the shower. He opened the shower door and Sage turned smiling. She was more than happy to help him relieve his tension.

Kris stood under the warm water and allowed Sage to wash and massage his body from head to toe. Kris rinsed and changed his position so Sage could receive the same treatment. They stepped out of the shower and dried each other. After using warming oils they relaxed in each other's arms and fell asleep forgetting the last drink Kris poured.

Chapter 49

Lamont went to visit Zach two days after the surgery. The nurses told him he was stable but his condition was weakening. Lamont decided to make an attempt to get Zach to tell the doctors who had done this to him. When he arrived at the hospital he called the number Dr. Norris had given him.

"Dr. Norris, yes, this is Lamont, Zach Blanding's friend. Yes, I'm here can I meet you in your office after my visit? Thank you, yes on the second floor. Goodbye."

Lamont got his visitor's pass, and as he went to the elevator, he felt the need to pray. He got on an empty elevator and pressed the floor's number on the panel. He was glad to have a moment to collect his thoughts. As the doors closed, he shut his eyes. Lamont prayed for Zach and asked God to give him the strength of a survivor. As the doors of the elevator opened, he ended with a resounding, "Amen."

Lamont looked on his visiting pass again to get the bed number. He looked at each door for 527A. When he arrived at the room he hesitated. Lamont noticed Zach's room was close to the nurse's station. All the rooms were closely watched on the floor but Zach's room was one of five that was on the television monitors at the nurse's stations. Lamont could seem himself on the camera as he entered Zach's room.

Zach opened his eyes and tried to smile. His entire head was wrapped in white bandages and his nose was still packed. He was still connected to an intravenous drip and monitors as he had been before the surgery.

"Hey, I won't even ask how you feel. How long have you been up?"

"Off and on since last night."

"They told me you were heavily sedated yesterday when I called and asked about you during the visiting hours. Otherwise I would have come by to see you."

"My head is killing me. Do you know if they got all the chips?"

"No, I didn't ask. Did you ask the doctor?"

"No, I didn't see him today yet."

"Hmm, don't think about that. They'll probably let you know today. Listen, Zach, maybe you should talk to the cops or something. Let them know about what Brian did to you. You don't know how bad this is gonna leave you."

"I don't want him locked in some jail over this."

"Zach, he needs help even you said so. If you don't say something he'll do it again maybe his next victim won't be so lucky. Just look what he has done to you and Demarest."

"He raped that boy?"

"Yea, and he wasn't a boy. He was just younger than us."

Zach listened to Lamont's words and relived running from Brian's apartment in his underwear.

"I thought I was pushing him to say he raped that, well you said he was a man."

"What made you think he was a boy?"

"Brian said he was a young boy in college, you know. I thought he had to be, to fall in love and do some of the things Brian said he got him to do. Lamont, Brian abused that man. I guess if I had the same demeanor it could have been me. He got upset with me because he couldn't get me that way. I guess I taunted him until he snapped. He needs help, not jail."

"How do we get him help without you saying something?"

"I don't know maybe after I get out of here. I'll talk to him and tell him, either he gets help, or I tell. Lamont I love him, I can't turn him in."

"If you love him, you'll find a way to turn him in."

"Whew, shit."

"What's wrong?"

"Pain man, my head is killing me."

"I'll get the nurse for you on my way out. You shouldn't be talking so much you need your rest."

"Lamont, thanks for coming."

"You're welcome. I'll see you tomorrow; rest now."

Lamont left and as promised, sent the nurse to Zach's room. He went to the elevator and pressed the floor for Dr. Norris's office. He got off the elevator on the second floor and walked through the doors of the main corridor toward the administrative offices. The door with the nameplate for Dr. Norris was opened. Lamont knocked on the door and Dr. Norris raised his head from the papers he was working on.

"Dr. Norris, good seeing you again."

"Lamont, good seeing you too, how's Zach doing today? I haven't made my rounds yet. I usually leave those on his unit to sleep, rest helps them heal."

"When I left, he was in pain. I told the nurse, she was attending to him as I was leaving. Will he be okay now? Were you able to get the chips that were floating?"

"I'll go check on him after we talk. No, there were two that we couldn't touch they were lodged in a bad area. It would have done more damage to remove them. We'll watch them while he's recovering."

"He'll have to go through this surgery again?"

"Unfortunately if the chips drift where we can get them safely it would be advised. He's in danger either way."

"Dr. Norris, he told me who did this. He wants the man to get help, mental help not judicial punishment."

"I'm afraid that if his condition worsens it won't be up to me to decide that. The cops filed reports when he was registered and admitted here. They have his clothes and his initial complaints, the treatment, everything. They'll investigate if something goes wrong."

"Doctor, what could go wrong now?"

"Let's just say he's not out of danger and just know that prayer works best in cases like these."

Lamont was silent, fearing the worst. Dr. Norris got up and closed his office door. He pulled a chair beside Lamont to talk from the front of the desk where he sat a moment before.

"Lamont, I don't want you to take this the wrong way. Its apparent Zach is gay. This man, is he Lamont's lover?"

"I guess you could say that. They were together at one time. I don't know if they had rekindled their relationship or what. I do know that Zach still loves him."

"What's your relationship with Zach?"

"He's just a friend. We've known each other for maybe a year. He doesn't have any family here, they live in Florida."

"What about the other guys?"

"They're actually my friends. Zach was trying to reach me when he called them."

"So you're really all Zach has right now. I mean, as a friend."

"Yea, I guess you're right."

"Lamont, if you know what happened to your friend you need to tell the police, so they can catch this man."

"Me? What could I tell the police?"

"Listen, if you wait this guy could get away with this assault. If he finds out how bad off Zach is I'm sure he'll leave town."

"Dr. Norris, I understand what you're asking but if Zach wants me to tell he'll ask me. I don't want to disrespect his wishes. If something should happen to him, I will tell."

"Lamont what he did is a crime. If you know you should tell."

"I'll try talking to Zach about it again tomorrow."

The doctor stood offering his hand to Lamont. Lamont rose to his feet and extended his hand. As the doctor opened the door his phone rang.

"I'll go and see Zach after this call. Good to see you again Lamont. We'll be talking."

Chapter 50

A week passed and Brian hadn't heard from Zach. He began to worry less about the police coming to his home. As he parked his car in his designated spot three men got out of a black sedan and approached him.

"Mr. Drakeford, we need to talk with you at the station."

The three flashed Baltimore Detective Squad badges, as though they knew what his reaction would be. They walked him to their car and the tallest officer of the trio opened the back door for him to get in the car. Brian remained silent as they rode to the downtown precinct.

The officers got out of the car and escorted Brian to a room on the third floor of the police station that Brian had only seen from the outside. The table and chairs in the dingy room told him he could say something wrong and become a guest of Baltimore's finest. Brian sighed realizing the visit he dreaded from the police, had become a reality.

"Would you like water, soda or coffee? Anything to drink?"

"No." Brian knew they didn't want to socialize. There was no need for refreshments.

"Mr. Drakeford, I'm Detective Griffin, that's Detective Childs and Mays. We need to ask you a few questions about an assault on Mr. Zachary Blanding."

"Why are you asking me? I don't know anything about an assault on Mr. Blanding."

"That's good, I mean, cause if you knew it would mean you were there or involved in some way."

"What do you mean by that?"

"Well, Mr. Blanding hasn't been able to call anyone since the assault. So it would be hard for you to know any other way."

"So where were you last Monday, Tuesday, or Wednesday?"

"He got assaulted all those days?"

"No but we'd like to know your whereabouts for those days."

"I've been home. I took a few days off from work. I've been a little worn down."

"I see. That is what his boss said also, right Childs?"

"I think he said he looked worn down."

"When did your boss see you Mr. Drakeford?"

"I think I saw him Tuesday."

Brian had started making mistakes already. When he didn't show up to work Monday and Tuesday his boss sent a car for his presentation that was needed in the office on Wednesday. The office courier Reggie Willis told the police Brian answered his door and looked worn on Wednesday.

"So you saw your boss Tuesday at the office?"

"Not Tuesday, I think it was Wednesday."

"Had you been drinking that day Mr. Drakeford?"

"No."

"But you went to work anyway?"

"Yes."

"So let me get this straight. This week you worked Wednesday, Thursday, and today."

Brian hesitated before answering. He realized his mistake. He hadn't seen his boss at all.

"Yea, but on Wednesday I stopped by the office to turn in a presentation. That's when I saw my boss, he sent me back home."

"I see."

Brian didn't think they would have talked to anyone at his job. The mornings are busy and there had been many days when he walked past the front desk and the receptionist never noticed he had signed in. Childs left the room and Griffin pulled up a chair and sat across the table to continue their discussion.

"Mr. Drakeford, Detective Mays is going to read you your rights."

"No he's not. You're going to let me call my lawyer, and then we'll talk. Until then talk to each other."

The detectives left the room and gave Brian the opportunity to make his call on the station's phone. There were no questions asked even when Mr. Silverman, Brian's lawyer arrived.

"Let's go Brian. They don't have any questions, you're free to go."

"What? They said they were going to read me my rights and question me."

"They're fishing."

"Fishing for what? What happened to Zach?"

Brian hoped he sounded concerned as he as his lawyer passed the front desk where the Detectives stood smiling. The two of them went out the front door before Mr. Silverman answered Brian's question.

"He's been hospitalized. Someone broke his nose Monday, maybe in the afternoon or early evening. Anyway the bones were chipped, and they're floating. According to the police, he's not out of danger. He could have some serious complications from the assault."

Brian tried not to show any emotions, but he wanted to go to the hospital and apologize. He fought back tears as he pretended he didn't know anything about the attack.

"What, what would make them think it was me?"

"I asked, they said you were free to go."

"They never answered you?"

"No. So why do you think they wanted to question you?"

Brian knew why. He didn't hesitate to give his prepared story to his lawyer. He told him about the dinner on Saturday skipping the reason for him going home. He told him about their plans to meet with each other on Sunday. But he told his lawyer; they changed their plans because of Zach's prior scheduled appointment to Monday. Brian explained when he didn't hear from Zach on Monday, he called him on both his cell and home phone. The lie sounded better each time he said it to himself and now that he had to tell it to someone he was convinced it was believable.

Mr. Silverman listened as they drove back to Brian's place. The lawyer parked his Mercedes next to Brian's car as Brian continued to paint his picture of what he hoped would pass as an alibi.

"Were you here alone all day Monday?"

"Yea, Zach never showed up."

"Brian, I'll check this out for you. There's a few things that don't make sense to me. The detectives coming here to get you and just letting you go tells me they want you to react to their actions. Secondly, I want to know who made the complaint. If Zach did then they know who assaulted him. If Zach didn't, who did and why? Did Zach tell them something? Yeah, let me do some research. Don't talk to the cops without me."

"Okay, I don't think they can get me on this. I didn't hurt Zach."

"You didn't hurt him or you didn't see him?"

"That's what I mean, I didn't hurt him cause I didn't see him."

"Yeah, remember that Brian. You didn't see him."

Chapter 51

"Greg, I don't think I had much of a choice. Zach is in bad shape. If you can get Demarest to talk to the police, that ass will be off the street."

"Lamont, that's up to Zach. Didn't he say he wanted Brian to get help? You know damn well the help he'll get in jail is not what Zach meant. What about his family?"

"What about them? Brian has been mistreating everyone, and it's about time somebody said ouch! I told the cops what I knew. They called me for questioning. I didn't call them."

"They called you? I thought you filed a report."

"Hell no, I told the doctor that I was going to talk to Zach again about filing one. There was a card from a Detective Griffin stuck on my door when I got home. I called him and they came to the house."

"What did they ask you?"

"What my relationship was to Zach? When was the last time I had seen him before going to the hospital to see him? How well did we get along? Who was he at the dinner with? That's when Brian's name was mentioned. I told him the same thing I told the doctor. I couldn't define their relationship. I knew they had dealt with each other in the past and that was it. Hold on Greg, hold on."

Greg held the phone thinking about how Kris would react if the cops wanted to talk to him. He locked the office door and walked to his car while waiting for Lamont to come back to the phone.

"I'm sorry. Douglas stopped by yesterday and of course left things he needed today. Anyway, I'm gonna have to take them to him later. What was I saying now?"

"Did the cops ask why Kris and I were at the hospital?"

"Yea, I told them Zach used the number, he had to reach me. It just happened to be Kris's number. They may want to talk to you or Kris. Just to verify if you know Brian or Zach."

"Shit, this is a mess. If they ask Kris he may tell them about Brian and how aggressive he's been about pursuing him. Look let me go, I need to call Kris."

"Call me back."

Greg hung up the phone and dialed Kris. Kris didn't answer and Greg dialed his office. When he didn't get an answer at either number, he dialed Sage's cell number.

"Hey Lady."

"Wow, you sound like Kris with that Lady thing."

"I think I heard him call you that once or twice."

Sage laughed thinking about what she would tell Kris about his secret name for her.

"What's up? Is everything okay with Zach?"

"So far. They've operated on him and Lamont said he's staying in the hospital so they can monitor his recovery."

"I feel so bad for him."

"Is Kris around?"

"He went to his office about two hours ago. I haven't heard from him. Did you try his cell?"

"No answer. Sage I think we're gonna be questioned by the cops."

"You and Kris? Why?"

"It seems Zach doesn't have much family. So we showed up at the hospital as friends and the only ones who may have known what happened."

"Kris won't be happy with that. I don't think he wants to talk to anyone about what has happened."

"If he calls, tell him to call me please."

"Sure, on your cell?"

"That's good. I'll wait for his call. Thanks Sage."

"No problem Greg, I wish things were different."

"It's not on you or us. I just want Kris to know what may be coming his way. The cops are moving slow though, it's been over a week since Zach has been in the hospital."

"I guess they weren't interested in the case until he got worse."

"You may be right. Anyway tell Kris to call me."

"There's my other line maybe it's him. I'll tell him Greg."

Greg drove to his condo to continue his cleaning project. There were two more weeks before Carla would be in town. He told her that there was plenty of room for her, Demarest and Carl to stay at his place. They accepted his invitation and he wanted to impress Carla while she was in town. They were due to arrive the night before the wedding, and they would be in town for a week. Both Demarest and

Carla had friends they hadn't seen in years and the week would be an opportunity for a quick reunion.

Greg pulled into his complex and noticed Kris was waiting in his car in a parking space close to his house. Greg got out of his car meeting Kris as he walked toward the front door.

"Man, what else is going to happen?"

"The cops called you?"

"They want to talk to me. I told them I had appointments scheduled. They'll meet me at my office around six."

"So I guess I'm next?"

"They didn't mention anyone else. What the fuck did Lamont say?"

"Nothing really, he told them how Zach used your number to reach him. He told them we were his friends, and we really weren't close to Zach."

"Greg, what am I supposed to tell them? If I say anything about Brian it will go into how I know him and so forth and so on. If I don't tell them, and they find out later, damn man, this can't be good."

"Listen, let them ask the questions. If they don't ask anything other than why we were at the hospital, don't volunteer any information."

"I told Sage and she said the same thing."

"So, where's your appointment."

"Shit, what's your house number?"

They laughed as Greg turned the key to the front door.

Chapter 52

"Mr. Randall, I'm trying to understand why Mr. Blanding called you the night of the attack and not someone he knew?"

Kris had heard three different versions of the question and his patience was wearing thin. Detective Griffin and Mays had been in his office for more than forty-five minutes playing good cop bad cop as though Kris knew what happened to Zach and why.

"I really don't know. I can't answer why he called me. As I stated over and over detectives, I don't know Zach like that."

"How do you know him?"

Kris looked directly at Detective Mays. He knew from the tone of the question what he was implying.

"I don't know him well enough to know what his reasoning would be. You have to know a person to be able to understand what makes them do what they do."

"Mr. Randall why do you think someone would attack Zach?"

"Again gentlemen, I don't know, and I don't know who."

"Mr. Randall, Kris. Can I call you Kris?"

Kris wasn't sure he was comfortable with Detective Griffin calling him by his first name. Griffin was playing the bad cop.

"Yeah, what's your question?"

"You said you were a liaison for various investors?"

"Yeah, I find property for them to develop or buy."

"How does that tie you in with Lamont?"

"Lamont?"

"Do you work with him in your line of business?"

Griffin's questions were beginning to agitate Kris. He didn't want to give them a reason to suspect he was hiding any information.

"No he works for a friend of mine."

"Would that be Mr. Gregory Tempts?"

"Yes, Greg Tempts."

Griffin didn't know where Mays questions were leading, but he wanted to know more about why Zach called Kris to the hospital.

"You said Zach phoned you, and he really wanted Lamont right?"

"That's right."

"Mr. Randall, why didn't he just ask for Lamont's number?"

"You'll have to ask him."

Kris had enough. His tone reflected sarcasm and his professional demeanor was vanishing fast. Detective Mays leaned forward in his chair across Kris's desk. Kris took it as an intimidation move and pushed his chair back and stood to his feet.

"I think we're done here. I can't help you anymore than I have."

Griffin stood holding his partners arm as though Mays had intentions on throwing a punch.

"If I could just ask one more question Mr. Randall."

"Sure."

"Does the name Brian Drakeford mean anything to you?"

"I know him."

"What do you know about his relationship with Mr. Blanding?"

"I don't know anything about their relationship."

Mays took the opportunity to ask another question.

"What's your relationship with him?"

"I don't have a relationship with him and that gentlemen, is your last question without my lawyer being present."

Chapter 53

Karen and Sage brought the bags in from the car. They had been grocery shopping and buying their accessories for the wedding.

"Girl, I think I forgot to get the sharp cheese for the macaroni."

"Listen you said that was for your Sunday dinner. We can get it during the week if you forgot it. You've been uneasy all day, what's up?"

"Karen, I don't know how this all is gonna play out. Trevon has been avoiding this type of visit for years and Dionne may not want to hear anything that puts Brian in a bad light."

"They're both adults and they should know. Look how long you've kept this. You shouldn't have to bear the weight of Brian's problems. You deserve better. Sage, you have to be able to move on. How can you move on if you don't leave the baggage behind?"

"You're right about that. I can't believe Brian's ass. If he assaulted Zach and Demarest, Karen, he's sicker than I thought. I thought his issue was his sexual orientation, but abuse, shit he needs help."

"So the plans are the same? I mean are they still coming for the wedding?"

"Girl, I don't know if he'll be at the wedding. Suppose the police arrest his ass. That's another subject I have to mention to Tre and Dionne. It's a mess Karen."

The conversation continued as they put up the groceries and repacked Karen's car with her items. They returned to the kitchen and Sage made a pot of coffee.

"So the cops are talking to anyone who knows Zach?"

"I think whoever visited him at the hospital. They spoke to Lamont and Kris. I guess they'll talk to Greg too. I told Kris it's routine when someone comes in after an assault. I don't know if they'll tie Brian in, unless someone tells them about him."

"Have they talked to Brian?"

"I don't know. He's an ass Karen."

"Why?"

"I mean, think about it. If he really loved Zach wouldn't he have gone to the hospital?"

"We don't know that he didn't Sage. But listen, they may not let him in. Wouldn't they have to ask Zach about his visitors?"

"You might be right. Maybe Brian doesn't know Zach is even in the hospital."

"No, I think he knows. But he might not be able to see Zach."

"Either way Karen, Brian is still an ass."

Chapter 54

Brian was getting nervous. His daughter was to be married in a little over a week, and he wasn't sure he would be in attendance. Zach hadn't called him and his lawyer said he was still in the hospital. He told Brian that Zach's condition was stable, but he wasn't out of the dark. The police had not called since they questioned Brian at the precinct. Brian took a leave of absence from the job and scheduled two sessions with his psychiatrist.

After his first session, the doctor gave him a prescription for medication to help him sleep. Brian claimed the lack of sleep was the reason for his sullen mood. He had the prescription filled and went home looking forward to a good night's rest. He thought about his last conversation with Dionne and realized he didn't know the time of the rehearsal or what time they had to be at the church the next day. He made a mental note to call her.

He checked his answering machine after he got settled. The monotone voice indicated he had three new messages. There was a message from Mr. Silverman. He was to return his call as soon as possible. Brian erased the message and listened for the other two. The next two held no message, there was only silence. He smiled as he listened to the sound of the person on the other end. He could hear the slow deliberate sound of the caller breathing. He had no way of identifying who it was. The caller id showed "unknown" in the lit identification panel. Brian smiled thinking it was Zach. Brian hung up the phone certain if it was Zach, he wouldn't speak, and he wouldn't be pressing charges. He waited until after he ate his dinner to return Mr. Silverman's call.

"Mr. Silverman, I'm returning your call."

"Brian, we need to talk. Zach is having complications and the detectives are becoming inquisitive about your relationship with him."

"They haven't called me. What do they want to know?"

"I'm your lawyer and they've been calling me. Apparently, they know the two of you were or are lovers. Their questions are legitimate; you and I need to be on the same page with the answers."

"I told you I don't know what happened to him. He and I were gonna meet and talk about our relationship. We never got together."

"So you were breaking up?"

"No, we were trying to get things back together."

Brian's reply had been rehearsed, as were other answers to the questions he assumed the detectives would ask. Mr. Silverman knew his answer wouldn't be believable.

"Brian, when can we sit and talk. I really don't want to discuss this on the phone."

"I can come to see you before the week is out. My daughter is getting married next week, and I really don't want to deal with any of this mess then. You know, relatives, friends and others will be coming and going."

Silverman listened to what he knew were poor excuses. He had been Brian's lawyer for years and knew Brian had problems with reality and his perception of reality.

Silverman knew with his attitude the detectives would bury him with questions that would lead him to deny the truth about his relationship with Zach. Eventually, Brian would be caught in his lies and on trial for aggravated assault.

"When Brian, when? The sooner the better."

"You want me to tell you now?"

"Yes, now." Mr. Silverman's tone changed immediately. "No let me tell you. It's Tuesday already; let's make it Thursday afternoon, about three o'clock."

"Okay."

"Brian, don't talk to the cops."

"I'm not understanding, what they don't understand. I didn't see Zach after the dinner, which was almost three weeks ago. I wanted to talk to him about our relationship and he never showed. I haven't heard from him since."

Brian smiled to himself assuming Mr. Silverman would push this point to the detectives the next time he spoke with them.

"Brian listen we'll talk, but you need to think about this. I understand what you're saying but there's some loose ends. Why haven't you called to check on him or even tried to go to the hospital? You wanted to rekindle a relationship, but you haven't shown any concern since the attack. It's hard to believe that you don't want to know his condition and show him that you care. It's just a question in my mind, and I know eventually they'll ask the same question. Have you checked with anyone concerning his condition?"

Brian's confidence was quickly fading. He hadn't thought about calling the hospital. He blurted out the first answer that came to his mind.

"I didn't even know he was in the hospital. How could I question about his condition, and I didn't know he was in the hospital?"

"Brian, they told you he was when they took you to the precinct. You said you hadn't heard from him. You were waiting to rekindle a relationship with someone you claim you love, and you didn't call to check on him then? Brian it's been almost a week since you spoke to them. He's had surgery on his head and may need more surgery. It causes reasonable suspicion."

"You handle that bullshit. I know what I did or didn't do. So what, I didn't call the hospital. Let me deal with my emotions about this. Did they check with any of his other lovers?"

"Brian, come and see me Thursday."

Brian hung up the phone and felt a surge of aggravation. He went to the kitchen and got a glass for his intended drink of Vodka and opened the bottle of pills prescribed for his well-awaited sleep. He took to pills and poured the Vodka over ice in his glass. Brian returned to the living room and cut on his television and looked for a movie to help ease him into a relaxed mode. It took him twenty minutes to dose into a deep sleep.

Chapter 55

Trevon's flight landed at the airport as scheduled. Sage and Dionne waved from the boarding lounge to get his attention as the other passengers pushed their way ahead of him. He quickened his pace to meet them. They hugged and kissed saying hello and Dionne praised the length of his dreaded locks.

"It looks good on you, how does the military feel about it?"

"If I was assigned off base I think they would have a problem, but I work with the education department now. I teach on base and wear civilian clothes; it gives me a chance to be me."

"So your days of travel are over?"

"Ma, you know better. If they want to send you, you go. I took the assignment on base because I enjoy teaching, and it keeps me home. It's a stable position and it holds my interest."

"How much luggage did you bring?"

Trevon usually complained when he traveled with Lynn and their children about the luggage they packed and carried. His reply was a smirk that brought on a bit of laughter as they walked to the baggage terminal and waited.

"So, it's not just Lynn and the children?"

"No, not this trip anyway. We'll be here almost a month before going home, I couldn't do it in two bags."

Trevon picked up his carry on, a suitcase and a garment bag and winked at Dionne. Dionne was glad Trevon showed no signs of anger because she hadn't returned his calls. They rode home updating Trevon on the neighborhood and his friends that still lived in the area. Dionne spoke about the final touches that had to be done or changed for the wedding.

Sage didn't want to spoil their first night with the problems that had mounted over the months, but she wasn't sure how Trevon and Dionne would react. Sage's thought was it might take days for them to digest the information, and she didn't want the look of shock to be shown in the wedding photos.

The three got out of the car and entered the house laughing about Jarad's first confession of his love for Dionne.

"He was so embarrassed. I don't know what made him want to stand up during Thanksgiving dinner and make a toast. Trevon kept saying it was one he hadn't rehearsed."

"Yeah, what was it he said."

"Something about, 'He'll never love this way again,' we all told him he was right and sit down." Trevon laughed mocking Jarad making the toast.

"Ma, that wasn't it though. He wanted to explain why."

Trevon quickly remarked why Jarad didn't explain.

"But Dionne wouldn't let him."

"I didn't know what he was gonna say."

"Child stop, you thought he was getting ready to confess to your activities the night before."

Sage and her children remembered the night and everyone's reaction. They laughed and talked about a few other memories. Trevon took his bags upstairs and returned to the living room hoping he hadn't missed much of the conversation. He was surprised he didn't feel overwhelmed for once. He actually felt better than he had in years about visiting, he hoped what he had to reveal to his mother wouldn't ruin the mood.

Dionne went into the kitchen to fill the ice bucket as her mother got each of them, a glass and the pitcher of ice tea. Dionne watched her mother smiling, contented with her children being with her for the evening. They both agreed to spend the night. Dionne prayed they would always remain close.

"I'm glad you both agreed to stay with me tonight. You know, this is the first time in years we've done this. I really think this will bring us closer. There, I wanted to say that first. Okay, get comfortable. What I have to say may be a little more than shocking."

"Ma, can I ask what's this is about?"

"Dionne, if I explain I might as well tell the entire thing. Some of this has happened recently. I mean, I found out recently. Some has happened within the past few weeks, but I should start from the beginning so you both will understand. It all has to do with your father and the reason we separated and then divorced."

Trevon and Dionne sat back. Dionne kicked off her shoes and tucked her legs under her on the couch. Trevon closed his eyes and said a prayer for strength. Sage took a long drink from her glass before she spoke again. She began where she thought was the beginning explaining Brian's romantic weekends away from home, his lies, their arguments and finally her walking in the bedroom that night.

"It was the worst feeling. I didn't know what to do or say. I was glad the two of you were away, and then I wasn't. If you had been home he would have been at a hotel somewhere and who knows how I would have found out about his sexual issues."

"Mom, stop. We know about Zach."

"Who knows?"

"We do, me and Dionne. From what you're saying we must have found out right before that happened."

"You knew?"

"We were lied to. He promised me was done with Zach."

"He promised you? When?"

Sage looked at Trevon and then at Dionne. She couldn't imagine Brian telling them about his periodic trysts. She refused to believe he would put them in that position. She wanted to know if Dionne knew and then she told Trevon. She wanted to know why neither of them told her. She could feel her emotions building into what would become an outburst of mixed emotions.

"Ma, dad had other problems. He may still have them. I knew and told Dionne three weeks ago. I reminded her I told her about Dad and Zach, but I didn't tell her or you about his other issue. I guess it's time you knew that as well."

"Knew what?" Sage took a deep breath trying to brace herself, preparing for the worse. She didn't know what else there could possibly be that equated to other issues.

Trevon told Sage about his father's late night entry into his room, the kiss and his attempt to have sex with him. Trevon kept the story descriptions short but Sage insisted on details.

"Trevon, why wouldn't you tell me? What the hell was he thinking? Oh my God!"

Tears welled in Sage's eyes.

"A week later I saw him and Zach in a car in front of the house. It looked like they had had a long conversation and were saying goodbye. Dad kissed Zach and got out of the car. Zach pulled off. I made sure Dad knew I saw the two of them. I had already stopped speaking to him, but he wouldn't let me in the house until we talked. I didn't have much to say so I just listened to his pitiful excuses of why he was in love with this man, and I would understand when I fell in love. He didn't know who to choose: us or Zach, us or his lifestyle that he had hidden for years — us or his happiness. He said he chose us and told Zach, although he loved him, he had a family that he loved more. Ma, he told me the same thing the night we fought. He lied. He told me he didn't want to hurt us. After that the two of you were on the outs for good. When you told us you were separating and getting a divorce, I knew you caught him with Zach, or somebody."

"Tre, how could you not tell me about this? Dionne, you knew and wanted to protect your father? Why?"

"Ma, I found out a couple of weeks ago. I thought Tre was lying about Dad and another man. It wasn't until he told me what happened that I understood the divorce, Tre's reactions and why Dad always said good things about you. Dad never mentioned anything about what happened to the relationship him and Trevon had. Ma, I just realized my father has serious problems."

Sage closed her eyes knowing the burden of the truth had just begun to show it's ugly face for them as a family. Each of them had their thoughts about Brian's indiscretions. The conversation continued into the early morning. Sage told them about her initial reason for dating Kris. She didn't spare the facts about their father stalking Kris; his affair with Carla or the child she carried. She paused before telling them the truth about Demarest and the attack on Zach. Silence replaced her voice and she knew they felt the same as she did. She needed to know what they thought about Brian being confronted at the wedding with more than just an appearance from Kris.

"It doesn't matter to me Ma. Its Dionne's wedding, Dad only cares about himself. He was that way before, and apparently he still is. He's done. If he assaulted Zach, he needs to be put away. He's lost it. Look at his track record. I mean that's my father but, whew."

"Wait! Shut Up! Just wait! He's my father too. You're both so ready to put him out there. Expose him for what he is. Where's your love for him, he's your father too, and your husband?"

"He's my ex-husband, for just the reasons that we've stated. He's selfish Dionne. If he thought more about who he claimed he loved, he wouldn't have mistreated any of us including Zach. Let's count the hurt Dionne; Trevon, me, Demarest, Carla, Carl and

Zach. How many more before he causes someone to kill him or themselves? What do you suggest, ignoring it?"

"No, ma, I don't know. I just don't think embarrassment is the best way to go about this."

"He won't be embarrassed. We're the only ones who know about them."

Trevon knew it would take a lot to convince Dionne of their father's problems. He didn't know how Dionne could want to still be by his side.

"What about Kris, Trevon?"

"What about Kris? He's a guest of your mother's not your father's. Dionne you can't help him this way. You want to help him? Tell him to turn himself in. Tell him to own up to what's he's done to some of us. Me and mom understand, we were hurt. Obviously, you didn't get a twinge of pain or shame. I go to the psych for counseling because of his ass. Excuse me ma. Yeah, Dionne, I'm still trying to deal with that night after all those years. I'd like to see him feel the way I felt or feel. We've got a brother? What was he thinking? He was married. You cover for him if you want to; he's done as far as I'm concerned. Ma, whatever you want to do that gives you peace in this matter, do it."

"It's your wedding Dionne. I don't want you to have a problem with them being in the audience. But they'll be here to meet you and Trevon and that's necessary for Carl even if they're not at the church."

"They say every wedding day has its own drama. My father has brought me mine."

Chapter 56

Detective Griffin removed his pad and pen from his inner pocket and pulled his chair closer to Zach's bedside. He had been visiting him off and on for two weeks. Dr. Norris had been interviewed twice as did the staff that was on duty the night Zach was brought in. None of them were told who had attacked Zach, but they knew Zach was well aware of who his attacker was. Griffin told his partners, Mays and Childs, it would take time, but he could get Zach to reveal who had done this to him.

Griffin arrived at the hospital at seven o'clock that morning. Dr. Norris called saying another chipped bone had moved, and it was causing blindness in Zach's left eye. They were taking him to surgery at nine. Zach was told about his need for surgery and the possible dangers. He asked Dr. Norris to call Detective Griffin for him. Zach didn't say why.

"Detective I called you here to clarify some things. Lamont and I are friends, we've never been the best of friends, but nevertheless, we are friends. I thought that Kris was dealing with Brian, that was my first thought. A person knows when their other half is out there. The problem is always with who. I wanted to know what this Kris looked liked and why Brian was acting the way he was. I agitated him detective. I started by throwing Kris Randall's business card at him. It escalated and I triggered a part of his character I had never seen before."

"So you did see Brian Drakeford that day?"

"Yes, I went to his house. We were supposed to talk about our relationship."

"Did he attack you?"

"I don't know if I would call it an attack. I don't want to call it an attack. We fought. He hit me in the nose."

Griffin gave Zach a look that told him he knew there was more to the story than what he told. Zach turned his head letting Detective Griffin know that was all he was willing to tell.

"A fight; have you had many fights with Mr. Drakeford?"

"No, none, as a matter of a fact. That's how I know this wasn't his intention."

"Has he been here to see you?"

"No."

"Has he called here or contacted Lamont about your condition?"

"No not that I know of."

"Zach, I've sat with you the past few weeks, when you couldn't hold your head up. When you went through the first surgery; and we've talked, laughed and prayed together for your recovery. Not once did the man you claim wanted you back in his life even ask about you? Doesn't that seem strange?"

"Yes, I guess it does. Why did you stay with me, visit, and gain my friendship? Was it to solve a case? Isn't that a little much? Some of that time was your own? I could ask, what was your motive?"

"Other than it being my job, you're a big boy you tell me."

Zach smiled, he realized Detective Griffin lived the same lifestyle that Lamont and Brian lived. Zach looked the well-dressed detective over. He was a good-looking man.

"I understand. What's your first name?"

"David, David Griffin."

"David, so you have a personal interest in this?"

"I do. I don't think anyone should feel subjected to the behavior Brian Drakeford displays. We've discovered some things about him that always touch the border of a crime. It's getting worse with each act. I want to stop it before he hurts someone seriously. Possibly, someone I know or care about."

Zach was glad he didn't make any implications that Griffin was interested in him. He would have felt like a fool. Griffin noticed how Zach repositioned himself. His features were no longer as relaxed. He took on a professional persona.

"Relax Zach. I do have an interest in you and what happened. I don't want to get myself put off the case. If they think I've become involved, they'll remove me. Did Brian do this or what? Tell me straight. You don't deserve this, unless my intuitions are wrong. Damn, no one deserves to go through this."

"That's what I'm trying to explain. Brian has done some fucked up shit, don't get me wrong, but he didn't mean for this to turn out this way. I know it."

"Did he try to rape you?"

Zach frowned and shook his head no frantically.

"What made you ask that? Who told you that? Is that what Brian said?"

"Zach, I do these investigations for a living. He hit you hard enough to crush your nose. It wasn't just a lucky punch. You refused him something."

"I fought him off. What happens to him now?"

"I've got to get a warrant for his DNA. We still have your clothes and maybe if I searched the bedroom, there's still a chance that your blood is somewhere in the room. You bled a lot. He might not have cleaned it well. The only problem is they may not give us a warrant."

"Is it really that serious? I'm okay."

"No you're headed to surgery. There may be complications. Your sight is already a problem. Zach tell me what went on that day."

Zach thought about it and began from the beginning. He told Griffin about the off and on relationship he had with Brian over the years. He told him about Sage, Demarest, and the Monday he went to hear what Brian had to say. Zach described the condition of the house and how he found Kris Randall's business card. He also told him he took Brian's cell phone. Zach waited for Griffin to respond.

"Thanks, I think we have enough to charge him with aggravated assault. I'll be here when you come out of surgery."

"Griffin, your interest is just in this case huh."

"I have to have an interest in the case, it's my job. I don't have to come back after the surgery. That's personal. Zach, get better and we'll deal with my interest in you. I'll see you this afternoon."

"Thanks Dave."

"You're welcome Zach."

Chapter 57

Brian drank the last of the fifth of vodka he had before dialing Dionne's number. It was Thursday, Dionne hadn't returned his calls, and he knew he would miss her again if he didn't call before noon.

Mr. Silverman had called earlier to inform him that Zach was blind in one eye and was undergoing surgery to remove the chipped bone that the doctor's thought was pressing on the optic nerve and causing the blindness. Mr. Silverman warned him that there were three possibilities after this type of surgery. The possibility of Zach coming out fine and their concerns would be resolved. He would be released from the hospital within the next week. There was the possibility of him permanently losing his sight and having complications from the surgery. Then there was the last possibility of permanent damage to the brain and him being in a coma. Brian listened pretending not to be concerned. Mr. Silverman told him his attitude wouldn't help him in court if Zach didn't recover fully. His lawyer was sure he would be brought up on charges in all the possibilities.

After talking to Mr. Silverman, Brian opened the fifth of vodka and had been drinking from it since. Brian gave up on cleaning again and called his psychiatrist to cancel his appointment. The doctor tried to convince him to come and talk with him but Brian used the excuse that Dionne's wedding was in two days and there were preparations he needed to be involved in. The doctor accepted what he knew was Brian's way of avoiding the appointment and made him schedule another appointment before hanging up the phone. After making the appointment, Brian dialed Dionne's number again.

"Hello."

"Hey, who's this?"

"It's Dionne's dad. Is this Jarad?"

"Yeah, how are you Mr. Drakeford?"

"Fine, are you ready for the big day?"

"As ready as I'm gonna get I guess. I pick up my tux this afternoon."

"Yea, I went by there yesterday. I was calling about the rehearsal."

"Oh, it's at five thirty tomorrow. We're going to rehearse at the church beginning at six. I think some people will be coming from work. Most of the ones from out of town are here already. Did you hear from Trevon? He's been here since last week."

Brian remembered that Dionne told him they were having a talk with Sage. It wasn't until then that he realized why Dionne hadn't called him.

"Jarad where's Dionne? I was trying to talk to her before the rehearsal."

"She's with the coordinator this morning. I think she'll be with some of the girls this afternoon. Did you try her cell?"

"I'll try it again. Could you call her and tell her to call or stop by, just in case I miss her?"

"Sure Mr. Drakeford, I'll tell her."

Brian clicked the phone to clear the line and dialed Sage's number. He was sure she would know why Dionne didn't call him back. His fury grew with each ring of the phone.

"Hello."

It was Trevon and Brian's thoughts changed to silence. He had prepared himself to question Sage not Trevon.

"Hello, who's this?"

Trevon repeated his greeting.

"Hey Tre, it's your father."

"Hello, what's up?"

"Well I, uh. Have you heard from Dionne?"

"She's here hold on."

Brian couldn't tell from Trevon's response, whether or not Sage had badmouthed him in light of Zach's attack. He was certain she knew and would be more than happy to use it against him. Trevon's passing off the phone with no conversation only indicated nothing had changed between the two of them. He waited for Trevon to return saying Dionne didn't want to talk to him. He was sure Sage had convinced them of the worse. He would talk to her before the ceremony and explain they had an agreement all of these years, and he expected her to uphold her end, even if she had a new love in her life.

"Hey Dad, how are you?"

"Fine baby girl, I was calling for more directions. Jarad told me the rehearsal time. Is there something else I'm supposed to know or do before the rehearsal?"

"No. Just be at the rehearsal and then at the church on Saturday. The coordinator will let everyone know what time to be there while we're at the rehearsal."

"Okay, I guess I'll see you then."

"That will be fine. Thanks."

"Uh, okay. I guess I'll talk to you then."

"Okay, bye."

The phone clicked in Brian's ear. He put the phone down convinced Sage had said something to Trevon and Dionne. He would call her on her cell phone. He looked in the cabinet for another bottle to open. He found a liter of vodka that he bought for card parties. The doorbell rang stopping him from pouring the first glass from the bottle.

"Mr. Drakeford, we have a warrant to search these premises."

"A warrant, what are you looking for?" Brian turned the knob feeling the weight of the officers on the door.

Detective Griffin entered while the other officers scattered throughout his home.

"Anything that may say that Zachary Blanding was here the Monday he was assaulted."

"I'm calling my lawyer."

"He already knows we're here."

The officers took more than an hour to take pictures, swabs and bag items that they felt had evidence of the assault. The detective wandered from room to room visually checking and pointing to items he wanted checked. Brian followed taking mental notes of the items they bagged.

"When will I get my things back?"

"They'll be released if they are not necessary for the charges. If they're needed, they will be labeled as evidence and kept until the court releases them."

"Detective, did Zach tell you he was here?"

"Mr. Drakeford, you said he wasn't here. If he wasn't these blood stains, hairs and other particles won't be his."

"He's been here before."

"We know. But he wasn't bleeding when he was here before or do you always assault your guest?"

Brian lunged toward the Detective and two officers stepped in restraining him from moving any further.

"Okay guys, we're finished here. Let him go, he doesn't need assaulting an officer added to his upcoming charges and he sure doesn't need his ass whooped. Have a good time at the wedding."

"I'll be seeing you again detective. It won't be under these circumstances either."

"You're right. You'll be on your way to jail." The officers left certain they would return.

Chapter 58

Dionne returned to the living room where her mother, Kris, Trevon and Lynn, were talking. She felt guilty that she had treated Kris so badly when they first met. He hadn't mentioned it to her mother, she could tell the way Sage smiled whenever Dionne spoke and Kris responded. Dionne asked questions about his business and his family. Kris was more than willing to share the information and pictures he had in his wallet.

"They're good looking children." Trevon passed the pictures on for Dionne and Lynn to look at them.

"They could be models. Excuse my question but are they mixed."

Kris laughed. He got asked that often.

"Yes, their father was white. My sister was as dark as me. I guess that's what you get when you mix milk with chocolate."

"They're beautiful."

"Your children are modeling material too."

Lynn spoke up waving her hand and shaking her head.

"Been there, done that. We went through that phase when they were … what was it honey?"

"About two or three years ago; they were four and seven. We thought it was cute too. They loved wearing the clothes, modeling you know; until our oldest Niecy got more offers to model than Londa."

"What are their names?"

"Treniece and Trelonda, don't ask how or why we came up with those names. You know females they just tell you the name."

Everyone laughed at Trevon as he raised his brow looking at his mother.

"What? I didn't have anything to do with that," Sage answered in her own defense.

"No, you just named me Trevon. Lynn loves the name but we don't have a boy so the girls are stuck."

The laughter broke out again.

"I don't see a problem Tre have a boy."

"Seems like I only make girls, man, I give up; I couldn't imagine three women in the house and me."

Through the laughter the bell rang and Dionne opened the door inviting Karen in to join the fun. They spent the afternoon talking and sharing family stories with Kris. Trevon really enjoyed another man's company. Dionne said her goodbyes about three o'clock as Trevon and Kris walked out the door with her headed to the store to replenish the sodas and snacks. They welcomed the moment to apologize for their father's behavior. Dionne had a separate apology to make.

"Man, I'm so glad to meet you. I'm glad you and my mother have a good relationship. I wish you the best."

"Kris, I want to thank you for not telling my mother what an ass I was the night I met you."

Kris tried to interject but Dionne continued to apologize.

"No, let me do what's right please. I really thought you had other intentions. I mean with all that was going on I didn't know where you fit in. I'm sorry for judging you. I agree with my brother. I'm glad you're here with my mother. She'll need more than just us and Aunt Karen to get through this. Kris, I'm afraid for my father, but I'm more afraid for my mother. Thank you and please accept my apology."

"Have you heard anything about the outcome of the surgery?" Trevon wanted to ask earlier but spared his mother what he felt would be an uncomfortable conversation.

"No, um, I'll call Greg while we're at the store. I don't want to upset your mother with any other bad news."

"I agree. Well, you guys have fun. I'll see you tomorrow my brother, and you on Saturday Kris." Dionne paused before getting into her car. "Hey, when are Carla and Carl getting in town?"

"Greg said sometime tonight. They'll be around tomorrow I guess."

"Okay, Tre call me. I'll make an effort to get over here before the rehearsal. I want to meet them before the wedding."

"Yeah, that may be best. drive careful."

Trevon and Kris talked going and coming from the store. Trevon felt good talking with another man who knew about his father's issues. Kris called Greg, as promised, but he had no word on Zach's condition. Greg told him Lamont went to the hospital and hadn't called. He would call Kris when he heard anything.

"Man, I don't know if I could have worked with an escort service."

"I didn't think I could either. Greg is a good guy. He runs a straight, well not straight, but legitimate business. It's all about business. He doesn't get into any personal matters, unless it infringes on his business. Your father used the business for his fantasies, it's okay as long as everyone agrees. I didn't agree."

"He should have backed off. My dad never showed that side of his personality to us. I guess he couldn't live hiding how he really felt. I've been told it's a part of who he has always been."

"I think so Tre. I'm glad he didn't show that side to you and your mother. Who knows how bad your home life would have gotten? You could have been Demarest and your mom could have been Zach."

The thought gave Trevon the chills. He understood what Kris was saying and just shook his head in agreement. A fogged memory of his last night crying in his bed crossed his mind.

"Man, I was young, thank God. I think if he had tried it again though man, I might have killed him, father or not."

"You won't get me to change your way of thinking. If it wasn't for your mother I might have changed his way of looking at things, or at least his way of looking at me."

The two men laughed as Kris parked the car and entered Sage's home. Karen and Lynn were talking in the living room and Kris took the bags from Trevon and entered the kitchen where Sage was talking on the phone.

"Brian, I'll call you back!"

Sage hung up the phone and shook her head. Kris knew better than to ask any questions. He walked to her and kissed her on her forehead. She returned his kiss by kissing his lips. The two stood in the middle of the kitchen holding each other until Sage calmed down.

Chapter 59

Brian jumped out of bed Friday morning awakened by the screams he heard over and over in his head. The voices started the night he was questioned at the precinct. He couldn't sleep knowing Zach was in the hospital. He could hear Zach then Demarest screaming, no begging him to stop. He heard their voices but he saw Trevon's face. It was becoming a recurring nightmare.

He got out of the bed and decided not to make an attempt to sleep any longer. The medication helped him doze but the nightmare was intense. The clock read seven but Brian had set it fifteen minutes fast giving him what he thought was extra time in the mornings. His phone was blinking indicating he had messages. It was odd he could sleep through the phone ringing. He pushed the numbers needed to retrieve the messages from the missed calls.

"Brian, this is Sage, I'm returning your call."

Brian remembered talking to her, although the conversation was sketchy. He listened for the next message.

"Brian, this is Silverman, call me."

Brian had no doubt in his mind he needed to call him immediately. He still wanted to know why the police invaded his home. *"What were they really looking for?"* Brian decided to visit Zach before the rehearsal. He would cover his tracks. The detectives and Mr. Silverman showed him he made a mistake not visiting or calling Zach. He could explain it as shock. He didn't want to see Zach the way they had described him. He would also spend the day calling mutual friends wondering if they had heard what happened. Brian was sure the questions would be asked again. This time Brian would give a list of people he spoke to about Zach and his condition.

As the time reached eleven Brian's plans began to unfold. He called Lamont first.

"Lamont, Brian Drakeford, how are you?"

"Fine, what about yourself?"

Lamont couldn't imagine how Brian mustered enough nerve to call him.

"I'm as well as to be expected. I mean with what has happened to Zach, I've been beside myself."

"I could only imagine."

Brian forgot how straightforward Lamont could be. It would take more than a phone call to break Lamont down. If Brian could get Lamont to understand his version of what happened, he could get anyone else to fall in line.

"Have you been to the hospital since yesterday? You know Zach had to undergo another surgery. I couldn't bring myself to go see him when he got hurt or during the first surgery and recovery. Every time I work up the strength to go and see him, it seems like something else happens."

"Maybe it would be best if you forget trying to see him."

"Do you think so Lamont, I mean I don't want him to think I'm not willing to be with him when things get rough?"

"I'm quite sure he doesn't think that. His mind is probably on his recovery and not you at all."

"You don't think Zach would find it abnormal that I didn't visit him."

"I don't think Zach would find anything you do abnormal."

Brian couldn't stand it anymore. The two men could play verbal judo for hours.

"Have you gone to see him?"

"What do you want Brian, really?"

"What do you mean?"

"Listen, you and I aren't friends, why did you call me?"

"Since you put it that way, I want to know what you and Zach talked about at the hospital. I know you visited him the day he was attacked. I want to know who did this to him. I've been waiting for the police to get a lead, but they just keep asking the same questions. It's gotten them nowhere. I want this bastard caught."

"Did Zach call you?"

"No, I don't think so, unless he called my cell phone."

"What's wrong with your cell phone? You don't answer it?"

"I think I left it at the office. I can't find it. Anyway, no he didn't call me."

"Why don't you call him or better yet visit? I bet he would be more than happy to tell you who did it."

Brian had his answer. He could tell Lamont knew what happened.

"I'll pay him a visit today for sure. Thanks."

Brian hung up the phone. He sat thinking about his cell phone. He dialed the number on his home phone. He waited to hear it ring. The phone was not in the house. Brian had to go pass the office on his way to the hospital. He would stop by and pick it up. It had to be in his desk. He cleared the line and dialed Sage's number.

"Hello."

"Tre, it's your father. Is your mother around?"

Trevon wanted to yell for Kris to tell his mother the telephone was for her. Kris was there early. They went to breakfast and had just returned to the house.

"Mom, phone."

"I've got it. Hello."

"Sage its Brian, listen, I don't want this ceremony to make either of us uncomfortable. I understand you're bringing a guest. Let's both be mature about this. We've been separated and divorced long enough not to play the sarcastic games. You know, the 'who hurt who', during the introductions and throughout the day."

"Brian, who said there would be any introductions. You're attending this wedding as Dionne's father not my husband. I'm not obligated to introduce you to anyone. I don't see the need."

"Damn it, I do. We'll be in each other's face all afternoon. The wedding and the reception, I would think you would have respect for Dionne at least."

"I've talked to Dionne and Jarad. They understand and it's their wedding. All others that don't understand don't matter. My guest is just that. He's attending to be with me in the celebration of my daughter's wedding."

"What did you tell them about us? What did you say about Zach and me?"

"They've known about Zach for years, and you knew that too. You tell me what else could I say?"

Brian was getting nowhere with Sage as he had done with Lamont. He was tormenting himself.

"Sage, remember your promise?"

"Sure I do and I've upheld my end. You make sure you keep your end of the deal."

"What are you talking about? The deal was you would have your divorce if you allowed me to keep a relationship with Tre and Dionne."

"Then act like we're divorced Brian. Don't call here again."

The operator's voice was the next he heard asking him to hang up if he wanted to make a call.

Chapter 60

"I'm sorry Mr. Drakeford, Mr. Blanding went under guarded care this morning. I can call to get you clearance if you would like but as of this morning your name is not on the accepted list of visitors."

Brian looked around the lounge of the hospital as though the police or security were watching him from cameras and hidden areas near the registration desk.

"Can you tell me his condition?"

"He's in the critical care unit."

"Critical? Are you sure you have the right patient? He was fine yesterday, I mean, he went into surgery yesterday, but he wasn't critical."

"Sir, these notes are updated regularly throughout the day. He was brought to this unit late last night. I guess he had a turn for the worse."

"Who do I speak to about seeing him?"

"It would have to be one of the officers in charge."

"Where's your security office?"

"I'm sorry Mr. Drakeford, not one of our officers. You would have to speak with Detective Griffin. I can give you the number if you would like to call."

"That won't be necessary. Thank you."

Brian left the hospital and went to his office hoping to find his cell phone. It was after twelve when he got there but the lobby was busy as usual. Brian went to his office greeting his co-workers and supervisors as he passed them in the hall. There were a few who told him they were keeping Zach in their prayers. He decided to call Mr. Silverman to tell him he tried to visit, but they wouldn't let him in and he had a list of friends who he spoke to about Zach's condition. That should satisfy the police. Brian's desk was clean, everything was in order, an indication someone went through his things. He sat in his chair and buzzed the receptionist.

"Mr. Drakeford, I'm glad to see you're back."

"Well, I'm not really. Listen, I noticed someone has been in my office, who?"

"Mr. Foster, and three detectives."

"Did they take anything?"

"No, they didn't take anything. They asked a few of the staff questions about you and Mr. Blanding but that was it. They snooped around for about twenty minutes."

"Regina, I can't find my cell phone. Are you sure they didn't take anything with them?"

"No, Mr. Foster was strict about that. He told them warrant or not they would have to list whatever they took from your office and leave a copy of the list with me. You know, just in case you wanted to blame one of us for taking it. The detectives looked through your entire office, moving things around and making a mess. I waited until they left and told Mr. Foster I would straighten things up for you."

"Did they tell Foster what they were looking for or why they were here?"

"I don't think so."

"Is he in, Mr. Foster?"

"No, he's gone for the weekend. I could call him for you, but he won't be back here until Monday."

"Thanks Regina, I'll see him Monday."

"Mr. Drakeford, will you be back to work on Monday?"

"Well, I hope so. I mean Mr. Blanding is not doing well at all. This will be a weekend of needed prayer. If he's doing better I'll be in Monday."

"I'll definitely pray for the both of you."

Brian hung up the phone. He made the point about Zach so he could add Regina to the list showing his concern about Zach's condition. It was then he remembered to call Silverman.

"Silverman & Whitehead. Good morning."

"Good morning, Mr. Silverman, please."

Brian listened to the music while he was on hold. The song was comforting and he hummed along not recognizing the jazz artist. It seemed as though he had listened to the entire song before Silverman picked up on the other end.

"Silverman. Good morning."

"Brian Drakeford, sir."

"Ah Mr. Drakeford, it's good to see you're still holding your spirits."

"Why wouldn't I?"

"They've got some evidence Brian that may or may not lead them to an arrest."

"Well that's what you're for; to make sure it doesn't lead to an arrest. Call it inadmissible; illegal search use that lingo that would squash what they got. Mr. Silverman, I told them when they came to the house that Zach had been there many times before."

"Brian they have blood spatter, and who knows what else."

"They shared the evidence with you already?"

"No, I have friends in the department."

"Doesn't that taint things? I mean them telling you about the evidence means we can get it thrown out."

"No, it means we can be a step ahead of them. I'm not revealing my source. You're not my only client. You tell me how the blood got there? Where are you?"

"I'm at my office."

Brian ignored answering the question about the blood and told Silverman about his attempt to get in the hospital.

"They said he was under guarded care."

"Detective Griffin left a message late last night. Zach didn't come around like he should have after the surgery. His vitals are weak and they don't know if he'll make it. If he should die, I'm sure they'll charge you with murder. If he survives, there's a list of charges you may still face."

"Based on what evidence?"

"The blood stains on your floor; DNA comparisons from his shirt and your bedroom, Brian you could do time if they connect you with this assault."

"So what am I paying you for if you're convinced already that I'll do time?"

"You pay me to keep your length of incarceration at a minimum. I can't get you off if the evidence can't be argued. I keep telling you to tell me the truth. The evidence tells a different story than yours Brian. Listen I get paid, as you know, whether you're guilty or not. The difference is, how long I perform in front of the jury. Give me a good script. I can work with any jury. I can get you and any other killer off. You give me footnotes, and they fill in the blanks. That leads to assumptions and convictions. It's up to you. The District Attorney is sharp, she won't go into court without thinking she has a win. That Detective Griffin and his squad specialize in what I call touchy assaults, the incidents no one else cares about because it takes work. They're good, Brian. If anyone can give us trouble it's them. However, working with you this way I can't win. You have to tell me the truth."

"I told you what I told them. Isn't it true if I change my story now I'm done? I even showed concern as you said. I went to the hospital. I have people here on the job that can tell you I've been out on leave because I've been so upset I couldn't work."

"Brian, we can work through anything if you tell me the truth. Listen, I'll try to keep them away from you for a day or so. Your daughter's wedding is tomorrow right?"

"Yeah, you sound like you know they're coming to arrest me. This isn't like the search warrant you never told me about is it."

"You tell me the truth Brian and we both can lay our cards on the table. I get inside information but I've got to let the process play out. We don't need you to mess things up, and they come back without the usual loopholes and errors. I can't do my job if you don't let me."

"So you want me to be arrested and hope that you'll pull a miracle to set me free?"

"Give me all I need to perform the miracle, that's all I'm asking. I need to know what really happened."

"Alright, we'll talk after the wedding."

"Okay, after the wedding. Call me if you need to."

Brian slammed the receiver on its base. Reality was becoming uncomfortable.

Chapter 61

The rehearsal went well. The coordinator explained the next day would be hectic, but it would be a beautiful ceremony with everyone's cooperation. Dionne and Jarad sat and watched laughing with Trevon's daughters, the flower girls and Jarad's cousin, the ring bearer. Sage, Brian and the Jarad's parents waited until the coordinator gave her final directions before quickly saying their goodbyes. The bridal party huddled in the pews across from where Sage and Brian sat.

"Dionne will make a beautiful bride."

Sage didn't add any comments to Brian's statement, pretending she hadn't heard him.

"This is what I'm talking about Sage. We should be cordial to each other because it is our daughter. Neither of us can change the fact that we will be brought together during certain times. We could at least agree to be civil."

"I haven't done anything that would indicate that I'm not able to be civil with you. Brian as usual you want someone to ignore your actions or decisions you've made. I can't do that and I won't. It's only for a day so let's get through this, and if I never see you again it will be fine with me."

Trevon and Dionne approached their parents. They too, agreed to get through the rehearsal and the wedding cordially.

"Lynn and the girls are headed to the car. We'll meet you at the house."

"Jarad is going to stop at his parents for a minute before he and the guys get together. I've got to stop at your house before I go home."

Brain felt left out. He made what would be his last effort to question what they knew.

"Can we all talk a minute before any of us leaves?"

The others in the bridal party and the coordinator told Sage and Brian good night as they excited the chapel. The best man excused himself and whispered in Tre's ear where the party for Jarad would be. He nodded good night to Sage and Brian. Tre, Dionne and Sage gave each other a look, a silent agreement to speak to Brian. Dionne led them all to an office in the back of the church. She told the Deacon, who was preparing to lock the church for the night, they would only be another minute.

No one sat down. All of them looked directly at Brian giving him a feeling of what it would be like to confront a jury.

"This will only take a moment, but I wanted to say this while we were together. I've done some things in the past that I am truly sorry for. I know that you're aware of Zach's condition and the fact that he's been in the hospital for almost a month. I wanted you to hear it from me. I didn't have anything to do with his injuries. The detectives have been around asking questions about me and our relationship, and they've made accusations about me causing Zach's injuries. I didn't want them asking you questions about me, and you wondering why I didn't tell you what was going on."

Trevon had heard enough. "So you're telling us this because you need us to tell them how great you were as a father, a husband, or what? What is it, you want us to tell them? Why don't you just give us the script? It's hard enough to deal with you, and now you want us, no me to pretend you couldn't have assaulted Zach. Ma, Dionne, I'll see you at the house."

Trevon walked out of the office. Sage stared at Brian waiting for him to respond.

"I'm as confused as Trevon. What do you want us to do or say? You chose your lifestyle and now you want to pull us in to paint a picture of who you are for the police. Brian we don't know who you are. You are not the man I married. You're not the man I chose to live my life with. That's what I will tell them if they ask; nothing more or less."

"You're misunderstanding my intentions. I just wanted you to be aware that the police may be asking you questions. It has nothing to do with you painting a picture of who I am. I can tell them who I am. You and Trevon have never understood that. I'm not trying to change who I am. I'm sorry about what has happened to us as a family and the fact that you may be involved in this because of my association with Zach, that's all. Listen, I'm not trying to ruin Dionne and Jarad's day. I'm glad you still want me to escort you Dionne. I'm honored. After tomorrow, I'll keep my appearances and contact to a minimum."

Sage refused to say what came to her mind, and instead she said a prayer. Dionne moved closer to Brian. Sage thought she was going to kiss him. Instead she lowered her voice certain only the three of them could hear. Sage knew her tone was to emphasize her statement.

"Daddy, make your last statement a promise you keep. If it wasn't for it being my wedding, I wouldn't want to see you tomorrow. After all these years, the ups the downs and your changes in lifestyles, moods and attitudes, you owe us tomorrow. Thank you for accepting the honor of escorting me down the aisle, but our ties are cut at the end of the day."

Dionne exited the room and Sage followed, leaving Brian standing alone. The deacon came to the door and noticed Brian watching what was left of his family leave.

"Sir, will there be anything else?"

"No I think that about finishes things for us."

Chapter 62

Greg told Kris they would be at Sage's house in less than thirty minutes. Sage prepared fried chicken, potato salad and tossed salad for them to eat before she left for the rehearsal. Lynn, Trevon and their daughters, along with Dionne and Kris anxiously awaited the arrival of their guests.

Trevon and Lynn talked about his comments and feelings after the conversation with Brian during the drive to his mother's. Though they didn't mention his uneasiness about seeing his father prior, Lynn knew it took a toll on him. Meeting Carla, Demarest and Carl only added to his internal stress. Lynn kept watching her husband hoping he wouldn't need his medication.

"Do you want me to get your medicine for you?"

"No, babe, I'm ahead of you. I took it. As a matter of a fact I took it before going to the rehearsal."

Trevon showed Lynn his pillbox and smiled.

"Don't leave home without it."

Trevon got terrible headaches and his blood pressure dropped when he had anxiety attacks. His attacks were prone to happen more during his visits home.

Sage and Kris talked between the kitchen and the dinning room while Sage set the table for buffet style serving.

"Did Brian admit to attacking Zach?"

"Now you know he wouldn't tell me that. He did just the opposite or tried to do the opposite. I think he wanted us to be character witnesses if he needed them. Kris, he sounded pitiful. I don't know what he thought we would say, but he'll have more to be upset about after tomorrow."

The doorbell rang and Dionne answered welcoming Greg and the others inside. Introductions were made and they proceeded into the living room. Sage and Kris greeted them, offering refreshments as everyone took a seat. Carl was grinning pleased he could have his choice of soda.

"I usually don't let him choose. He always leaves half a can." Carla gave Carl a look of warning. Her son responded coyly as he popped the can of Sprite.

"Wow, Ma. That's Trevon at a younger age isn't it?"

"I'm looking; he does have a resemblance."

"Carl how old are you?"

"I'm twelve. How old are you?"

Everyone laughed waiting for Trevon to answer.

"Man, don't ask. I'm your older brother though, did you know that?"

"Yeah, my mom told me, and I know how old you are too. You're twenty seven and Dionne is twenty nine. You're married to Lynn and have two daughters, my nieces Treniece and Trelonda. Dionne is marrying Jarad tomorrow, and they don't have kids yet. Your mother's name is Sage and our father's name is Brian. Greg is my mother's new friend, well old friend but new boyfriend."

"Okay Carl, that's enough."

"Oh yeah, Uncle Demarest is still gonna live with us."

"Okay, I guess we can relax since we know he's aware of what's going on."

The children left the adults to talk. They went into the den and cut on the television. Carl found an interest in the piano. He played a few keys which sparked questions abut his ability to play.

"He plays for a group at his school; mostly at concerts and plays. He also plays for the church we attend. He's pretty good."

"That's alright where did he learn to play."

Carla smiled proudly. Demarest stood and asked Sage which way was the bathroom.

"Demarest taught him. I didn't even know he played until he told me he wanted room enough in his part of the house for a piano. He has one in his music room. You guys didn't see his side of the house we're in. He doesn't play as often as he did when we first moved in. Maybe later he'll play for you. He plays beautifully."

It was close to nine o'clock when Greg's phone rang. He looked at Carla as she rolled her eyes at him. She was assuming who the caller was. When he saw it was Lamont, he didn't ignore the call.

"What's up, how's things at the hospital?"

"Greg, Zach's slipping deeper into a comatose state. He was responding to the treatment a little this afternoon. They finished some other test and the results weren't what they expected. I'm leaving now and so is Detective Griffin."

"The cops are still there?"

"They've been here since he had the surgery. Detective Griffin comes and goes but there's always one on duty."

"Damn, why?"

"Detective Griffin said they're considering the attack a bias crime because Zach is gay."

"That's deep. Does it mean Brian can get serious time?"

"They have to prove he did it. I think Detective Griffin is on the DL."

"Lamont you hope he's on the DL."

"That is a thought. Greg you didn't look at him did you. Oh I forgot you're trying to find yourself with Ms. Carla. How's the introductions going?"

"Everything is fine. They'll be fine. We'll see how Mr. Drakeford handles the reunion. Listen I'll call you after the wedding."

"You better."

Greg told everyone about Zach and the reason for his police protection.

"Greg do you think my father will be arrested?"

"Dionne, I don't know. I would think if they had all the evidence they needed, they would have arrested him already. I don't know what they've found or who they've asked questions. I guess they're waiting for Zach's condition to stabilize."

"What would they charge him with?"

Sage couldn't imagine Brian getting time for breaking Zach's nose.

"He could be charged with a few things. Attempted aggravated sexual assault or aggravated assault and who knows what else."

"Did Zach press the charges?"

Demarest was remembering how he felt when he was assaulted by Brian. He couldn't bring himself to press charges because he loved Brian. He knew Zach did too.

"Demarest, what difference does it make as long as someone stops him."

"Carla, I should have stopped him. If I had pressed charges this would have never happened."

The mood in the room was changing. Each person had his own thoughts about what Demarest said.

"No, Demarest, I should have said something way before you. If I had to go through it again I would have done it differently."

Tre had already told Carla and Demarest about his father's attempt to molest him. He explained he didn't understand everything about people who live the alternate lifestyles, but he hated those who forced themselves on others.

"Tre, be careful what you ask for, according to Lamont the cops may be asking us questions."

"Greg, Brian said the same thing."

"Will they wait until after my wedding? I would hope so, this is too much."

"Well sis you'll have a police escort from the church to the reception."

"Me, no, that would be your father."

Dionne's comment was a welcomed tension reliever. They all laughed although they knew her answer wasn't far from the truth.

Chapter 63

Brian stood at the top of the church stairs waiting for the limousine to pull up. He stood at the back of the church smiling at the guest as they arrived as long as he could. The guest list didn't include many of his relatives. Brian didn't have many names or addresses to give Dionne, he and his family weren't close. The church was filled with Dionne and Jarad's college friends and co-workers. Brian was greeted by a few of Sage's staff and friends, neighbors and those who associated with him before their divorce. Guests he did not recognize acknowledged him, Brian thought, only because of his tux and boutonnière. The whispers and glances after they took their seats made him uncomfortable. He felt like an outsider at his daughter's wedding.

Brian didn't recognize the Mercedes that pulled up in front of the limousine, but when Sage got out, he assumed it was her guest that was driving. Sage had a beautiful dress on that added to her air of elegance. Karen got out of the back seat as Vince opened the door for her. Brian was surprised that Karen and Vince were still seeing each other. He shook his head at the thought. The door of the limousine remained closed. Sage walked up the stairs smiling. Brian returned her smile and gave a sigh of relief knowing she was willing to put on a show for the audience inside.

"Good afternoon, have you been inside?"

"Off and on, I've been here about forty five minutes."

"I hope everyone showed up. Dionne bugged me about invitations and the guest list for months."

"Seems like they did; it's pretty packed."

"Good, good, did you see the coordinator?"

"Yes, she's in the back with Jarad and the other guys. She told me to hang out here for the limo, so here I stand."

"You followed directions? That's a good sign."

"A good sign c'mon Sage, I do know how to act sometimes."

"Let it be all day today okay?"

"You got it. You look good. You look beautiful. The dress, your hair, everything; you're beautiful."

"Thank you. Wait until you see Dionne. I almost cried again."

"Again?"

"I've been crying all morning."

The church door opened and Trevon smiled and nodded to his mother. She knew that meant Carla, Demarest and Carl were in the audience. They had parked their car in the rear and entered in the side door.

"Are they ready to begin?"

"I believe so. Dad, you should be with Dionne until the coordinator calls for you."

"Thanks man."

"Mom, they're waiting to seat you and Jarad's parents."

"Alright, let's get this started."

Trevon and Sage went into the church and Brian remained on the church steps in thought. He had called the hospital again that morning only to hear that Zach had been in and out of sleep but never for more than fifteen minutes at a time. He was still on the Critical Care Unit under protective watch. Brian didn't understand who they thought had attacked Zach and why they were watching him, as though he was a celebrity or state official. Brian wanted to talk to Detective Griffin, but he changed his mind. He didn't want the police to think he was scared of their investigation. Brian heard the music that indicated the ceremony was about to begin. The bridesmaids, flower girls and ring bearers got out of the limousine and passed him saying their hellos. Brian went to the limousine and peeked inside.

"Come in and sit a minute."

"No, I don't want to wrinkle the tux. I'm fine. How are you holding up?"

"Okay, I guess. They said I was supposed to be nervous. I guess it's a bride's thing. Anyway, it will all be over in a minute. How are you holding up?"

"I'm okay. No, I'm lying. It's all hitting me fast. This day, the last few weeks, months, years; I've got some serious thinking to do. But today, I'm okay cause you're okay, and I'll get through it."

"Dad, you've got to get through this and get the help you need to get through everything else."

Brian didn't answer as Dionne's phone buzzed.

"That's the sign. They're ready. Take me father, to my husband."

Brian smiled and helped Dionne out of the car. The church doors opened and Brian thought he was in a different world. All eyes were on them. He felt guilty and the guests looked on. His head spun, the beginning of a headache. He scanned the audience as smiles and nods of approval were given. As they got to the middle of the church Brian's eyes made contact with a face he thought he would never see again. Demarest smiled and then nodded as though he was sending silent message saying, *"It's not over."* Brian thought his mind was playing tricks on him. Next to Demarest stood Carla and a young boy who resembled Trevon at a younger age. Brian felt weak in his knees. Questions began to run through his mind as they got closer to the altar. Brian stood as the words from the minister became muffled and the visions of Demarest, Carla and the child repeated again and again.

"Mr. Drakeford."

The minister was whispering indicating it was his turn to acknowledge giving the bride to the groom.

"Yes, I do, I do."

Brian stepped back to return to his seat. The face he saw sitting next to Sage hit him in the chest like a shotgun blast. Sage and Kris moved over giving Brian room to sit on the pew. Brian wanted to refuse the seat but the entire church seemed to be watching. Demarest and Carla were sitting at the end of their pew, two rows behind where Brian was expected to sit. Brian sat down, holding his head in his hands. He couldn't believe he was set up. He wanted to ask Sage what was on her mind dating Kris Randall. Brian realized the link. Kris Randall, they would definitely settle this before the reception. Brian had no intentions of spending the afternoon looking at his past.

The ceremony continued and as the bridal party passed and the family procession began. Brian was the first out of the pew. Sage looked back and smiled at Kris. Demarest and Carla watched Brian pass and turned to Sage for confirmation. Their plan worked. Brian knew all his secrets were revealed. Sage remained on the stairs where the parents were expected for pictures and greetings. When Brian saw Kris leave Sage's side, he took his position on the stairs. He stood next to Sage as instructed by the coordinator and whispered in her ear.

"We need to talk. Right after these pictures, before we go to this reception. We need to talk."

Sage responded through her smile.

"Sure. Smile they're taking pictures."

Brian felt trapped. Sage had done what he never thought she would have the nerve to do. She was destroying the only thing Brian valued, his relationship with his children. Brian knew, after the wedding his ties with them would indeed be cut forever.

The picture session on the stairs and in front of the church was over in minutes and the bridal party opted to take more photos at a park near the reception hall. The parents and guests were getting into their cars en route to the reception. Sage told Kris she would meet him at the car. Brian watched as Sage and Kris talked. Demarest, Carla and the boy approached them. Sage and Kris greeted them with hugs saying goodbye. Brian could hear them as they agreed to talk later. Sage walked over to Brian as Kris went to the Mercedes and waited.

"What the hell is this about Sage?"

"What are you talking about?"

"You know damn well what I'm talking about?"

"Brian, tell me, so I'm clear. I'm no longer willing to guess the pieces and put them together later."

"Is that what you're doing? Piecing my life together and putting on display?"

"No, you should have displayed it earlier. When we could have dealt with it and been at peace with knowing what fell out of your closet."

"So, I guess Dionne and Trevon know all of this?"

"They know as much as I know. No one wants to live this lie but you. Live with it Brian, you have this far. You can use all the excuses you want, but we know the truth and it feels good. I can sleep now, not wondering what I did. Brian I went for years thinking I could have done something different to make our marriage work; to keep you at home. I thought I could change your mind about being with Zach. I had no idea there was any truth to your involvement with Demarest. Lord knows I didn't know about Carla. What excuse could you give me about Kris? Damn that Brian, what about our son? You tried to molest our son? And today, you have the nerve to ask me what the hell this is about? As usual, it's about you. This is your shit and I served it to you in one plate, not in bits and pieces."

Brian took a deep breath. The church was closed and the parking lot where they stood held only a few cars. His first thought was to take his anger out on the only woman he loved and the only woman who ever loved him. Kris stepped out of the car when Sage's voice got louder; although he remained propped on the hood. Brain understood his stance meant he would react if he needed to.

"Sage today isn't a good day for this. You've made a mistake bringing this in the open like this. What happened to me explaining my position in all of this?"

"There's no need to explain Brian. Really, just live your life and leave me alone. This will be the last day I want to have to deal with you on any level."

"Sage, tell me who the boy is." She realized he must have felt a twinge pain at the sight of his youngest child.

"Ask Carla."

"You know damn well she won't tell me. Who is he Sage?"

"His name is Carl, he's Carla's son."

"Am I his father?"

"Brian, our daughter's reception is beginning shortly. We need to deal with that right now. You can talk to Carla about your questions later."

"I won't be humiliated at this reception. I can't sit there with Carla, Demarest and Kris; oh, and a child that looks like Trevon."

"You won't they're not coming, and if you don't escort Dionne into the hall ... Kris will."

Sage walked away and Kris smiled as she reached for his assistance stepping into the car. Brian's anger grew. He definitely would talk to Kris at the reception. He watched them pulled out of the parking lot before he got in his car.

Chapter 64

The reception was as beautiful as the wedding and none of the guests suspected that Brian and his family were at odds. Trevon and Brian spoke while greeting the guest who admired the resemblance between the two of them. Brian took their small talk as an opportunity to talk more privately.

"Trevon, I want to spend a few hours with you and Dionne before you go home."

"I don't know what Dionne's plans are, but I'm going to visit Lynn's parents with her. We'll be leaving from there going back to Oklahoma. That leaves little time for us to get together."

"Are you saying if Dionne agrees, you'll see about making the time?"

"No, I'm saying I have plans and very little time to deviate from those plans. We've already had to change our plans, and it's really not fair to Lynn."

"I see. I don't know what Dionne's plans are either. You're right everyone has plans already. Are you leaving Sunday?"

Trevon didn't answer. He knew it was the last time for him to be this cordial with his father. He promised his mother, he would be civil because of the wedding.

"Yeah, talk to Dionne, see what she's doing. I know we're both supposed to get with Carla and Carl before they leave."

Another shot hit Brian's heart. Trevon's words answered the question he asked earlier. Carla's child was his. He had no way to contact her but through Sage or Kris. Trevon walked away to talk to Kris, who was talking to Trevon's daughters. The girls were smiling and laughing when their father joined in. Brian's head began to throb again. He looked at his watch wondering how much longer he would have to pretend he wasn't angry. After talking with Trevon, Brian knew it would be useless to ask Dionne about having a family talk. Dionne's attitude was the same as Trevon's. She had ignored Brian for most of the afternoon. Brian returned to the table marked reserved and waited for the cutting of the cake. He would have a few words with Kris and leave after the cake was cut.

The D.J. slowed the music down for the couples in attendance and Brian went to the bar to replenish his drink. Karen walked over to the bar and ordered her drink ignoring Brian's stare.

"Nothing to say Ms. Thing?"

Karen knew Brian had more than his share of Vodka and decided that answering him would be better than pretending he hadn't spoken.

"I have plenty to say, it's just not the right place or time to say it. The day and ceremony have been too beautiful to ruin it with my thoughts or opinions on something that really doesn't matter."

"She speaks words of wisdom. Why didn't you give advice to your girlfriend?"

"Didn't know she needed any, Sage is doing well. She's got her self esteem back; sales are fine; and excuse me for saying so, she's even got a real love life."

Karen took her drink, thanked the bartender and walked away before Brian could make a comment. As the music blended to another slow song Kris and Sage moved to the dance floor. Brian watched from the bar. His eyes scanned the room as he imagined that every conversation, whisper and sound of laughter were a result of his wife dancing with another man while he stood to the side watching. He began to hear the voices and imagined conversations getting louder and louder. Brian moved closer to Kris and Sage. Dionne saw him from across the floor and interrupted his attempt to stop their dance.

"You haven't danced with me other than the father daughter dance. Have you been ducking me?"

"No, I need to dance with your mother one last time."

"I don't think so. You need to dance with me one last time. The reception is almost over. C'mon don't deny the bride on her wedding day."

Trevon saw that Brian wasn't willing to dance with Dionne and was still making an attempt to get to the other side of the dance floor where Sage and Kris were still dancing and talking softly to each other. Trevon didn't want Brian to draw attention to his efforts to cross the floor.

"Dance with Dionne or sit down."

Trevon spoke softly but firmly. Brian gave him a disapproving glance but Trevon's stare told him he meant what he said. Brian stopped trying to move.

"Is that what I had to do to get you both to pay attention to me?"

"Man, today ain't your day."

"Your mother made me the center of attraction. She invited them to the wedding and that punk ass to the reception."

"I invited them. It's my wedding."

Dionne looked at her father as he hung his head. He looked at Trevon and Dionne and they both knew he was drunk and anything they said would not be remembered.

"Listen, how are you getting home? You can't drive."

"What the fuck do you care?"

Trevon answered before Dionne could say anything.

"Man, you can get nasty if you want. I'll drop you where you stand. Drunk or not, you won't disrespect us anymore. I'll say it one more time. Dance with your daughter or sit your ass down. You choose."

The house lights came on and the coordinator called the bride and groom to the center of the room to cut the cake. Brian went back to the bar. He positioned himself where his vision wouldn't be blocked from any angle. Trevon returned to the family table. Kris excused himself and went to the men's room. Brian saw his opportunity.

Chapter 65

Brian waited outside the bathroom door for Kris. His thoughts went to his past when his father pleaded for him to be quiet as he muffled Brian's cries. Brian shook his head as he relived the nightly bedroom invasions his father put him through. Brian's screams and cries changed to Demarest's and then to Zach. Brian heard his father's voice change to his telling them both to "shut the fuck up". Brian clenched his fist and took out the pills in his pocket hoping to relieve the pain in his head. He walked over to the water fountain tossing the pills in his mouth. He sipped enough to wash down the pills. The door to the men's room opened and Kris stepped out into the hall. Brian had his opportunity to speak with no one to hear him but Kris.

"So you're fucking my wife?"

"No, again you got the wrong man."

"No, don't play me Kris. You're here with her or did you use her to do your dirt!"

"Dirt? What dirt? You did the dirt. You're right I'm here with her. Am I fucking your wife? No, she's not married to your sorry ass remember?"

"I ought to beat your ass."

"You've been trying to beat my ass, one way or the other, for months. That's what's got you into all this trouble; beating men in the ass. Go home Brian. You served your purpose. Take your sorry ass home."

"How did you find Carla and Demarest?"

"I think I told you before, you and I aren't friends, associates, or lovers. Don't talk to me as though we are, or that I owe you any reason for my actions. If I had my way this would have been over long before they stepped back in the picture. Brian I'm glad it didn't happen that way. I may have been in jail if I had done what I wanted to do."

"Kris, I still say you're confused. You're just like me my brother. You like men and you'll be just as uncomfortable as I was with Sage. It will come out sooner or later no matter how fine the woman is. They don't satisfy us, you'll see."

"She's been quite satisfying and I'm sure it will only get better. I'll call you in the morning and let you know. Now that the stress is over, she'll really relax. You know soft as a kitten. The type you just want to go deeper and deeper into. You wouldn't know about that though. You're more of the tight ass type."

Kris went to walk away. Brian pulled his shoulder swinging him around to deliver a right-handed punch. Kris blocked the punch and countered punching Brian in the face. The two continued to fight until one of Jarad's friends noticed the fight and broke them up holding Brian back as Kris returned to the reception.

Sage saw Kris adjusting his suit as he returned to his seat. She frowned turning to the entrance of the hall wondering what could have happened. Kris took a deep breath ignoring the looks from the guests at the other tables. He shook his head and downed the remainder of his drink. Vince, Trevon and Jarad spotted Brian coming into the hall yelling Kris's name.

"Faggot ass, get up Kris. You want to fight c'mon. You come to my daughter's wedding with my wife, and you want to fight me?"

Trevon stood and walked toward his father followed by the other groomsmen. The possibility of a fight caused the guest to move leaving room for Kris and Brian to confront each other. Kris remained in his seat and took another drink from the glass in front of him. Sage yelled for her son to intervene.

"Stop him Trevon, he's drunk."

"I'm not drunk. I'm celebrating, just like everyone else here. Tell him to leave, Sage; he's no longer welcomed here. Time to go playa, she'll sneak out and be with you later, she's going home with me. We have some making up to do. Tell him Sage. Now that everything is in the open we can get on with our life. Kris it backfired my brother. Why do you think she never dated all these years? She still loves me."

Dionne was apologizing as her guest gathered their things to leave. Trevon didn't move and hoped Kris would remain seated. Kris ignored Brian and touched Sage's hand. Tears fell from her eyes. Detective Griffin and Mays entered the room.

"Who called the police?" One voice echoed another as the officers entered scanning the room.

Dionne broke down crying and Jarad went to her side.

"Who called the police Jarad?"

The Chandelier Banquet Hall manager came over to the table where they all stood watching the police handcuff Brian.

"Ms. Monroe, I am sorry. It is our policy to contact the police whenever there is a disturbance. I'm just the night manager. I would lose my job if something happened, and I didn't call the police. I'm sorry."

Sage was in shock and didn't know what to say. Kris acknowledged him and told him they understood.

"Tre, let's get them out of here man."

Trevon agreed it was time to go.

Detective Griffin walked outside the reception hall leading Detective Childs and Mays to the unmarked car where two police stood waiting for their passenger, Brian Drakeford. The team had been waiting until the reception was over. Detective Griffin got the warrant for Brian's arrest Thursday and convinced his team of his certainty that Brian wouldn't leave town before the wedding. They were to pick him up two blocks away from the reception hall to prevent the family from being embarrassed. Griffin would follow him from the time he got into his car and Childs and Mays would make the arrest at a cross street. They didn't want it to turn into a chase if he left the hall headed for the highway. The call of a disturbance at the address made the arrest easy.

"Mr. Drakeford you're under arrest for aggravated sexual assault and aggravated assault against Mr. Zachary Blanding."

Childs waited for his response. Brian didn't answer. Before they put him in the car, he was read his rights. Brian looked beyond the officers watching his family go pass the car to their cars in the parking lot.

"Detective Griffin?"

"Yes, sir."

Brian wanted them to understand he really was concerned about Zach.

"How's Zach? Did the hospital tell you I tried to visit him?"

"We got word you did."

"You say it like it doesn't matter."

"It doesn't. Put him in the car."

Chapter 66

"Kris, did Trevon say he needed someone to pick him up at the airport?"

"No, Jarad and Dionne picked him up this morning. They'll meet us at court."

"What about Carla and Demarest?"

"They stayed with Greg, Sage baby, calm down. Everything is going to be alright."

"I'm nervous. I guess I want this to be behind us. I don't want to have to go through any of this again. Kris our relationship for the last year has been nothing but drama."

Kris walked closer to Sage giving her a smirk.

"Good thing I love you. Most men would have ran as fast as they could; proves my love baby that's all."

"I love you too, I love you more."

"And I am a lucky man."

Kris kissed Sage and looked at his watch while holding her in his arms.

"Lady, it's close to the time. Anything else you want to check before leaving?"

"No, who's bringing Zach?"

"He's under police escort."

"What? Why?"

"Detective Griffin. Lamont says he's got a personal interest in this case, Greg and I agree; it's Zach."

"You're joking."

"No joke. Griffin has been by his side since he started the investigation. We'll know for sure after the trial. He probably won't let it get beyond professional until this is all over."

"Damn, are all the lookers into the life?"

"No, didn't you and Karen say I was a looker?"

Sage pushed Kris toward the door. They were headed to the court. The State of Maryland vs. Brian Drakeford was scheduled to begin at nine o'clock.

Throughout the preliminary hearing and the first two days of the State's presentation Brian and Mr. Silverman didn't seem concerned about the testimonies heard by the jury. Today would be different. The state submitted a list of people they subpoenaed and Mr. Silverman immediately asked for a recess. The judge granted them two hours, time for Mr. Silverman to talk to his client.

"Brian, we've got a problem. The State gave me this list of names. These are the people that will be testifying on their behalf. The state is closing their side of the case with them today."

Silverman handed the list to Brian. He looked at the list. He shook his head slowly. It had been almost a year since Zach had been attacked. Brian still had not told Silverman the truth. After the wedding and the arrest Brian shut down completely. He had a few months of psychiatric treatment. Although Mr. Silverman made protests that his client was incompetent and couldn't stand trial, the doctor's reports reflected, he was not only competent, but denied his needing any further treatment.

"You tell me Brian, what am I supposed to do?"n

"I thought Zach was still under doctor's care. He was in and out of sleep, what could he remember that couldn't be debated.

They have nothing. These others, their testimonies won't have anything to do with that night."

"What will they say Brian? What will they uncover that will bury you or your character?"

Brian looked at the list. He realized his freedom was over. He wouldn't walk away from this act, and reflect on it later. He shrugged his shoulders.

"Do what you can do. If you can't perform a miracle, how am I to blame you? You're not God. Only he can save me now."

Silverman looked at his client. Brian still hadn't confided in him. He had defended guilty men before but none of them gave up until the judge's gavel pounded before the verdict. Brian Drakeford had been different from the start. Silverman's experience taught him how to decipher senseless cases. He couldn't pour water on the fire the case created.

The two men returned to the courtroom and waited for the judge's entrance. The case resumed with the court calling Demarest Graves to the stand. Ms. Pamela Struthers, the prosecutor, began with general questions and Mr. Silverman stood, off and on, protesting and debating the relevance of the witness and his testimony. Ms. Struthers set the stage for the jury and as the questions asked revealed the personal relationship between Demarest and Brian, Silverman knew why Brian decided not to tell the truth. Demarest told his story, cried and explained the torment he went through.

"Your Honor. This testimony is meant to taint the mind of the jury. Although this may be the truth as told by Mr. Graves this has nothing to do with Mr. Drakeford's case today. We are here because of Mr. Blanding's assault. There is no link between Mr. Graves and Mr. Blanding."

Silverman sat down. He was certain the testimony would be disregarded.

"Your Honor, they both had a romantic relationship with the defendant. If Mr. Graves had pressed charges Mr. Blanding may not have suffered by the hands of Mr. Drakeford."

"Your Honor, I object!"

"Ms. Struthers are you finished with your questioning of the witness."

"Yes, sir."

"You may cross examine Mr. Silverman."

"Mr. Graves, have you been in contact with Mr. Drakeford?"

"No, I haven't."

"For how many years?"

"At least five years, sir."

"So this happened eleven years ago, and you stayed in touch with the man you say raped and harassed you for six years afterward, why?"

"He paid me not to go to the authorities."

The jury shifted. Silverman noticed their reaction to Demarest's response.

"Do you have proof of that Mr. Graves?"

"Yes. He sent checks each month. I have the copies and my bank statements of the deposits."

"Mr. Graves do you still love Mr. Drakeford?"

"No, I did for a long time after that night but through counseling and treatment, I've gotten over our relationship."

"Mr. Graves so it can be concluded that your only reason for testifying today is revenge isn't it?"

"No, Brian Drakeford raped me and his violence has continued to someone else. He needs to be stopped."

"Your Honor."

The court audience had begun to give their verbal reaction. The jury was shifting and grumbling again. Brian held his head in his hands and shook it slowly. The judge banged the gavel for order. Silverman returned to his seat. Demarest's testimony was over.

The doors to the courtroom opened and Zach entered the court with a patch over his eye. He took his seat on the witness stand and was sworn in. As he testified, the jurors watched Brian and Silverman whispering at the table.

"Mr. Silverman, please refrain from interrupting the testimony. Do you need to approach the bench?"

"No your honor."

"Advise your client, he will be removed from the court if he can not refrain from sideline comments. Continue Ms. Struthers."

Zach told his story ending with his last operation that left him blind in one eye. Mr. Silverman stood slowly asking his questions looking at the jury.

"Mr. Blanding, why didn't you press charges immediately?"

"I didn't want Brian to be arrested. I didn't want him to be in trouble like this."

"So why now?"

"I realized he deliberately hurt me. At first I thought it was an accident. The result of a lover's quarrel, you know a bad argument. Honey, he tried to kill me. I realized that after the doctors started talking surgery. I was in and out of sleep so much I couldn't press charges. I wasn't coherent enough to talk to anyone about what happened."

"So you stumbled into the hospital and didn't tell the staff or the police about Brian Drakeford attacking you?"

"No, I didn't. I told you I didn't want him to be in trouble. It doesn't mean I didn't know he did it."

"Your Honor, please ask the witness to stick to only the question."

"Mr. Blanding, answer the question only."

"These questions need not be vague than judge. This man took my eye out or haven't you noticed."

"Your Honor, please."

"Get on with it Mr. Silverman."

"Mr. Blanding, who did you tell first about Mr. Drakeford doing this to you?"

"I told Lamont Ward, Kris Randall and Gregory Tempts."

"You told them and didn't tell the doctor's or the police."

"No, not then. I told them the night of the attack and I told the doctor and the police later."

"I guess I have to ask again. Why them Mr. Blanding, they couldn't help you? Why not tell the police?"

"The police couldn't help me either, the damage was done."

"Mr. Blanding, you say you were at my client's house when this attack happened. The state has stood by you but there is no proof of your visit other than your word."

Zach gave a questioning look to Ms. Struthers. Ms. Struthers stood, knowing she submitted results of Brian Drakefords' cell phone records.

"Your Honor, may we approach?"

"Yes."

The attorneys approached the bench and the judge covered his microphone, so they would not be heard.

"Your Honor, we submitted evidence. Mr. Drakeford's cell phone records the day of the attack."

"Your Honor, what the records show are calls made by Mr. Blanding on that day. He could have had the phone from anytime prior to that date. The records prove nothing."

"Your Honor, the records prove that Mr. Blanding took the phone from Mr. Drakeford on the day of the attack. Calls to Mr. Blanding were made from that phone the morning of the attack and the night before. Mr. Blanding would not have called himself. If Mr. Silverman would like to question Mr. Blanding about those calls the state has no problem with it."

"Mr. Silverman, you may question the witness about the calls if you like."

Silverman and the Prosecutor returned to their prospective places. The questioning continued.

"Mr. Blanding you took Mr. Drakeford's phone the day of the attack. Why?"

"I wanted to check his calls. We had been having problems for a few months, and I thought he was seeing someone else. I found evidence around the house that made me want to check the numbers he had called recently."

"Was Mr. Kris Randall one of those numbers?"

"Yes, but that number had a block on it. So he couldn't call him from his cell phone. The only other calls were business calls and mine."

"You were able to check all of that the night of the attack?"

"No, I checked it before I turned the phone over to the police. They thought it was my cell phone and didn't take it with my clothes and other items. When I told them it was Brian's, they took it. That was a week or two later."

"So, you said your number had been called?"

"Yes."

"You called your home before calling Mr. Randall from the hospital?"

"I was in the hospital, why would I call my house?"

The audience laughed. Zach was getting annoyed with Silverman's questions and his professionalism was wearing thin. The gavel sounded and the court came to order.

"Mr. Blanding. My client could get ten years on one charge and ten or more on another. You've already stated your love for him prevented you from turning him in. Is it safe to assume you don't love him anymore?"

"No, it's never safe to assume anything. I still love Brian Drakeford. Unfortunately, the man who sits here is not the Brian Drakeford I fell in love with, and he can go to hell."

The court broke into an uproar. The judge pounded his gavel and called for a lunch break. Silverman returned to his seat and looked at Brian. The lawyer knew his client's case was at the mercy of the court.

Chapter 67

Court resumed at one o'clock. Everyone was in place waiting patiently for the judge. Brian returned with Mr. Silverman smiling as though he had no worries. There were only a few other witnesses on the states list and Brian told his lawyer that he was ready for whatever they would throw his way. Silverman wished he had the confidence his client portrayed.

"The state calls Trevon Drakeford."

Brian frowned and snatched the paper with the list of witnesses from his lawyer. He had overlooked Trevon's name. When he read it again for the third time he realized he assumed it was Sage. Sage's name wasn't on the list. Trevon took the stand and was sworn in.

"Mr. Drakeford please state your full name and your relationship to the defendant."

Silverman deemed Trevon's testimony just as irrelevant as he had Demarest's. The questions revealed his relationship with his father as an adult and then the prosecutor probed into his childhood. Brian began to shake his head and hold it in his trembling hands. It was as though he was in severe pain. He couldn't look at his son as he told the story of Brian's attempt to molest him and their fight.

"...We haven't had a father son relationship since."

"Mr. Drakeford do you believe your father, Brian Drakeford could have assaulted Mr. Blanding?"

"Objection, your Honor, the witness is not qualified to analyze his father or any actions he's accused of."

"Overruled, Mr. Drakeford you will not answer that question. Ms. Struthers rephrase your questions or move on."

"Mr. Drakeford, your father is on trial for Aggravated Sexual Assault and Aggravated Assault do you think your father could have done either of these acts?"

"Your Honor!"

"Ms. Struthers, I'm warning you."

"Mr. Drakeford, has your father shown you any signs of this type of aggression since he attempted to assault you?"

"Not against me. My father has always been aggressive and I guess it's reached a peak. He needs help and if this is it. So be it."

Brian pulled Silverman to his seat so he could whisper in his ear. Silverman sat back in the seat to listen to his client.

"Man, stop this shit. I'm guilty."

Silverman asked to approach the bench. The attorneys and the judge concluded there was no need for the proceedings to continue. Brian Drakeford was facing serious time behind bars.

Chapter 68

The sentencing was set for three weeks later. Brian's family decided they wouldn't be attending the proceedings. It would be mid July and they all agreed they needed a vacation from Brian's life and a chance to live their own. Trevon, Lynn and the children left for Florida when the girls got out of school; Dionne and Jarad took the first two weeks in July and went to Myrtle Beach; Greg, Carla, Sage and Kris spent the same two weeks in the Cayman Islands.

Lamont called Zach after closing the office to confirm they were meeting for drinks.

"Hey, Zach, it's Lamont. Are we still on for dinner?"

"Yeah, definitely, did you reach Doug?"

"That damn man will drive me crazy. He's gonna meet us there."

"What's up with that?"

"Zach, don't ask. Anyway we'll see you about seven."

"Thanks Lamont. I mean including me as a friend in your life has been a more than what I expected."

The two had become close almost inseparable since the trial. Lamont showed no pity. He knew what Zach would have to go through if he had no one who understood him. There were few programs that dealt with rape and the victim being gay.

"Don't show up dressed to impress either. It's a casual thing."

"Yeah, yeah, I can't help what makes me, me. Take it or leave it. I am who I am."

"Yeah, a conceded bitch."

They laughed teasing each other and hung up the phone promising to meet at eight o'clock.

Lamont went home, to shower and get dressed. Doug left a note on the dining room table. Doug would be waiting for Zach and Lamont to arrive at the club. Lamont called Zach again and told him there was a change of plans and he would pick him up and take him to the club where Doug would have a table waiting. There was to be a live performance, a DJ, drinks and a promised night of fun. Lamont explained Zach couldn't drink and enjoy himself if he had to worry about driving home.

As promised Zach was ready at seven thirty. The two arrived at the club and asked for their reserved seating. Zach was surprised to see the place was nicely decorated and the music was better than most of the clubs he frequented.

"Have you ever been here?"

"No, how long has this been open?"

"Oh, maybe five years, Doug and I come here off and on. It's a place we can relax without the whispers and stares, you know. I think you'll like it."

They walked through the tables. The dim lightening made it hard to spot Doug, who put his glass in the air to get their attention. As they approached the table he stood pulling the chairs out for both Zach and Lamont.

"Zach, how are you doing?"

"I'm good. Lamont has been watching over me like a mother hen."

"Please, you love every minute of it."

"I thought you didn't notice it. He's really been a good friend. Saying thanks is not enough. You know, I owe you both."

"You don't owe us. We just want you to continue to get better."

"Can I join you?"

The voice was familiar. Doug stood and greeted Dave Griffin with a handshake.

"Good evening Detective."

"It's Dave, Lamont. Just Dave, I'm off duty. Hey, Zach, it's good to see you."

Zach was in shock. He hadn't talked to Dave since the start of the trial. There were no phone calls or visits. Zach had a difficult time dealing with losing another friendship and not understanding why. He didn't return Dave's greeting. Lamont and Doug recognized their need to be alone for the moment.

"Excuse us. Do either of you want a drink?"

"I'll have a Hennessy and Coke. Zach what would you like?"

"The usual Lamont thanks sweetie."

"Are you going to speak to me or is this gonna be a long night?" Dave's question annoyed Zach.

"Why haven't you contacted me?"

"Zach, I told you I couldn't afford to lose the case. I wanted Brian behind bars. He deserved it after all he had done. If you and I looked as though we were interested in each other they would have dismissed the case. It would have been a mistrial. I separated myself so you could win. That case was important for you and others that may fall victim to that type of abuse. I told you I had an interest in you, Zachary Blanding. So is it gonna be a long night?"

Zach was relieved. He looked forward to having a friendship with the detective. He wasn't sure how far it would go but he wanted to be his friend.

"I owe you an apology. I have cussed you more than you can imagine. I've even asked God what was wrong with me. I mean first, going through life with the problems of society not accepting me for me. Then of course there was the thing with Brian, the court case, the humiliation and the lost of my sight in one eye. Then you coming into my life and disappearing. I was giving up. I don't know what I would have done if Lamont hadn't kept my spirits up. He is a royal pain in the ass but he's such a good friend."

"I heard you can be difficult."

"You stayed in touch with Lamont?"

"I'm a detective but I'm not psychic. I planned this evening. Listen … tonight is a new beginning. Again I ask you, is this gonna be a long night?"

"I'm all for a new beginning."

Other Novels by Nanette M. Buchanan

Family Secrets Lies and Alibi's

A Different Kind of Love

Bruised Love

Gossip Line

Bonded Betrayal

Scattered Pieces

The Stranger Within

The Perfect Side Piece

The Hustler's Touch

Duplicity

The Corner Pew

Purchase Your Copy Today

www.NanetteMBuchanan.com

Books are available in Kindle, Nook and other ebook formats

www.ingramcontent.com/pod-product-compliance
Lightning Source LLC
Chambersburg PA
CBHW061558100726
47898CB00002B/427